GADFLY

BY: M. LEE PRESCOTT

Published by Quicksand Chronicles

Cover Design by Ashley Lopez

For my family

CHAPTER 1

Many would say that fifty-eight is old. Young, old or somewhere in between, fifty-eight was still much too young to die. As the minister droned on about the deceased, Ron Harp's civic mindedness and his "life of the mind," I wondered how long a fidgety atheist like myself could survive without breathing. My name is Ricky Steele and I am fifty-eight, a sort of jill-of-all-trades, mistress of none. Some months ago, following my involvement in a murder investigation, I applied for a private investigator's license. I'm still very much in training. I'm single, of average looks and build and no longer in possession of the breasts with which I was born. So far, I've survived breast cancer, mastectomies, reconstruction, divorce, and numerous relationship breakups. Still standing and still an optimist, even on a dark day such as the present one.

"Freak biking accident" was how Karen's mom described it. What kind of accident? What manner of freak? And where was his helmet? These questions pounded "rat-a-tat-tat," drawing my attention from the minister's homily as I sat wedged between a trembling octogenarian and a ruddy-faced teenager. Granny's eau de mothballs clashed violently with junior's "fresh scent" aftershave.

The sanctuary's austere wooden pews were packed with mourners. At the front of the church, I spied Ron's wife, Karen, my dearest childhood friend, sitting motionless and straight, flanked on either side by a Harp brother. To the left, at the far end of the pew, was Milly Spenser, Karen's mom. Where was Alex, Karen and Ron's twelve-year-old?

Ronnie dead. Incomprehensible. I thought back to four years earlier when we'd run in the Ocean State Marathon. Ron's stolid silence had been both a comfort and an annoyance. I like to think it was my incessant chattering that got him through mile twenty-six, when he doubled over, seeing stars. Despite twinkling asteroids dotting my own vision, I had mopped him up and dragged him onward, biting back the urge to scream "I told you so" for his refusal to drink anything at our previous three water stops. I slurped like a water buffalo at every stop, necessitating two detours into the woods during the final five miles. As we limped toward the finish line, I recited every joke and amusing anecdote my depleted brain could dredge up. Ron never again mentioned that mile, and my almost carrying him through the chute. Maybe I'd dreamed the whole thing, including Karen at the far end, holding up my birthday/survivor's cake, fifty-four candles burning merrily in the sweltering heat of a breezeless day.

Gazing around the church, I spied a few familiar faces in a sea of strangers. As is often the case in small towns, everyone looked alike. Out the east window, the church cemetery stretched for a quarter mile. The graveyard dated back to the 1600s and held many of the village founders including Libby Chase, daughter of Simeon Chase, one of the town founders. Beyond the graveyard, Rushing Brook road wound two or three miles to Nauset Point and Nauset Light perched at edge of the cliffs.

For an oceanfront village within commuting distance to Providence and even Boston, Windy Harbor was remarkably unspoiled. In fact, its longtime denizens worked round the clock to conceal its existence from the rest of the world. A number of times, Hollywood had come calling, approaching the Town Council and church deacons about using the village or church as film settings. Such offers were always rejected. Bunny Stark, a childhood friend who owned a real estate company fifteen miles away, once made the mistake of featuring a Windy Harbor property as the *Providence Journal*'s "House of the Week." For months afterward, she was besieged with hate mail and nasty phone calls.

As we filed out of the church, I heard murmurings from the throng behind me. "What's Karrie gonna do? Alex, almost a teenager, and that big place to keep up? Ron might not've been a real go-getter, but he did do most of the work. Not to mention taking care of Alex. What in the world will she do? And by the way, where the hell are Alex and Jolie?"

When I turned back, a sea of strange faces greeted me. Just ahead, I spied Karen Spenser Harp patting the arm of her brother-in-law, Jay as she stepped away to greet a fellow mourner. Circles lined her hazel eyes, her skin pasty white, light brown shoulder-length hair limp. Her black sheath hung from her body like a gunny sack and she looked as if one gust of wind would blow her away. As mourners came forth to hug her, I cringed, afraid their hardy embraces might snap my friend in two.

His velvety voice caught me off guard and I almost toppled over. "Ricky Steele, isn't it? Been a while."

I swung around to find chestnut eyes studying me, hand extended. "Jay, hi. Yes, it has." I reached out to grasp his hand. "I'm so sorry about Ron."

He nodded. "A real shocker for all of us."

When I gazed up, I found eyes glistening with mischief, not grief. All three of the Harp brothers were tall and good-looking, but Jay was downright gorgeous and he knew it. He held on to my hand, all the while drawing me close enough to be surrounded by his scent, a spicy cologne that might have intoxicated a lesser mortal.

As I watched Karen stroll off in a cluster of women, my hand grazed the soft black cashmere of his overcoat. I gathered my strength and pulled back, exhaling with a whoosh. He smiled, delighted at my discombobulated state. Nineteen years and the man still made my knees turn to jelly. Irritated, I turned away, pretending to search for my friends. Fortunately, at that moment a well-wisher embraced him and gave me time to escape. I really did need to date more often.

Nineteen years ago, in our roles as best man and maid of honor for Karen and Ron, Jay and I had worked closely in the weeks leading up to the wedding. During that time, we had enjoyed a brief, passionate affair. However, once the festivities ended, Jay returned to his fiancée, Sheila, and I to the single life I did so well.

I watched as a blonde fortysomething in a short, tight-fitting black business suit seized Jay, pressing herself against him, ostensibly in grief. Had she no shame? I spied Karen standing alone and moved to her side, my arm circling her waist. "How you doing?"

Pale eyes lit up, her expression haunted. She grabbed hold of my wrist and steered me away from the crowd. "Ricky, can you stay?"

"Yes, of course. I'm coming back to the house. Can I help with something? Food? Serving, anything?"

"No, I mean, can you stay overnight?"

"Well, I—"

Her fingers dug into my skin. "Please! I really need to talk to you, alone."

"Karen, what is it?"

"I can't talk here…but it's—"

"Karen, for heaven's sake." Milly Spenser appeared out of nowhere to lay ahold of her daughter's wrist. Even at seventy-nine, she was a force. "Come along, dear. You and Dorothy can catch up later. Your guests will be waiting."

Karen hugged me. "Please say you'll stay."

"Of course, but what's wrong?" A stupid question considering that we had just come from her husband's funeral.

"It wasn't an accident. Ronnie, I mean. It wasn't an accident."

I started to speak, but Milly pulled Karen from my grasp, steering her toward the waiting limo. As I watched their retreat, I spied Bobby Harp, Ron's younger brother, helping his wheelchair-bound father down the steps. Bobby's much younger wife, Betsy, trailed behind, a towheaded child on each hand. Tan and weathered from his life as a lobsterman, Bobby didn't look a day older than he had a decade earlier.

The Harp boys had inherited millions from their maternal grandparents. The money allowed each to live the life he wanted. Bobby had chosen the sea, Jay the law, and Ron the life of a country farmer. Ron also ran the Harp Foundation, a charitable trust based in Providence that gave away millions to educational and community service projects every year.

As the limo pulled away, I headed to my car, an ancient Jeep Grand Wagoneer.

Chapter 2

By the time I reached Macomber Lane, cars lined the drive a quarter mile from the house. Undaunted, I putted down the tree-shaded drive until the house came into view. On a farm, there was always room to squeeze in one more all-terrain vehicle. I spied a nice, open spot beside the barn and maneuvered in next to Karen's dark green Land Rover.

I soon discovered why my convenient spot was empty when I stepped into a mudhole, sinking ankle deep, my hundred-and-sixty-dollar pumps disappearing with a slurp.

Stuck fast, I grabbed the cane I keep for my unsteady knee, flailing against the side of the jeep, hoping for leverage. My knee twisted painfully, and I stopped struggling. "Shit!" I said aloud.

"You're lucky that's not what it is." I looked over my shoulder to find a vaguely familiar person. He chuckled as he extended his hand. "Here, grab hold and I'll pull you out."

I grasped his hand. After several minutes of sloshing and slurping, my knee wrenching painfully with every move, I broke free, scrunching my toes so as to bring my new heels along with me. I needn't have bothered since one look at them told me they were ruined. That's what I get for buying expensive shoes. Ordinarily I pay no more than fifty dollars for dress shoes since I'm apt to wear them once and throw them to the back of my closet, never to be seen again. Probably for the best. With my unsteady knee, I had no business wearing heels.

"Better get in and wash those off."

"Beyond hope, I'm afraid." Gingerly, I took a step.

"You okay? Your leg, I mean?"

"Fine, just feeling a bit foolish."

"You're Karen's friend, Ricky, the detective, aren't you?"

"Private investigator, yes. Hi."

"Will Ramsey. My wife and I live in town. Karen needs you, that's for sure."

I studied his expression. The Ramseys were new friends of Karen and Ron's. When she had mentioned them last summer, Karen referred to Will as "one of Ron's activist buddies." It was on the tip of my tongue to ask him if he was part of IMPACT, the group Ron had started to work with on various civic projects, when we were interrupted by the appearance of a short, mousy woman who emerged from behind a maroon minivan laden with baskets and bags. "There you are. Willie, I could use some help, please." She smiled, first at her husband, then me.

Will rushed to her side, taking several bags and the largest of the baskets. "Val, guess who this is. Ricky Steele, Karen's detective friend."

"Oh, yes, hi. What a relief for Karen to have you here." She stepped forward to shake my hand, then spied my shoes. "Oh dear, what happened?"

"Dumb parking. Luckily your husband came to my rescue."

"Will's very gallant." She patted his arm, pretty when she smiled. "Can they be salvaged with soap and water?"

"Doubtful." A sloshing sound made me turn round just in time to see the jeep's tires disappear, mud lapping at the door frames.

Will laughed. "They don't call this area Quicksand Pond for nothing. But don't worry. The garages in town are used to it. They'll have you out in no time."

"That's a comfort."

"Give Billy Mederois a call when you get inside. Come to think of it, he's probably in there. He works on Karen and Ron's cars. They're pretty good friends. Come on. I'll see if I can spot him."

I tossed the ruined pumps into an open trash barrel and hobbled after the Ramseys into the house. My gray linen suit was now wrinkled and dotted with mud and my legs sported lovely mud anklets. Will introduced me to Billy Mederois. If he was horrified at the vision standing before him, Mederois never let on. He promised to arrange for a tow as soon as he got back to the garage. I thanked him and excused myself to go in search of a private spot to remove my blackened panty hose, wash my feet, and ponder what Karen had meant about Ron's death not being an accident.

CHAPTER 3

I limped down a narrow hallway, its twenty-foot ceiling painted in three shades of yellow, marveling, as always, at the home the Harps had created. Built ten years ago by Ron, his brothers and friends, it was one of a kind. "No right angles, no square rooms" had been their instructions to the designer, a friend in her last year of architectural school. The friend had not only won an award for her plans for the Harps' dream house, but had landed a job at a prestigious California architectural firm because of them.

A maze of curves, winding passageways and wide, airy rooms, the home's surroundings were every bit as spectacular as the interior. The house's glass-walled south side faced the river. To the east and west lay acres of fields and woods and to the north, three rustic outbuildings—a barn, chicken coop and small shed that housed gardening tools.

Karen had done all the interior painting, sometimes enlisting friends and neighbors to help with ceilings and large projects. The living room's vibrant blues gave way to the verdant greens, yellows and reds of the kitchen and crescent-shaped breakfast room. Each bedroom sported a different color, sometimes several, the walls either stenciled or adorned with fanciful murals.

Karen's gaily painted furniture was everywhere, from the built-in kitchen benches and bar stools to the bureaus and chests in every bedroom. Her painted rugs were scattered throughout the house across wide pine floors, and her hand-painted tiles graced the walls of the three bathrooms and the kitchen backsplash. In the dining room, now crowded with mourners, the walls were painted with floor-to-ceiling murals, depictions of the village, the beach and local landmarks.

Beautiful as the rest of the house was, Karen's masterpiece was Alex's room, where I now retreated to wash my feet in his tub. His walls mirrored the terrain surrounding the house, creatures of the field and forest peeking out from behind bush, tree and rock. Careful scrutiny revealed over sixty different local birds and woodland creatures— woodchucks, squirrels, chipmunks, foxes (the three varieties indigenous to the area), rabbits, moles, voles, mice, deer, and even a mother coyote and two kits.

The room had been photographed and written up in magazines from *Audubon* to *Rhode Island Monthly*. Karen had been asked many times to recreate Alex's murals, but she always declined, explaining that it was one-of-a-kind gift to her son. Alex, I thought, remembering Sally's comments. How would Karen cope? Between her travels and other projects, Ronnie had shouldered ninety percent of the parenting duties. Who would she find to take his place?

Alex's bathroom walls were covered with hand-painted tiles depicting every nursery rhyme character imaginable. As I washed and dried my feet, tossing the black, encrusted panty hose into the wastebasket, I studied my surroundings. Adorable, but what did almost teenage Alex think of this homage to Mother Goose these days?

I stood up, running fingers through my hair in a futile attempt to tame the frizz. Finally, turning away from the alarming vision who stared back at me from the mirror, I hung up my towel and made my way toward the hum of voices. As I neared the crowd, I felt one of my killer migraines creeping across the top of my head. Resigned to twenty minutes of agony, I stopped in the kitchen for a glass of water, and swallowed two of my miracle pills.

CHAPTER 4

As I stepped into the living room, Val Ramsey spotted me and waved. "Are you okay? You look kind of pale. And you're limping."

"Headache. It'll pass. A bad knee, nothing to do with my wallow in the mud."

"Can I get you something?"

I shook my head, managing a grimace. "Just took something. It'll be working momentarily."

A couple approached. Both short, dark and round, the woman was dressed in a red sweater, long black wool skirt and brown clogs. The man, who appeared to be much older, looked uncomfortable in a gray suit two sizes too small. Val introduced them as Alonzo and Ramona Souza. Souza, a lobsterman, told me he worked with Bobby Harp. Ramona cheerfully introduced herself as a "stay-at-home mom." After loading plates with smoked bluefish, lobster salad, and thick slabs of buttered bread, we retreated to a window bench in the kitchen to eat.

As they ate, I nibbled a piece of bread to fight off waves of nausea. Ramona chattered on about the Harps and her son's school until her husband interrupted. "How do you know Karen and Ron?" he said to me.

"I'm a childhood friend of Karen's and erstwhile running buddy of Ron's."

"You're the one who ran the marathon with him, aren't you?" Ramona's dark eyes twinkled. "The detective, right?"

"Private investigator."

"Karen must be so relieved."

"Is there a reason she'd need a private investigator?"

Alonzo shot his wife a warning look. "Ramona means it'll be good for Karen to have close friends with her."

At that moment we were interrupted by Rebecca and Peter Morse. "Hi, Ricky," she said, stooping to peck my cheek. Her sandy hair pulled back by a black velvet headband, Rebecca wore a Stewart plaid shirtwaist dress that looked like a throwback to the fifties. Her red-haired husband dressed, in a brown corduroy jacket over a gray sweater vest and khaki pants, looked uncomfortable and ready to get back into his overalls.

Peter extended his hand. "Don't get up. Nice to see you, Ricky. Wish it was under better circumstances."

I nodded. As Peter talked to the three of us, Rebecca stared out the window, her gaze vacant and dead, eyes puffy and red-rimmed, white skin covered with red blotches. The closest of Karen and Ron's friends, I'd met Peter and Rebecca many times over the years. He was the fourth generation of the Morse family to be running a large, prosperous greenhouse and nursery business. Rebecca, who had also grown up in Windy Harbor, was a public defender serving Newport County. Serious and down-to-earth, they had always impressed me as people devoted to home and career, while their passion, like Ron's, was IMPACT. IMPACT had brought many of these people together, creating a liberal, activist family in ultra-conservative Windy Harbor. Rebecca and Ron had worked on a number of civic projects together and Rebecca provided legal advice and expertise to the Harp Foundation.

"You planning on staying around a while?" Peter asked.

"At least for tonight."

"Karen will be glad of that." He stared toward the door, affable expression clouding over.

Following his gaze, Val turned to Ramona and shook her head. "The nerve of the woman."

I followed their gaze and spied a sandy-haired matron in wool skirt, a white blouse with a Peter Pan collar, and tan cardigan sweater open except for the top button. She was on the arm of a younger man, bleach-blond hair close cropped and spiky, his charcoal suit tailored, expensive. She looked to be in her early seventies, her companion, twentysomething.

"Who are they?" I asked to no one in particular.

Ramona looked as if she had bitten into a lemon. "Ruth Bowen and her son Tripp."

"What a hypocrite," Val said, pursing her lips. "She hated Ron. Did everything she could to turn townspeople against him. How dare she come here today."

As she spoke, we watched Ruth Bowen greet Karen, pecking her cheek, her son following suit. Karen's expression was blank, as if unaware of their presence. At her side, Jay ran interference and the Bowens moved away, heading toward the buffet table.

Rebecca Morse stalked off. When she reappeared several minutes later, she held a quart-size tumbler of straight bourbon, no ice. Peter gave her a look, then turned away. Dick Chaffee and his wife, Myra Rollins, came by to say hello as they worked the crowd room by room. Myra was pencil-thin, with long, dark hair parted in the middle, her black dress hugging every inch of her. She looked as if she'd out of a Charles Addams cartoon. Her husband followed, red-faced and tweedy, salt-and-pepper hair in need of a trim. I had heard Dick was running for Town Council.

The Chaffees were also members of IMPACT, but their commitment had always seemed a little wishy washy to me. Both had high-profile jobs in Providence. Dick was a tax attorney and Myra a divorce lawyer, partner in one of the largest firms in the city. They talked a good game, but maybe their passions lay outside town? Like Rebecca and Peter, I'd met Myra and Dick many times at Ron and Karen's summer parties.

CHAPTER 5

Val and I rose. As we made our way toward the dessert table, Val tapped my arm. "So, Ricky, are you still single?"

"Yup."

"Steady boyfriend?"

"Not at the moment." Not for many moments, I thought, my nonexistent love life becoming more depressing by the minute.

"Find an older man, that's my advice. Look at us, and Myra and Dick. Why, he's got to be ten or fifteen years older than she is. A bit vain, won't tell anyone his age. And Peter and Becca. He's, what? At least ten years older, maybe more. Come to think of it, Ron and Karen are the only ones of our crowd who married people close to their own age. Alonzo was already an old man when he married Mona. Of course," she whispered, eyeing the Souzas over her shoulder. "Alonzo was probably an old man when he was two." We laughed as we sidled up to the dessert table to load our plates with brownies, cookies and mini-cheesecakes.

Plate piled high, I spied the Bowens at the far end of the room. "The other side," Val whispered. She proceeded to identify the Bowens' companions, a trio Val called "Ruth's lackeys"—Tippy Bingham, a twenty-one-year-old college dropout Ruth had installed on various town boards and committees to vote her way, Sedgewick Montgomery, the town solicitor, and George Wilbur, a grade-school classmate of

Ruth's, whose main function, according to Val, was to support and defend Ruth's policies to the Town Council she had presided over for forty-three years.

I watched the group, all of them exchanging furtive looks, as they glanced around the room. My headache had loosened its grip and I was halfway to la-la land, thanks to my miracle pills. Emboldened by my euphoric state, I strode up and introduced myself.

Bowen's grip was firm. "How nice to meet you, Miss Steele. And where are you from?"

"I live in Ocean Grove, but my office is in Fall River."

"How nice." Translation: *So sorry to hear that you live in the slums.*

"What line of work are you in?" Her son stepped forward. "Tripp Bowen." I reached out and shook his hand receiving a dead fish in return.

"I'm a private investigator."

"Really? What kinds of cases do you handle?"

"Mostly insurance investigations and the occasional domestic case."

"Snooping on errant spouses, peeping in motel windows, snapping incriminating photos, that sort of thing?"

I decided his questions did not deserve a response and turned back to his mother. "Were you and Ron close?"

She blanched. "This is a small town, Miss Steele. Everyone knows everyone here."

"I was referring to social friendship. I've been out of touch with the Harps the past few years and—"

Suddenly enthralled by something behind me, she waved to someone in the next room. "Would you excuse me? Town business. I'm sure you understand. Come along, Trippie."

I watched as they greeted Karen's sister-in-law, Betsy Harp, like they hadn't seen her for years. Town business, indeed. Betsy looked stricken, clearly unaccustomed to such an effusive greeting from the Town Council President, never mind her fish-faced son.

CHAPTER 6

October sunlight faded as the last guests trickled out and quiet descended on the house. The Harp family, myself and the ladies of the community center group shuffled from room to room, cleaning up. The food had been catered, but the serving and setup had been handled by four stalwart women in white aprons, who were now operating an assembly line from sink to pantry, washing, drying and storing china, glasses and cooking utensils. Karen had gone to her room to lie down and Bobby and Betsy's children were squabbling in the front hall, their parents distracted and irritable as a result.

As I wiped a spill from the tiger maple coffee table Ron had built for Karen's fiftieth birthday, I heard Jay on the phone in the study. He sounded angry, but his words were lost in the cacophony from the front hall. A few minutes later, he joined Bobby and Betsy in the dining room. "Why don't you two take off? We're all set here and it sounds like the kids have had enough."

"I hate to leave Karrie."

"She'll be fine, Bets. I'll hang around a while and Ricky's spending the night. You guys go, really. You can check in first thing in the morning."

Not wishing to disturb the family conference, I skirted the dining room to bring the last of the trash to the kitchen. I was just in time to bid the ladies goodbye. I decided to escape to the study, where I shut the door behind me. No sooner had I stretched out on Ron's leather couch and closed my eyes than the study door opened and shut again. Before I could make my presence known, Jay began talking on his cell.

"It's me again. Sorry, where were we? Oh, yes, I've decided I should stay the night, then head straight to work in the morning." A long pause ensued, punctuated by several sighs before he got another word in. "We've been through this already, Marty. This is all I can manage right now. No, I'm not negotiating, I'm trying to be honest. It has nothing to do with Sheila. That's completely over. I told you that. Karen? Are you crazy? She just lost her husband, for Christ's sake. Now, hold on a second, that's not fair. I never promised marriage." Another long pause, this time accompanied by pacing, his Italian leather loafers clicking over the wood floor at the carpet's edge.

"Marty, I can't do this right now. I just buried my brother, for Christ's sake. No, I'm not breaking it off, I just don't think it's the time for us to— Okay, that's it. I'm hanging up. I'll see you in— Marty? Marty? Shit."

He stuffed the phone in his pocket and crossed the room to the desk, just in time to spy me rising on one elbow. He sank into a chair, head in hands. "Terrific. This is all I need."

"Your secret's safe with me, Tiger."

"Why don't I find that comforting?"

I gripped the back of the couch and rose unsteadily to my feet. "Look, I'm sorry. I took some really strong medicine for a migraine and it knocked me out. I needed a place to shut my eyes and didn't know if a bedroom was free."

He shrugged. "Life sucks, doesn't it?"

I wasn't sure if he was referring to his own or mine, but I nodded anyway. "Sorry to hear about your divorce." I sat back down with a thud.

"Ancient history. Sheila and I split up six years ago. I'm living with someone now, but, as you heard, things aren't going so well. Guess I'm not the domestic type." He grinned sheepishly. Distress suited him. "What about you? You seeing anyone?"

"Not really."

"That's a shocker. A woman like you, still unhitched? Can't believe you haven't had offers."

"I was married once, for about thirty seconds. I think I'm too independent for most men."

"No one in the picture right now?"

I shook my head, unwilling to go into the details about my nonexistent love life.

"So you're a P.I. now? What's up with that? You weren't sleuthing when you and I had our thing, were you?"

"No. I kind of fell into it."

"How's it going?"

I shrugged.

"That good?" He rose and came to sit beside me on the couch. "I like the barefoot look."

My hand shot out. "Whoa, Tiger—you've got enough trouble. Besides, I'm not myself at the moment."

"All the better." He slid closer, grinning wolfishly.

"Back off," I squeaked, feeling light-headed and vulnerable.

He laughed, putting a little space between us. "You kill me, Ricky, you really do. While the rest of us slog along in boring jobs, you're out there, aren't you?"

I sniffed. "Depends on how you look at it."

"So, how does one fall into becoming a P.I.?"

"Long story for another day."

"I'll look forward to hearing it. What's up with the limp?"

"I messed up my knee a few months ago. I'm waiting, hoping things will heal so I can avoid surgery."

"You may want to rethink that. I've had four knee operations, and everything's been fine. Just have to get the right surgeon."

"She's excellent. It's just I'm kind of tired of surgeries and hospitals."

"Yeah, I heard about your breast cancer. You okay now?"

"So far, so good. Been four years, almost five." I smiled wanly, grateful he had had the sensitivity not to stare at my chest while offering his condolences.

"Glad to hear it."

I leaned back, closing my eyes.

"Well, I'll leave you to your nap. Better see if I can help Bobby and Betsy get their rug rats into the car."

I closed my eyes and when I woke, the room was dark and Karen's voice called softly from above.

CHAPTER 7

"Ricky? You awake?" Karen flicked a desk lamp on, its soft green light casting shadows across the room. She held a tray of tea and cookies.

"Hey, you." I sat up, patting the couch beside me. "Sorry about the headache. Took me by surprise. Took two of my horse pills and they really knocked me out."

"Is it gone?"

"Mostly, and along with it millions of brain cells. Why are you whispering?"

"I'm hiding from Jay. He's driving me crazy. Thinks he's a mother hen. My mom's got Allie so it's just you, me and Jay. I wish he'd go back to Boston."

"I don't believe that's the arrangement he made with Marty." I grinned wickedly.

"Oh, God, have you met her?" I shook my head. "What a bitch. Jay knows how to pick 'em, doesn't he? Marty makes Sheila look like Mother Theresa."

"Even at sixty-two, he's too cute for his own good."

A smile played at the corners of her mouth. "You interested? He's always asking about you, you know."

"Tempting, but under the circumstances, probably best to keep my distance, at least until he's split with Marty."

"Oh, Ricky, I'm so glad you're here. I've got spare clothes, toothbrush, toiletries, anything you need."

"A nightshirt and toothbrush and I'll survive till tomorrow."

Her eyes filled up and she collapsed against me. I held her a long while, her sobs eventually quieting to sighs. Finally, she sat up and fetched a box of tissues and a pack of cigarettes from the desk. She placed the pack between us and lit up, dragging deeply, then leaned back to exhale.

"When'd you start up again?"

She took a long, deep drag. "Last week, right after they found Ron. Have one." She threw the pack across the table, pouring us each a cup of tea.

I accepted the tea, but put the pack aside, not willing to risk the resumption of a nasty habit that had taken me years to kick. "I'm sorry I haven't been around much, Karrie."

She shrugged. "That's life, isn't it? How have you been, anyway? I should have been in touch more after your surgeries. Are you okay?"

"Yes and no. Not much I can do about it. The reconstruction has helped."

"Have you been dating?"

"Not much."

"You deserve someone nice after that drunk, then that lying, cheating Michael."

"Now, now."

"He was your worst, I think. Just the right combination of snobbery and uselessness. None of us liked him."

"Thanks, I feel so much better."

"I mean, he was so arrogant and in love with his own voice. No one could get a word in edgewise. And he would drone on and on about the most boring things. Come to think of it, with his Libertarian views, he'd have fit right in with Ruth Bowen's crowd."

"Let's not talk about Michael, okay? My headache is finally going away."

"Are you seeing anyone?"

"Actually, I sort of met someone recently. I've been tailing him for his girlfriend. Name's Mark Fallon."

"That doesn't sound promising. Was he cheating?"

"Sort of."

"Ricky!"

"He's a nice guy. First one I've met in a long time. Now, now, don't get excited. It's not going anywhere. He's at least twenty years younger."

"Oh, boy."

"We had a beer one night. Period, end of story."

"I'd keep it that way, if I were you. You don't need another cheater. Have you been busy with the P.I. work?"

"Some insurance cases, research, online searches and stuff. Had one missing person case that kind of solved itself in six hours. I do glass commissions and repairs now and then, and some writing."

"Do you like it, the P.I. stuff?"

I shrugged. "How's Alex? I was surprised he wasn't here today."

"Poor thing. Keeps crying for Ron. He's twelve, but still acts as though he expects his father to walk through the door at any minute. What am I going to do, Ricky? Ron was everything to him. They were inseparable. I'm never home between the business and everything else and, let's face it, I'm a lousy parent. I'm not like homemaker Betsy or Earth Mother Val. Did you meet Val and Will?"

I nodded.

"I'm glad. They're nice people and they've been so helpful this past week since the accident." Her voice trailed off and I thought she might break down again. Instead, she squared her shoulders and sat up straighter, her mouth set as she flicked ashes into her hand.

"Want to tell me about it?" I said.

"Ron was on his way to get the papers. He always rides his bike into town on Sundays while Alex and I are at church. One of my few motherly duties—Alex's religious education. They called me out of the service. They had already taken him to St. Anne's in Fall River. He never regained consciousness. One of the women at the church took Alex, but by the time I got there, Ron was gone." Tears snaked down her pale cheeks, but she sat ramrod straight, determined to go on.

"I called Bobby and he came right up. Took care of everything, then drove me home. I asked him to stop where it happened. It was on Willow Road, just before the turn-off to Bridle Falls. A local woman, Mindy Church, found him and called the police. Cal Ripler responded, called the rescue and rode with Ron to the hospital. When we got to the scene all we found were papers scattered all over the place. It was obvious where he'd fallen. There was quite a lot of blood."

"What about the bike? Had the police already taken it away"

She shook her head. "Cal said they left it at the side of the road. Said that after they got Ron to the hospital, he sent Skip Burrows back with his truck to pick up the bike, but it was gone."

"What did the police say about that? Doesn't the missing bike suggest that the death might be suspicious?"

"No, Cal swears it was an accident. Claims he could tell by the way Ron fell. Says it looked as if he hit a patch of sand, skidded, then flipped over, hitting his head on a rock at the side of the road."

"No helmet?"

"The dog chewed it up a few weeks ago and he hadn't had time to replace it. Poor Gumbo. It wasn't his fault, but I haven't been able to look at him since it happened. He's Alex's puppy, a golden Ron bought him for his birthday. Bobby's taken him home for now."

"Karrie, what makes you think it wasn't an accident?"

"You know Ron, Ricky. He was the most cautious cyclist in the world. He always rode straight down the middle of the road and if a car came, he would usually come to a complete stop till they passed. There's no way he skidded."

"Maybe the car surprised him."

"Never. Ronnie's hearing was excellent."

"Have you told the police about your suspicions?"

"No."

"Why not?"

"I don't trust them and neither did Ronnie. They hated him and he hated them."

"You're not saying that they—"

"No, I don't believe Cal or Skip or any of them would do this, but I do believe that if someone they knew killed Ron and it was in their interest to keep quiet, they would."

"Are you sure about this, Karrie?"

She rose, pacing back and forth, arms folded across her chest. "I'm not sure about a lot of things right now, but I am absolutely certain Ron was murdered. You know what a gadfly he was. Always asking questions, stirring things up. It's been very ugly the last few years, but this past summer things grew downright nasty. It started last Memorial Day when Skip Burrows left an effigy of him on the steps of the Community Center just before the parade. It was horrible. We have photos of it somewhere. Bloodied face, swords through the heart, a sign round the neck saying 'King Harp.'

"He talked to Rebecca Morse and they thought about suing, but then Skip sent a long, heartfelt apology, admitting that he was trying to impress the veteran cops, his new colleagues."

"And the town didn't fire him?"

She laughed. "This is the Harbor, my dear. They don't fire 'up and coming' native sons who've wanted to be cops since their playpen days. It's not like they couldn't have spared him with the number of police in this town."

"How many are there?"

"Twelve, I think, including the chief. Chief Sisson is part-time, only works a few hours a day. There are actually two guys whose only job is to race around the shoreline in their sixty-thousand-dollar S.U.V.s and fancy Boston Whalers, all purchased with the drug forfeiture monies. You remember the drug bust about six or seven years ago? Netted millions of dollars for the town and it all goes to the police department. Those monies pay for exorbitant salaries, and they bank-rolled the construction of the new police-fire complex. Have you seen it?"

I shook my head.

"It's one of the many things Ron's been researching."

"I'd say you've got eight cops too many for Windy Harbor."

She nodded. "It's a scandal, really. A real embarrassment for the town when you think about it."

"So, if Ron was killed and the cops didn't do it, then who?"

"Have you got a month? It's a pretty long list."

The study door opened and Mother Hen appeared, carrying a tray of sandwiches and coffee. "Okay, ladies. Gotta keep up your strength. I've got turkey, lobster and chicken salad, and I think this is a portabella mushroom." He had changed into sweatpants and a faded Princeton tee shirt, his hair wet and rumpled, fresh from the shower.

Karen smiled and reached up to squeeze his arm. "What would I do without you, darling?"

Jay took a seat beside her. "Don't get too excited, sweetie. I just stuck 'em on the plate."

Karen selected a half of a turkey sandwich and a mug of coffee, neither of which she touched. Jay and I both ate a sandwich and a half, washing them down with mugs of strong coffee.

It was obvious Karen did not wish to discuss Ron's death with Jay so we talked about Alex, the farm, and plans for the next few days. Jay had already hired two village men to handle routine yard work. Alex was comfortably ensconced at Granny Spenser's, where he could stay indefinitely. Jay also told Karen that Granny Harp was ready to take over if reinforcements were needed.

Finally, the conversation dwindled and we retired, Jay to his attic loft and me to the guest room, grateful that there were two floors separating us. When I woke at seven he was gone, the house quiet and Karen still asleep after taking two sleeping pills.

CHAPTER 8

When I returned from a morning bike ride, I propped Karen's bicycle against the barn. I banged into the house, shirt soaked through with mist and sweat only to find Milly Spenser in the kitchen. She was alone, no sign of her daughter or grandson. I suspected that a game of cat and mouse was afoot. Guess who was the mouse?

"Morning," I said, grabbing paper towels to mop my brow, sitting, unstrapping my heavy knee brace, stretching both legs, my knee warm and surprisingly flexible.

"Dorothy, I'm so glad to see you getting around all right. How well you look, dear."

Milly never called me "dear" unless she wanted something. One time she thought I was encouraging Karen to smoke pot and had her husband offer me a thousand-dollar bribe if I'd find a new friend and leave Karen alone. Little did she know that Karen's boyfriend at the time, Dustin somebody-or-other, was our main supplier, with Karen getting a nice commission on every score. How did Milly think Karen afforded all those gorgeous designer clothes on the measly allowance she gave her? Maternal myopia, an interesting condition.

"Milly. Nice to see you. Where's everyone else?"

"Alex has a riding lesson and wanted his Mommie to drop him off. Karrie went into town to do a few errands. How's your knee today?"

"Much better, thanks." I guzzled several glasses of water, aware of her eyes following me as I hobbled round the room. She wanted something and was willing to bide her time to get it. Curiosity finally got the best of me. "Something I can do for you?"

"Yes, Ricky dear, there is." Milly never called me Ricky. She wanted something all right, and wanted it badly enough to use what she always called a "horribly common boy's name, instead of the lovely name your dear mother gave you."

"You can help us, help Karrie to find the truth."

"Excuse me?"

"Look into it. Stay here in Windy Harbor and make inquiries. See if there's any truth to my daughter's suspicions."

"Do you believe there is?"

"Frankly, I don't know what to believe, but that doesn't matter. Right now Karen believes Ron was murdered and we need to help her get through this." She reached down, heaving her Vera Bradley handbag to the table. It was one of the big ones, a bright yellow floral pattern with loads of pockets—de rigueur for the bridge and garden club set. "I'd like to give you a retainer now. I understand you charge one hundred dollars an hour plus expenses with a thousand up front. Am I right?"

"How did you—"

"I know the Biddles," she said, referring to a couple whose daughter had gone missing a few months ago. I'd managed to locate her two miles from home, shacked up with a guy from the wrong side of town. "Frankly, when Hazie Biddle told me your fees, my first thought was, 'highway robbery,' and it is, but I'd do anything for Karrie." She scribbled out a check, holding it out to me.

Three thousand dollars. "Milly, this is a little—"

"No, please." She raised her hand, willing me to silence. "Allow me to finish.

"I am asking you to drop everything and take this up. I've arranged accommodations at Peg and Bob Crawley's guest house. It's near the center of town. You can have it for two weeks. That should be sufficient time for you to wrap up your investigation and give us a complete report."

Is that so? I bit back a host of sarcastic remarks tickling the tip of my tongue. "Milly, I'd like to help, but this is way out of my league. If you'd checked any further than the Biddles, you'd know I've only been at this a few months. You need someone with experience."

"Dorothy, please, this is your oldest friend. What could be more important than helping her? This isn't the city, just a small, safe little town. It's not as if you'd come to any harm and it would put Karen's mind to rest, help her get on with grieving. Please, say you'll help us."

While I hated to give Milly what she wanted, I couldn't turn my back on Karen. Karen, who had sheltered me in the days and weeks after my mother's death. Karen, with whom I'd shared my deepest secrets, my biggest fears, my soulful longings. And I was between projects if I ignored the stack of work currently on my desk. Most of the current projects could be handled by phone or online. If I grabbed some materials from the office, I could probably spend a couple of weeks working out of town without dire consequences. "Let me see what I can do and I'll get back to you."

"Thank you, dear! I knew we could count on you."

"Now, wait a minute, I—"

"I'll let Karrie know immediately. No one knows about this except myself and Karrie. I'm going to call Jay, too. I think we ought to keep it very quiet, don't you?"

I smiled through gritted teeth. No one knew unless you counted the Ramseys, Morses, and all their fellow IMPACT members. For a second, I thought Milly meant to hug me, but my sweaty self must have warded her off. Gathering her things, she swept from the room, announcing that she was going to collect Alex from riding camp.

CHAPTER 9

I showered and left a note for Karen. The mud-encrusted Wagoneer started right up and I headed home, a thirty-minute drive. I live in the seaside community of Ocean Grove. Contrary to its name, the Grove, as it's known to locals, is many miles from the ocean, but does have a very nice, if slightly polluted, river running along its banks. My ricky-ticky cottage is right on the river, my neighbors to the south an elderly couple who love cocktails and entertaining, and to the north, a bodybuilder named Vinnie. Vinnie helps with most of my endless home restoration projects while Maddie and Fulty keep us well-supplied with cocktails and canapés. All in all, it is a perfect neighborhood.

The following morning, I rose, took a six-mile bike ride, then loaded my bike into the back of the jeep. I rummaged around, gathering piles of things I needed for a two-week stay. After packing two bags with clothes, Ace bandages, a light knee brace, and every pain medication I could lay my hands on, I rang Vinnie and arranged for him to feed Beaky, my cat.

Beaky did not take kindly to my absences and usually rewarded me with a week's worth of scratches upon my return. "There's my pretty girl," I cooed, reaching down to pet her as I flew out the door.

"Ra-ra-rah," she replied, turning up her nose as she strutted towards the living room to take up her favorite perch in the bay window. Beaky spent most of her daylight hours in the window, stalking seagulls. At night, if I let her out, she became

Beaky the Huntress, preying on blind, defenseless mice, moles and voles. In the morning, I'd find headless carcasses displayed like trophies on my back doorstep.

It was late morning when I got to my office. I have two rooms on the third floor of an old mill. The plumbing's iffy and the bottom floors crawl with outlet shoppers most days, but my space is cheap, quiet and private so I can't complain. I spent an hour listening to and answering phone messages. Then I went online, checked email, completed three reports for recent insurance cases, and rifled around for the papers and files I needed. It was after five when I finally finished up. I gave Karen a call, letting her know I was on my way. She invited me to dinner, saying that seven or seven-thirty would be fine. That would give me time to meet the Crawleys and move into their guest house.

I wrote a note to my assistant, Janice Cotter, who comes in Tuesdays and Thursdays to do typing and light office work, running documents to clients, handling the mail and cleaning up. There were four more reports to type up, but they were straightforward. Janice could easily finish up using my notes. In my note, I promised to call with a local number, but Janice had my cell phone number.

Janice had been working for me for two months and her presence was a real luxury. Thanks to a good year, some financial support from a family trust, and my relatively low overhead, I could afford her. And Janice possessed important qualities that I did not possess, but admired in others. She was quiet, efficient, and discreet. She was also itching to help with investigations, but so far, I hadn't pressed her into service. In her twenties, she had worked as a bank teller, secretary at a friend's insurance agency, and various other odd jobs before becoming addicted to Zumba and step aerobics. She taught six classes a week, making pretty good money, and she lived with a slightly seedy guy with a hefty income, so working two days for me suited her just fine.

As I rummaged in my tiny fridge, searching for a bottle of water for the drive, I heard footsteps, first on the stairs, then in the hall. Men's dress shoes, probably loafers. Not a sound one often hears in these parts. He knocked and shoved the door open all in one motion. I couldn't have been any more surprised if the Pope himself had stopped by. "Jay? How did you—? Why did you—? What's wrong?"

His face was flushed, probably from the exertion of taking three flights of stairs two at a time. His gray pinstriped suit was rumpled, tie loose, his hair mussed as if he'd been running his fingers through it in frustration, anger, or whatever emotion had seized hold of him. "Are you nuts?"

"I might ask you the same question. How did you find this place? And why in the world are you here?"

"Because at noon I received a call from Milly Spenser telling me you were 'on the case,' that's why. Are you, crazy? You'll only stir up a lot of trouble and—"

My hand shot up in a defensive pose. "Whoa, let's back up a little, shall we?" Motioning him to a seat, I asked if he wanted coffee or water. He shook his head simultaneously, grabbing the bottle of water I held out to him. "Now, what seems to be the problem?"

"My parents and brother live in Harbor. You go poking around, accusing people of things, and pretty soon they're taking the heat."

"What heat? What are you talking about?"

"It's a small town, Ricky. It's a delicate balance, you know? Ron wouldn't leave it alone, but the rest of my family would rather live quietly beside their neighbors."

"Even if one of those neighbors killed their son and brother?"

"Now, you know that's bullshit. This is Karen's grief and paranoia talking."

I tended to agree with him, except when I pictured the look of certainty I'd seen in Karen's eyes. There was a lot she hadn't told me, but she hadn't looked the least bit paranoid. Grieving, of course, and resigned in her belief that Ron had been murdered, but paranoid? No. "What about the bike? Karen says it's missing. How do you explain that?"

"It'll turn up."

"That's hardly the point, is it? It was a suspicious death. The police should have impounded that bike immediately."

"My brother fell off his bike. He was still alive when they got there so they rushed him to the hospital, trying to save his life for Christ's sake. It was an accident, Ricky. Ronnie had the bad luck to hit his head on a rock and—"

"His death should be investigated."

"I'm sure Chief Sisson is doing everything he can to see that a careful and thorough investigation is conducted."

"Yes, I've heard about him. Semi-retired, isn't he?"

"Sarcasm. That's just great. Ricky, for Karen's sake, leave this alone. It will only cause her more grief and it will drive my parents and Bobby's family crazy."

"Listen," I said quietly, my interest aroused by such impassioned pleading. "Milly's hired me for two weeks. I'll look into things quietly, then be on my way. Give me a little credit. I'm not planning to run around giving people the third degree. I do know how to be discreet." A little white lie never hurt.

He was still perched on the edge of his seat, but his expression softened. Dropping head to hands, he ran fingers through his thick, dark hair. When he looked up, chin on hands, hair mussed adorably, he was smiling. "I'm sorry. You must think I'm a world-class idiot."

"Grief will do that."

"I miss him," he said, so softly I barely made out the words. Tears rimmed his dark chestnut eyes, the first genuine sign I'd had that he was mourning his brother. "He was the family's conscience. Always fighting the good fight, never giving in. I wish he'd been happier. The fight cost him his marriage, his health, everything."

"He wasn't well?"

"Chronic ulcers for one thing. He also had skin problems, headaches, back problems. Guy was a mess and it was all stress. When you look at the three of us, you'd guess Ronnie's running would've kept him in better shape than Bobby or me, but not so. I mean, I've had my aches and pains, but I'm okay. Bobby drinks too much, but he's hardy as a horse."

"Where'd it come from?"

"Uh?" he looked confused, as if waking from his recitation of Ron's medical woes.

"The stress. Where did it come from?"

"Everything. You name it. He was always fighting with the Town Council, the police, people on town committees, wherever he thought he'd found corruption. It was endless."

"What were the fights about?"

He shook his head. "He didn't confide in me. All I know is what I read in the papers. You'd have to ask one of his IMPACT buddies about it. Someone like Becca Morse. She and Ron were thick as thieves. Have been for years, ever since high school."

"Rebecca Morse and Ron went to high school together?"

He nodded. "I'm surprised Karen never told you about that. Ron and Becca dated all through high school and college. My mother had already had one of Granny Harp's diamonds set as Becca's engagement ring."

"What happened?"

"Your friend happened. I was away in England that year, Ronnie's last at Yale. When I got back, Becca was ancient history and Ron was gaga over the beautiful artist he'd met in Providence. They met through a friend of yours, didn't they?"

I nodded, remembering the New Year's Eve party where Karen Spenser and I had first been introduced to Ron Harp. Tad Halsey's party on the East Side of Providence, not two blocks from the RISD campus where Karen had gone to college. Karen was instantly smitten, my reaction to Ron Harp less enthusiastic. Yes, he was handsome, but a little aloof and serious for my liking. But then, what did I know? I usually fell for drunks, cheaters or loudmouthed guys with beer bellies who knew how to have a good time and were invariably gone by morning.

"It was a great party," I said, talking more to myself than him. "The beginning of the affair, as they say. But I had no idea about Rebecca. Were she and Ron really over, do you think?"

"Far as I know. When Karen and Ron moved back to the Harbor, the Morses were living in Chicago. Becca was just out of law school and Pete was writing for a magazine, I think. I don't think they intended to come back here, but then his uncle had a stroke and duty called. Becca's a public defender in Newport and a damn good one from what I hear."

Interesting, I thought, wondering if the high school romance had been rekindled, but not wanting to ask him. Somehow, it felt like a betrayal of Karen.

He rose. "Look, I've kept you long enough. I'm sorry if I flew in here half-cocked. You heading home or back to the Harbor?"

"Harbor. You?"

"Not tonight. Gotta get home. This past week the work has really piled up. I'll try and get down Friday for the weekend. Can I take you to dinner Saturday? I know a really great place."

I studied his expression, his gaze friendly, not a trace of the "come hither" charm of the previous day. The man was a study in contrasts, which made him even more appealing. "Sure, that'd be great."

"I'll call you. You'll be at the Crawleys', right?"

No flies on him, I thought, amazed at the Harbor grapevine. I was going to have to be the model of discretion or I'd be run out of town on a rail. I handed him my card. "Not sure of the phone, but you can leave a message on my cell."

"I know the number." He smiled, the wolfish grin resurfacing. "Walk you to your car?" He watched as I rose slowly. "Or, can I give you a piggyback?"

"No thanks. I do it every day. It's just slow so you may want to make your escape."

"I'm in no hurry." His eyes watched my every move as I gathered my things. While we wended our way down three flights of stairs, I babbled on about the history of the building. He feigned interest, keeping up the friendly chitchat until we reached the parking lot. I heaved myself into the jeep, his hand on my elbow, then he slammed the door behind me.

I cranked down the window to say goodbye. "Thanks for the lift."

Winking, he turned, heading for his B.M.W. parked on the street. I was going to have to be careful, I thought, chugging out of the city, the lights twinkling on all round me. In my weakened, vulnerable state, I was going to have to be very careful indeed.

CHAPTER 10

After leaving I-195, I drove along country roads, small towns giving way to stretches of woods and fields as I came into Windy Harbor. Most Harbor homes are invisible from the road, hidden away at the far ends of long gravel or clamshell drives. This leaves the main road to open fields, woods and farmland, the landscape punctuated every mile or so by the occasional house, roadside stand, or greenhouse. I passed Harbor Vineyards, three hundred acres of woods, fields and vineyards just south of the village center. Beyond the vineyard, the Bluestone River emptied into the sea, curling round Nauset Point, site of the future Harbor Club.

The natives guarded the Harbor's treasures fiercely, its tawny fields surrounded by tumbling stone walls and five points of granite and shale coastline jutting into the Atlantic. Blue-green expanses of pond and wetland lay between each point and smaller ponds, lakes, and acres of woodlands stretched for miles in every direction.

Following Karen's directions, I turned off the main road at Red Gate Farm, heading down a long gravel drive to the Crawleys'. As I drove up, I spied both Crawleys in the yard of the main house. A friendly, middle-aged couple, soft around the middle, Bob was an insurance agent, Peggy a self-described "dabbler in real estate, antiques and other interesting ventures." He was in blue jeans and a sweatshirt, trimming bushes while Peggy, in a flowing mustard-and-black-patterned caftan, sat in a lawn chair, hooking a rug. They welcomed me like a long-lost relative.

After exchanging pleasantries and going through my all-too-familiar explanation of why I was limping, Peggy hopped up to give me a tour.

We breezed through the main house, filled with Shaker and colonial antiques, Peggy's collection of hooked rugs everywhere on floors, walls and tables. Finally, she led the way to the side yard and poured me a glass of iced tea, saying, "Here, this should perk you up. Now, come on back and see the cottage. I'm sure you want to settle in."

The cottage was several hundred yards from the main house. She suggested we take the jeep so she could show me "just where to park it." Bob stayed behind as Peggy and I drove round to the rear of their property. A separate driveway branched off to the barn and guest house. All the buildings were sided in weathered gray shingles, with shutters, trim, and doors a bright winterberry red that matched the farm's gate. Trees and hedges separated the main house and cottage, shielding each from the other's view.

The cottage's furnishings looked worn, but comfortable. A sagging couch and chairs covered in matching floral chintz faced the living room's fieldstone fireplace. The hearth was a massive granite millstone salvaged from a local grist mill. Bookshelves held an assortment of light summer reading, a few poetry books and paperback novels.

To the right of the living room were two tiny bedrooms, one with a bath. A galley kitchen was at the rear of the house, its window over the sink affording a lovely view of the fields and woods beyond. The house's nicest feature was an addition, an octagonal dining area added the previous year, according to Peggy Crawley. The room had floor-to-ceiling windows on six sides, while the seventh side held a pine hutch and the eighth the doorway to the rest of the house. She stood in the middle of the octagon, arms outstretched. "Lovely, isn't it?"

"Incredible." And it was, a beautifully crafted space, the vaulted ceiling solid mahogany. "Who built this?"

"Ralph Boardman. A bit of an odd duck, but he's a master builder. Does all kinds of carpentry projects, but these octagon rooms are his true art. He's built a couple of octagons for folks in town. Ruth Bowen has one, and Dickie Chaffee and his wife. Chaffees' is the largest. It's incredible. You'll meet Ralph soon enough. He's doing some work on the cottage. Exterior mostly, putting up storm windows, some minor sill repair. Milly said you wouldn't mind."

"Of course not," I said, wondering what other decisions Milly Spenser had made on my behalf.

"Well, now that you've got the lay of the land, how about some dinner?"

I explained that I was dining with Karen.

"Tomorrow night, then? We won't take no for an answer."

"Well, I don't want to be any trouble."

"Nonsense." She waved her hands. "We always wine and dine our guests when they arrive. Then it's hands off. Come to supper and we won't bother you again for the rest of your stay. I'll leave you to settle in. Remember, tomorrow, six thirty," she called over her shoulder, swishing out, her caftan a streak of flashing color. For a big woman, Peggy could move.

CHAPTER 11

After throwing my things in the cottage, I jumped into the jeep and headed for Karen's. When I arrived, I found Karen and Alex on the porch swing. They waved, coming to greet me. I hadn't seen Alex in six months and he looked as if he had grown a foot.

"Hey, big guy. How are you?" No response. I hugged his mom, peeking over her shoulder to wink at him. He rewarded me with a half-smile, then walked ahead of us into the house.

Karen started to call him back, but shrugged, leaning against me as we strolled up the flagstone walk. "He's a mess like his mom."

"Give him time. It takes a while and everyone has their own way of grieving."

I thought back to my own mother's death. My sister, Annie, and I had been older than Alex when we found her, in the closet under the stairs, gun at her side, blood everywhere. No ambiguity there, yet for six months, Annie still threw open our front door and called "Mama" every day after school, running from room to room, hoping to find Mama waiting, arms outstretched, for her "golden baby."

"I'm getting a nanny, one who's experienced with teens. She arrives Friday. She's coming from my college friend, Lila. 'Member her? Her kids are grown. The youngest just left for boarding school. Carly, the nanny, has been like a family member, so she stayed on till she could decide what to do next. She's great. We're very lucky to get her. I know, I know…he needs me. Don't say it, Ricky."

"I'm not saying a thing, Karrie." I shuddered inwardly, recalling the string of nannies and housekeepers my father had employed in the years before Annie and I were old enough to ship off to boarding school, but what did I know about Karen and Alex's life? Maybe a loving nanny would help ease the pain for both of them.

We ate in the kitchen, grilled chicken salad, warm rolls and butter, leftovers from the funeral. Alex ate two bites, then asked to be excused. Karen started to protest, but then sat back and let him go. After dinner, she went to find him and I cleaned up, made tea and went to sit in the living room.

Karen joined me shortly after and we sipped our tea in silence, the sweet warmth of almond and honey a soothing tonic. "Ricky, thank you for this. I hope my mom wasn't too obnoxious." I smiled, shaking my head.

"Should we get started, do you think? I have some things you should look at. They're in the study. Ron kept detailed files on everything and there are his computer files, too."

I wondered if I should tell her about Jay's visit, but decided to hold off. I followed her into the book-lined study with its leather coach, matching chairs and Oriental carpet, marveling at her late husband's tidiness. The books were categorized and alphabetized, not a volume out of place, the desk as trim and polished as a general's. In fact, until Karen began pulling files and folders from desk drawers and cabinets, I was having difficulty imagining any work taking place in such a rigidly ordered place. As I watched, she moved in staccato, like a pinball careening from side to side, no apparent rhyme nor reason to the materials she was pulling out and slapping on the desk. Finally, I grasped hold of her arm, leading her to the couch. "Karrie, let's sit down a sec, okay? I can go through all this later. Why don't we start at the beginning. Who do you think might have a strong enough reason to hurt Ron?"

"Lots of people and no one. That's the simple answer. To tell the truth, I've stopped listening these past few years. Ronnie hardly ever confided in me. I mean, he would have, if I'd asked him. It's just, I've been so busy and away so much and…he…"

Tears welled up in her pale eyes. Shaking herself, she straightened up, smoothing her chinos, wrapping her mauve silk cardigan tightly around her.

"In the past, his battles were mostly with Ruth Bowen, the Town Council President. You met her yesterday, right?"

I nodded.

"Ruth has her own little fiefdom here in town. Over the years she's parlayed a largely volunteer position as council president into a full-time, forty-hour-a-week job. Pays herself a salary through various contingency accounts. She's been on the Town Council, as its president, for over thirty years.

"She drove Ronnie crazy. He believed a lot of what she does is questionable, but so far she's proven herself to be untouchable. Most townspeople love her, think she does a great job and are grateful she's willing to put in the time for the town. So she keeps getting re-elected, most times by a landslide. She's a Republican. There are four on the council and one Democrat. They give the lone Democrat, Laura Morrow, a really rough time, but so far she's hanging in there.

"Did you meet her yesterday?"

I shook my head.

"She's a peach. A social worker. Husband works down at the navy base. Laura's a fighter, but she gets really discouraged. Without Ron and the others cheering her on, I'm sure she'd have given up long ago. She's been the top vote-getter the last three elections, but she desperately needs friendly faces on the council.

"Ronnie ran one year. Do you remember that? Lost by a narrow margin. That had Ruth in a panic. She circled the wagons, begged her supporters to come to the polls, and they didn't disappoint."

"So, how much of a threat was he?"

"Big-time. If Ron and another Democrat had gotten in, Ruth's life would have changed overnight. She spends eight hours a day at Town Hall ordering everyone around. If Ron had gotten in, that would have stopped the day after the election."

"So, he wasn't her favorite person?"

"Hated him and she was scared of him."

"Bad combination. So who else, besides Ruth Bowen, might've wanted Ron out of the picture?"

"Any of her lackeys, I suppose. If the Queen Bee went, they'd all be out before long. You saw them yesterday, trailing behind her. It's disgusting. At town meetings, one look from Ruth and Al Shortliff, the town moderator, cuts off any dissenting discussion. Then there's Tippy Bingham, a complete moron Ruth's installed on various committees. Went to college with her son, Trippie, lives in her guest house, an illegally built guest house, I might add. Doesn't that sound cozy? Tippy's a simpering toady, firmly under Ruth's thumb. But the most despicable of the bunch would have to be Sedgie Montgomery, the town solicitor. Wait till you meet him. I guarantee he'll make your skin crawl. 'Conflict of interest' is almost a religion with Sedgie. At the moment, he's pushing the council to okay building plans for the Harbor Club, a huge project at the point. Sedgie's wife is one of the principal investors."

"How much money are we talking about?"

"Millions. If the project is approved, the investors stand to make millions in membership fees alone. Apparently, they've already got over a million in signed membership agreements."

"And if it's defeated, Montgomery and friends stand to lose a bundle, right?"

She nodded. "I haven't been following this closely, but Rebecca could tell you. She's been helping Ron with that one."

"What about other investors?"

"You'd have to ask Becca, or Will Ramsey. He's been working pretty closely with Ronnie on a bunch of things. I've been away so much the past year, I'm really out of it, but I have a feeling most of the club's investors were from out of town."

"Anyone else I should know about?"

She laughed, leaning back on the couch. The Karen of our younger days peeked through for a fleeting second. "Have you got all night? This town is such a tangled mess going back four or five generations. Ruth Bowen's schoolmates, cousins, neighbors. The list goes on and on. She has this one guy, Georgie Wilbur—a perfectly harmless old guy. Sweet as a lamb when you talk with him, but there he sits on the council, nodding his head whenever the Queen Bee speaks. There've been rumors since his wife died he's romantically involved with Ruth, but I don't believe it.

"And let's not forget Patty Boardman. She definitely wasn't there yesterday. She's one of my sister-in-law Betsy's best friends, but she wouldn't dare set foot in my house. She and I nearly had a knockdown drag-out a few years ago. She's someone you have to see to believe."

"What was the problem between you two?"

"She runs a concession stand at the town beach—one of her many lucrative sidelines made possible through permission granted by the Beach Commission, of which she is President. My friend Connie's daughter, Kit, wanted to sell picnic basket lunches to boaters at the pier, and take orders from beachgoers as well. It was a small operation that wouldn't have hurt Patty's greasy hot dog stand one bit, but she blocked it nonetheless. Pushed for a special ordinance first through the Beach Commission, then the Town Council. I went to the council meeting to speak on Kit's behalf.

"Afterward, Patty and I got in a shouting match. It was awful. She actually shoved me. If Will Ramsey hadn't been there to hold him back, I'm certain Ronnie would have punched her. And, I fear my brave husband might have had his ass whipped. Patty's one tough cookie. Doesn't hurt to have a cousin on the police force. Cal Ripler, another charmer. You'll meet him."

"What about the police? Where are they with all this?"

"Useless. The only one I trust is Roger Demaris. He's on loan from Old Harbor. Young guys don't like him. According to Ronnie, Cal and Ruth have tried to get Roger fired a couple of times, but, Roger and the Chief go back a long way. As long as Chief Sisson stays, Roger does, too, or until Old Harbor insists he come home."

"Did you talk to him after the accident?"

"He's been in Virginia on vacation the past two weeks. Got back last night."

Karen's eyes fluttered closed. She leaned back, her brow etched with fresh lines, cheeks dark chasms in the soft light. I rose. "I'm going to head home and let you go to bed. I have plenty to get me started. I'll come back and have a look at all this tomorrow."

As I drove back to the Crawleys', I thought about Ron. Ron Harp, the relentless gadfly. His intelligent, reasonable convictions about right and wrong must have driven Ruth Bowen and Sedgie Montgomery crazy, but crazy enough to kill? That depended on the stakes, I decided, shaken back to reality by a battered van that nearly ran me off the road. I screeched to a halt at the entrance to Red Gate Farm, swiveling round too late to catch the license plate. It was a white van with a red "I Love Windy Harbor' (a heart substituted for "Love") on its rear bumper.

I drove on, a bad feeling settling in my chest. Sure enough, when I opened the cottage door, my few belongings were thrown hither and yon, the house a mess of open drawers and scattered furnishings. "Shit," I muttered, eyeing the contents of my briefcase strewn all over the bedroom. It appeared to be malicious mischief rather than a methodical search, but it was still a pain in the neck. I went out on the porch, craning to see the main house through the hedges. The windows were dark.

I slammed back inside, intending to pick things up, then stopped. Grabbing the phone, I dialed 911 and gave the dispatcher my location. I told her about the break-in and asked for Roger Demaris.

"Hold on a sec and I'll see if he's here." She set the phone down, returning several minutes later. "On his way, hon. Hold tight."

CHAPTER 12

I made myself a cup of tea and sat down to wait, calculating how many hours it would take to reassemble the files and records scattered round me. There was nothing related to Ron's death. The intruder had made a mess for the sake of making a mess and now it would take a day to sort through the hundreds of tiny notes and scraps of paper strewn on the floor, bed and furniture.

A few minutes later, a knock rattled the screen door. I opened it to find two men waiting on the stoop. The first appeared to be in his late thirties, early-forties, about my height, dark, wavy hair, deep blue eyes. He wore khakis and a windbreaker. Aside from a slight paunch round his middle, his wiry frame exuded power and strength. His companion, in uniform, looked to be in his twenties, carrot-red hair, about six-two.

"Detective Demaris, I presume."

Demaris clasped my extended hand firmly, gesturing to his companion. "This is Pete Dugan." The other nodded, but remained silent. "Now, what seems to be the problem?"

I stepped aside, gesturing. "I just moved in this evening. Went out to dinner and returned to this."

"Don't s'pose this is just messy housekeeping?"

"In my wildest moments, I've never been this messy. Not a very friendly welcome on my first night in town."

Dark eyes scanned the room. "Anything missing?"

"Not that I can tell."

"Thought not."

"Excuse me?"

"Looks like a prank. You know, kids foolin' around."

"Is that what the kids in this town do for kicks?"

"Hold on now. Don't get yer knickers in a twist. That's not what I'm sayin'. Just that this looks like someone was fooling around, not looking to steal anything."

"That's exactly what I thought."

"Any idea who?"

"It's your town. You tell me."

"Why exactly are you here, Miss…?"

"Steele, Ricky Steele."

"Ms. Steele, what brings you to the Harbor?"

"A friend's husband just died. I came to be with her for a few weeks."

"Ronnie Harp? So, you're the friend of Karen's everyone's buzzin' about." He walked through to the bedroom, eyeing the papers scattered around. "What kinda work do you do?"

I suspected he knew the answer. "I'm a private investigator. Insurance work, mostly."

"What's with the Ace bandages? You planning to host the track team?"

I looked around, noticing the unraveled bandages thrown hither and yon. "I have a bad knee. Never know when it'll need extra strapping."

"What're all these papers?"

"Clients' records, case notes, everything I needed to finish my current cases. I brought everything down to work on while helping Karen."

"Not very organized, are you?"

"Look, Detective, if you've nothing to add here, I'll just clean up and go to bed."

"Why'd ya call me?"

"I felt it was my civic duty to report a break-in."

"Bullshit." He arched his brow, calling to his companion. "Pete, run out to the car and get the print kit, would you?" Pete hesitated. "Go on. I'm not gonna dust the place, but I need somethin' in there."

As soon as Dugan stepped out, Demaris turned to me. "You want my help, don't you? And you were willing to make this god-awful mess in order to get it."

"You think I did this? That's perfect!"

"Well, didn't you?"

"No."

"Why'd you ask for me?"

"Karen said you're the only cop she trusts."

"How'd ya know I was on duty?"

"I took a chance. Now, tell me about Ron Harp."

He laughed, hands on hips, regarding me. "Lady, I don't know shit about this. I've been out of town."

"But you have to have questions."

"Not my case. Was an accident, from what I've heard."

I studied his expression, but my scrutiny told me nothing. "Where's the bike? Surely you don't think it wheeled off on its own?"

He shrugged. "Could be lots of explanations, but let's leave 'em for now, shall we? Here's Pete."

Taking the bag, Demaris made a show of removing a pad of paper, jotting down a few notes. When finished, he looked up at me, expression softer. "Want us to help you clean up?"

"No, thanks."

"Gonna be a job what with that bum leg and all."

"Thanks, but I can handle it."

"We'll make some inquiries, check with Bob and Peggy in the morning. Don't s'pose they saw anything."

"The house was dark when I got back."

"They go to bed real early," Pete said. The first words he'd spoken since their arrival. I wondered who else knew about the Crawleys' early bedtime.

"Pete, why not just take a flashlight and shine it round the backyard. See if you spot anything unusual. I'll be right out." The door closed and Demaris turned back to me. "Ronnie was good people. A little over zealous at times, but a good guy."

"So you were friends?"

He smiled, zipping his windbreaker. "I knew him, but we weren't bosom buddies. I'd like to hang on to my job and Harp wasn't one of the department's favorite people."

"Why are you telling me this?"

"Because I don't like messing with people and sometimes this town goes too far. I'd watch yourself, Miss Steele. You're not gonna be popular if you start pokin' around askin' about missing bikes, especially missing bikes that went missing in the middle of a police investigation."

"But you could look into it, couldn't you?"

"Have you been listening to a thing I've said?"

"There's something wrong here and you know it. Ruth Bowen and her crowd don't scare me and neither does malicious mischief."

"That's the spirit. Go get 'em." He was smiling, but I sensed a seriousness in his gaze. If I played my cards right, I might have an ally in Roger Demaris.

Dugan returned, having found nothing. "Well, that's it for now, I guess. We'll head out, let you get to bed. I'll send someone over in the morning to take another look around outside. Come on, Pete." Demaris slipped me a card on his way out. "Use the home or cell number if you want. Pete's is there, too."

The wind howled as I cleaned up, finally flopping into bed shortly after midnight. A loose shutter clattered against the house as I dozed off to dreams of gremlins running back and forth over the bedclothes, scattering Post-it notes in their wake.

CHAPTER 13

Exhausted after a fitful night's sleep, I rose sore and achy from my bed 'o rocks mattress. I pulled on sweats and sneakers, did a few yoga stretches and pushed my bike out the back door. After the malicious mischief episode, I decided it was safer in the cottage. It's a lightweight but rugged mountain bike, with wide thick tires and a very comfortable seat. Peggy had mapped out a "beautiful route" the evening before, so I headed off in the early morning fog for a ride through the woods behind the property, following a four-mile dirt path that circled Long Pond.

I returned to the cottage, my body tingly, revived and ready to face the day. I showered, changed into jeans and a tee shirt and warmed up a blueberry muffin, which I had with a large mug of tea. After breakfast, I limped up to the main house, my knee stiff from the bike ride.

Peggy was in the kitchen, Bob nowhere in sight. She offered coffee, donuts and fruit, but I declined, telling her I was saving myself for dinner. She hadn't heard a thing the previous night, but promised to ask Bob when he got back from town. "Of course, you know we're dead to the world by eight thirty. And I mean, dead. We hear nothing unless Skeeter barks. And she's getting deaf, poor old girl."

Back in the cottage, I spent an hour organizing and sorting the mess of notes and papers from my briefcase. Finally, I gave up, grabbed my bag and headed into town. My first stop was the scene of the accident. Karen had described the place exactly, drawing me a small map. Once I drew near, the map wasn't necessary. A brown stain, two feet wide, marked the place where he'd fallen, several feet from the side of the road.

Nearby, a ridge of rocks defined the shoulder, beyond which the grass was torn up. Why? Had the bike flipped over onto the grass, and if yes, then why hadn't Ron gone with it? Skid marks ran off the road into a large patch of sand. Why was the sand here in such quantity? Surely this was more than the leftovers from winter snowstorms. And why had it accumulated in that particular spot, just as the road dipped down into the shadows? Why not at the bottom of the dip where he'd fallen?

Remnants of last Sunday's newspaper clung to bushes and branches at the edge of the woods. It hadn't rained since the accident so in addition to the spot on the road, Ron's blood dotted several boulders. Why were these rocks scattered so close to the road, a good ten feet from a crumbling stone wall? One couldn't have devised a worse hazard for such a spot. At this point, a cyclist would be moving, trying to build momentum for the steep hill ahead.

I sat on a rock. The distant bark of a dog and the intermittent chirping of a warbler were the only sounds to punctuate the silence. Kicking a stone with my toe, I reached for a stick to draw pictures in the sand, a favorite childhood pastime. Instead of wood, my hand pulled up a thin metal spoke partially wedged under the rock. Hollow and light, it was bent and broken at one end. Scrambling around, I scoured the grass around the rocks, but found nothing more. At last I stood up, my jeans grass-stained, knee throbbing. As I limped back to the jeep, I slipped the spoke into my purse, deciding that for now at least, it was finders keepers. What kind of an accident would cause spokes to pop off? It could have lain there six months or a year, of course, since aluminum doesn't rust, but I would bet a month's salary that it came from Ronnie's bike.

Unlike on the main road, a number of houses on Willow were visible from the street. Two homes stood within sight of the crash. I considered knocking on their doors, but since no cars were in the drive, I decided to head into town. Hoping to speak to Mindy Church, the woman who had discovered Ron, I parked in the library lot. I found her behind the desk, a stack of returned books in front of her. She appeared to be running bar codes under the scanner. Fortyish, I guessed, a few streaks of gray in her short brown hair, reading glasses perched at the end of her nose. Totally absorbed in her task, she did not notice my approach. When I cleared my throat, she jumped. "Oh, dear, sorry." She blushed, clutching a Ruth Rendell mystery to her chest.

I identified myself and she said, "Yes, I heard about you."

I asked if we could talk for a few minutes and she apologized, claiming she was late for a staff meeting. "You've caught me on a bad day. I'm running in fifty directions, trying to get my work done."

"Just a few minutes, please. For Karen's sake, I'm trying to understand what happened to Ron Harp."

"Isn't that the police's job?"

"I'm helping out a dear friend, trying to ease her mind. Please, just a few minutes."

"Ms. Steele, I can't. I just can't today. My family's leaving for a long weekend at two this afternoon. I have no time. Please, you do understand, don't you?"

I smiled, graciously accepting defeat. "Maybe we can chat when you get back?"

She nodded and returned to her work.

CHAPTER 14

I pulled into the parking lot of the police-fire complex, marveling at how the spanky new building fit into its surroundings. Despite strong opposition from groups like IMPACT and Harbor Conservation, the construction had been financed with funds from the multimillion-dollar drug forfeiture case. Perched on a grassy knoll, the rambling shingled structure looked as if it had been erected and lovingly maintained by the village founders for centuries, the church's white spire just visible to the east over the rooftops.

As I strolled into the airy, open reception area, a beefy young man with a florid complexion eyed me from behind the desk. His name tag read, "William Larabee." I nodded and asked to see Chief Sisson. "Not in. Can I help you, Miss? I'm Billy, Billy Larabee."

I smiled my innocent *helpless little ole me* smile. "How about Cal Ripler?"

"Out."

"Skip Burrows?"

"In the gym, liftin'."

"Excuse me?"

"This must be your first time in the building?"

I nodded. "Don't s'pose you'd have time to give me a tour?"

He shrugged, heaving himself off his stool. Officer Larabee showed no visible signs of having availed himself of the gym. I followed as he led the way down a hall of offices, all unoccupied, the doors open except one at the far end. Stopping at this office door, I read the name plate, Detective Demaris, and peeked through the glass window. The empty office provided a sharp contrast to the sterile, largely vacant and spotless offices of his colleagues. This space looked lived-in, his desk a mass of papers, empty coffee cups and takeout food containers.

We descended the stairs to the basement hallway, doors on the right leading to the fire station garage. To our left was another hallway, which Billy headed down, passing men's and women's locker rooms and a glass-fronted, fully-equipped weight room. Empty, no one in sight. At the end of the hallway, Larabee threw open double doors, revealing a full-size basketball court. "Pretty nice, huh?"

I whistled.

"We were s'posed to get a pool, but the town got stingy."

"Imagine that. This must be a great community resource. Is it well-used?"

"Only members of the force have access."

"You're kidding."

"Nope. Security, you know? Can't have the general public running around in a police facility."

I bit back a sarcastic remark, asking instead if we might pop back into one of the other rooms to see if Skip was around.

"You sit tight. I'll see if I can find him."

He disappeared through the next set of doors and returned in less than a minute. "Sorry, Miss. Skip's in the showers. He's gotta go out on a call right after. Says he'd be happy to chat if you stop back later."

I'll just bet he is, I thought, smiling at Larabee, wondering if he was as clueless as he seemed.

CHAPTER 15

I fared no better at the Town Hall, where I was informed that Mrs. Bowen was out of the building at a meeting. Frustrated, I wandered around the town green and into the cemetery. I strolled back and forth, reading old gravestones, the damp, oaky smell of freshly fallen leaves reviving my spirits. My knee felt stable and strong, nary a limp. As I emerged at the far end of the graveyard, I spied Will Ramsey, newspapers under one arm, coming out of the general store. He waved. "Hey, Ricky, I heard you'd moved in. Welcome."

We chatted for a few minutes as cold seeped into my thin jacket. I shivered, rubbing my arms.

"Hey, you look frozen. Come on, I'll buy you a cup of coffee."

I followed him into the Lunch, the greasy-spoon establishment attached to the general store. As we settled at a table in the corner, I gazed around, recognizing several faces. Ruth Bowen held court in a booth in the far room, five admirers surrounding her. At an adjacent table, a group of policemen and firemen, HFD stitched on gray uniform shirts, feasted on mountains of eggs, potatoes, johnny-cakes, and country-style hash. "So this is where everyone is," I whispered as a red-haired waitress, Tessa, her name emblazoned over her ample left breast, arrived to take our order. I ordered tea, Will a decaf. Several minutes later, Tessa returned, setting down our drinks. "Get you folks anything else?"

Will winked at her. "Thanks, Tess, I think we're all set." Tessa winked back, waving over her shoulder as she sauntered toward the far room.

Noticing my gaze, Will blushed. "It's all a game. Makes it easier if you work in town."

I gestured toward the far room. "I've been trying to find these people all morning. Is this where they spend the day?"

"Most of it. Ninety percent of the town's business happens at the Lunch since Ruth Bowen usually eats breakfast, lunch and dinner here."

"I hope they give her a discount."

He leaned forward, whispering. "She runs a tab. Rumor has it her monthly bill is less than a single dinner for a family of four."

"Some tab," I replied, sipping my tea. As Will and I chatted, I continued to glance at the group in the next room. Invariably, one of Ruth Bowen's co-conspirators was staring back at me.

Returning my attention to our table, I said, "Will, tell me about Ronnie's recent projects."

"Not here. The walls have ears. Why don't we take these and head back to my office? It's just up the street." He rose, leaning over the counter to retrieve two Styrofoam cups. After transferring our coffees to takeout, he threw a few dollars on the table and we headed out. Will kindly offered to carry my cup after watching it slosh and spill as I limped.

CHAPTER 16

Will's office occupied half of a one-story cape across from the parsonage at the far end of the green. The other half of the building was used by Harbor Realty, owners of the building. Kitty Collias was the sole owner and full-time realtor. Will and Kitty shared a receptionist and secretary, an arrangement Will said worked fine except at tax time and the height of summer rental season.

Will introduced his receptionist, Lotty Mendoza. She greeted me coolly, looking relieved when the phone rang and she could turn away. We stepped into the office and he closed the door behind us, clearing piles of file folders off a chair. "Lotty's okay, just married into a mess, the whole Mendoza family. Hank's a jerk. Don't know how she stands him. He's one of Ruth's appointees, part-time police officer assigned to animal control. Useless in most cases. Sit, please. Sorry about the mess. I had just started a massive rearranging project when Ron died. It's thrown me for a loop, I'm 'fraid. I don't seem to be able to get back to my routines."

"Talk to me. What's going on?"

"Nothing…a lot of things…it could be…I honestly don't know. Truthfully, I'd have been less surprised if something had happened to Ron or one of us last year when things were really nasty."

"How so?"

"It's a long story. Ron's been fighting these people for years. If it's not one thing, it's another. Last year the biggest fights were about the open meetings law. Ruth's notorious for making all her decisions behind closed doors. That way everything's decided before the Town Council meets. Then she just puts on a show, the vote's taken, and it's a done deal.

"Ron and a group of us went to the state attorney general. Becca, Rebecca Morse, prepared a report or some kind of statement. She and Ron were the spokespersons, but I went, and Dick and Myra. Peter Morse, Becca's husband, went too. At great personal and financial risk to himself, I might add. Could have lost a lot of local business for the greenhouse. Fortunately, a good seventy percent of Morse's business is out-of-towners or summer people now. Ten years ago, an action like that would have ruined them.

"Anyway, the attorney general supported us and the Town Council was cited for the violation of the open meetings law. Got a big fine, too. You can imagine how happy that made them. Anyway, since then, all meetings have been videotaped, even lesser committee meetings like the Beach Commission, Budget Committee, and of course, the School Committee. And Ruth has to post notice a week in advance when she meets with more than one council member on an ad hoc basis between meetings."

"Does she do it?"

He laughed. "Did you see who she was with back there? Tippy and George are on the council. Sally's not, but she's pretty tight with them."

"Sally?"

"Sally Williams. She and her husband Patrick are the unofficial town archivists/historians. She's an open-minded, thoughtful person, Patrick, too, but unfortunately, most of the time, they take the party line."

"How does Bowen get away with it?"

"Says her time at the Lunch is social. There's only so much anyone can do. We all work full-time. We can't follow her around, eavesdropping on her conversations. And if we did, I'm sure Cal or Skip would be happy to slap us into one of their shiny new jail cells."

Why hadn't Billy Larabee showed me these shiny new cells on my tour? Hmmm. "So open meetings are happening, sort of. What else?"

"Well, there's the ongoing battle over the Harbor Club. We've only been peripheral players in that. Ron objected, as we all did, but he was less concerned with blocking the club than he was about public access, and Sedgie's involvement, of course. In fact, those are the only reasons he got involved in the first place. Ron and Becca backed by someone at state petitioned for guaranteed public access, once the club was built. They also cited conflict of interest related to Sedgie. This forced him to remove himself from Harbor Club discussions. He's now got a colleague from his law firm representing the town on any matters pertaining to the club."

"No conflict there."

Will laughed. "Oh, he's still got his hands all over it, believe me. Sedgie has a lot riding on that project."

"What else was Ron involved in?"

"There was the land dispute at Button's Marsh. Big developer from Boston trying to put twenty-five houses on the bluff. Someone called Ron, asked him to get involved."

"Who?"

"Not sure, but Karen or Becca would know. And it would be in his notes. Ron was meticulous about recording everything. I honestly don't know anything about that. Happened last year during tax season and I was buried. I think Myra and Dick were helping out one since they live quite near Button's Marsh."

"What else?" I asked, my head swimming in small-town squabbles, none of which sounded like motive for murder, except perhaps the millions tied up in the Harbor Club.

He removed his glasses, rubbing his eyes. He looked younger without them, like a teenager caught sitting behind his dad's desk playing office. "The list goes on and on. There's Karen's fight with Patty Boardman."

"She told me about that."

"Vicious woman, very tight with Bowen and her crowd. And, of course, the building inspector. I don't know much about that, but his name came up at one of the IMPACT meetings last summer. One of the group—I think it was Ramona Souza—had a complaint from a new property owner. Again, you should ask Becca or Mona."

"What's the inspector's name?"

"Carl Acevedo. About once or twice a week you might find him at Town Hall. Otherwise, he's at home. Operates a semi-illegal pig farm on West Shore Road. He's not a pleasant fellow. DEM fines him once or twice a year for some violation or other as his pigs create a terrible stench. Neighbors are always complaining. Oh, and one other interesting fact about Acevedo. He's Ruth Bowen's second cousin."

"Cozy."

"There was also the Memorial Day parade last year and the very ugly episode with Ron's effigy. Pretty horrible. Ron and Skip Burrows nearly came to blows in the post office several weeks after it happened."

The phone rang and Will picked up, listening for several minutes. "Thanks, Lotty. Tell him I'll be with him in five minutes."

I returned Will's files to their place on the chair. "You've got work to do. I'll get out of your hair."

"Just set those folders on the floor, would you? I've got a client coming in. Thanks."

As I turned back, I found Will scanning materials on his desk, taking thirty seconds to prepare for his client. "I'm sorry, Will. Can I ask you one more thing?"

He looked up, folding his hands over the papers. "Shoot."

"What I've heard so far sounds like typical small-town turf wars, you know, old guard versus the newcomers. Ugly and stupid, but murder? Do you really think any of Ron's work would get him killed?"

He regarded me quietly for over a minute, his gaze soft and faraway. "Honestly, no, but then, I'm not sure I'm the best person to ask. I've been very involved with

IMPACT, but I've only known Ron and Karen a few years. There are other people who'd know better."

"Thanks, Will. See ya."

When my hand was on the doorknob, he came from around the desk and stood close, whispering. "Ask Becca about the permits for the golf course. Also, I know she's been helping Ronnie sort through how Ruth pays herself a salary when there's no line item in the budget for that. And better check with Dick Chaffee about the Conservation Commission, too. He used to serve until Ruth had him kicked off. They've been involved in some questionable land purchases. Dick, Myra or Becca would know."

As I passed the reception desk, Lotty Mendoza kept her eyes glued to her paperwork. I wondered if she had just raced back to her swivel chair after listening at the keyhole.

CHAPTER 17

As I made my way to the jeep, I spied Cal Ripler emerging from the Lunch and waved. "Lieutenant Ripler, hello!"

Confused, he studied me for a second, his expression soon clearing. He knew who I was. How nice. He swaggered toward me, body language screaming, "Watch out, I'm the law." In plain clothes—dark slacks, navy sweater, a lightweight gray police department jacket slung over his shoulder—he towered over me. I guessed him to be in his late thirties, at least six-six, broad shoulders, hefty gut, short, dark hair, cold chestnut eyes. "Miss Steele, isn't it?"

"Yes, hi." I extended my hand, which he shook firmly, then returned hand to hip, resting it just under a bulge I assumed was a shoulder holster.

"What can I do for you?"

"I wonder if you'd have a few minutes to talk to me about Ron Harp's accident. I'm a friend of the family and—"

"Honey, I know who you are. Aren't you a little long in the tooth for this kind of work?"

I smiled through gritted teeth as every part of my body longed to lunge for his throat. "I do all right."

"Well, babe, I'll give you a tip. We don't much care for private dicks. Police force takes care of things around here."

Biting back so many sarcastic remarks I nearly choked myself, I kept my smile firmly in place. "I understand completely. I'm really just helping a friend work through her grief. You understand, don't you? After a death people seek closure in many different ways."

He studied me for a long minute, as I struggled to keep a smile plastered on. "Sure, why not? Follow me back to the station and I'll give you a couple minutes. Unless that heap of yours needs a rest, in which case I'll give you a lift. By the looks of things, you need a lift, too. Should I call for a stretcher?"

I wondered how long I could keep my temper without bursting blood vessels. "No, thanks. I'll follow you."

He winked, heading to his car, a shiny black S.U.V., "Harbor Police and Rescue" emblazoned on the door. When we arrived at the station, he ushered me into the second office on the corridor, promising to return "in a sec." Fifteen minutes later, he sauntered in, apologizing about the "urgent police business" that had delayed him.

"So, hon, what can I do for ya?"

Usually people who call me "hon," "honey," or "babe" do it only once. In this case, I grimaced, again holding my tongue, the adage *catch more flies with honey* running over and over in my head like a mantra. "I'd really like to hear about Ron's accident. Who found him, what the scene looked like, the bike, the road, the rock."

"Have you been out there yet?"

I nodded.

"So you've seen the road. We've had bike mishaps along that stretch before. Light's poor. Biker comes outta bright sunlight into deep shade in the middle of a steep downhill. Mindy Church found him. She's our assistant librarian. Have you met her?"

I nodded.

"Was pretty shook up. Found him lying there on her way back from church. Goes to the Episcopal service. It lets out a little earlier than the white church. Mindy ran to Cliff Wright's just down the road. Cliff called me then came back with Mindy to stand watch over him. We were there in less than five minutes. Rescue, too. He was still breathing. Rescue bundled him up and took him to St. Anne's. My guys cleaned up the road, got Mindy home safe, and that was that."

"What about the bike?"

"Ended up at the dump, I s'pose. There was no savin' it. Wheel was wrecked, frame all bent. He hit a rock and flipped right over. The bike was all twisted, one of those new, lightweight pieces of shit. Built to go fast, but not much else."

"Didn't you think the family might want it?"

"Nothing left. Thought it might upset 'em."

Incredulous, I willed my voice to remain friendly, neutral. "What about the possibility that it might be evidence? Don't you usually investigate when an accident results in death?"

"Hon, what did I just tell you? We did investigate. It was an accident. A terrible, unfortunate accident, that's all. The town is still recovering from the murder last year, our first in forty years. I wanted to wrap this up, get things in order quick as possible. Let the family grieve and the town move on."

"But—"

"Listen, hon, I'd love to sit here chatting, but I do have work to do. If there's nothing else?"

"Of course," I said, rising. I had a hundred more questions, but it was clear the answers would be the same. At the door, I turned back. "When you cleaned up, did you bring anything back to the station?"

He hesitated for a second, staring at me before replying. "Nope, not a thing. All Harp's things went with him in the ambulance."

"Who was on duty in the van that day?"

"E.M.T. was Pat Reid. Aggie Bruner was the aide. She's one of our volunteers. Not a trained E.M.T., but she helps Pat."

As I stepped out of the office, I heard Roger Demaris's voice at the far end of the hall. He appeared to be on the phone. I poked my head back in. Cal looked up from shuffling a stack of papers. "Did you know I was broken into last night? The Crawleys' guest house where I'm staying?"

He nodded. "Rodge and Pete filled me in this morning."

"Any idea who might have done it?"

"Search me. Sounded like kid stuff."

"Think you'll catch them?"

He shrugged. "Better check with the investigators on that case. I'm up to my eyeballs in other stuff."

"About the bike. I work for several insurance companies and I've been involved in a lot of accident investigations. No one ever takes evidence from the scene to the dump."

"Who said we did?"

"But you said the bike was probably in—"

"Listen, Miz Steele, maybe where you come from, the cops hand any broad off the street evidence in an ongoing investigation, but that's not how we do things in the Harbor."

"You're saying you're still investigating, then?"

"Nope."

"Are you saying you do have the bike?"

"No." Red blotches were creeping up his neck.

"Then who does?"

"Look, I'm really busy, so if you don't mind."

"It was gone when you went to pick it up, wasn't it?"

"Get out. And close the door behind you."

CHAPTER 18

I closed Ripler's door and made my way toward the front door. Roger Demaris sounded like he was still on the phone so I did not drop in to say howdy-do.

It was nearly noon so I headed back to the Lunch, hoping to catch a glimpse of Bowen and her co-conspirators. As I chewed my BLT very slowly, I listened to a couple of farmers discussing crop rotation, the assistant minister and sexton arguing about placement of spring bulbs, and two housewives describing their children's Halloween costumes. I was just paying my check when Peter Morse arrived with a half-dozen men in overalls and work boots, the crew from the greenhouse.

As the gang headed for back booths, Peter came to greet me. "Hey, Ricky, how's it going? Hear you've taken up residence." Pale blue eyes regarded me warmly.

"Word travels fast." I resisted the urge to reach over and wipe a smudge of dirt from his freckled cheek and smooth his curly red hair tamped down with a bad case of "cap head." When I'd first met Peter, he was thin with the pale faced look of academia. Now he was a robust, rosy cheeked farmer, his shoulders and arms sinewy and strong.

"You're welcome to join us."

"Thanks, but I just ate. You better go. Looks like the guys are ready to order."

He shrugged. "They'll order for me."

"Peter, I'd really like to talk to Rebecca. Is she hard to reach during the day?"

"This week, yes. Sometimes she has open office hours, but she's in the middle of a trial. She expects it to end by Friday or early next week. But come by the house anytime in the evening. She'd love to see you."

"Thanks. I'll give you a call."

CHAPTER 19

I drove back to the Crawleys' for a half-hour nap. Then, tea in hand, I spread all my paperwork on the kitchen table and spent the rest of the afternoon sorting and organizing. I typed two reports, and since I had no printer, emailed both to Janice with instructions to mail them out. It was just before six when I remembered I had nothing to take to my hosts for dinner, so I buzzed back to town and stopped at the liquor store for a bottle of wine. I also ran into the general store for some breakfast supplies, snacks and a few staples to keep me from starving until I got to a real market.

At exactly six thirty, I presented myself at the Crawleys' back door, wine in hand. Bob greeted me and we followed our noses to the kitchen, where Peggy was putting the finishing touches on dinner, a leg of lamb prepared with garlic and rosemary. Looking around, I marveled at the spacious farm kitchen with its deep expanses of wooden countertop, enormous black slate sinks, and massive cast-iron cookstove. A long maple deacon's table ran the length of the room. Above it hung a rack of the gleaming copper kettles and cast-iron pans. Walls and ceilings held an extensive collection of antique cookware, from hammered tin pie plates to shiny copper ice cream and candy molds. I thought about the hours of polishing, my own copper pots blackened beyond salvation after years of neglect.

We had drinks in a cozy, wood-paneled den, a fire blazing in a field stone hearth identical to the one in the guest house. Peggy served dinner precisely at seven in a spacious dining room, the walls adorned with murals depicting a small town that was clearly not Windy Harbor.

"Karen Harp originals," Bob said, noticing my gaze. "Had 'em done as a surprise for my bride in '82, the year we bought the place. That was before I retired, so we were only using it summers and weekends. The murals are of Duxbury, actually kind of an idealized Duxbury of yesteryear. Town's changed quite a bit the last twenty years. Peg grew up there, hated to leave, so I had this done to ease her separation anxiety."

Peg smiled, taking her seat. "Took me longer than Bob to see the charms of the Harbor."

"But now you do?"

"Oh, yes, but if you'd asked me five years ago, I'd have said, 'Get me out of here.' It's pretty and all, but it takes a while to break into things, if you know what I mean. We had so many friends in Duxbury. But luckily there are lots of us transplanted newcomers, so we kinda stick together. We even have our own garden club, a friendly, down-to-earth bunch of gals, if you'll pardon the pun. And we finally got into the golf club. That helps. Takes ten or twenty years now and the initiation fee is exorbitant, so we were lucky."

I groaned with pleasure at my first bite of lamb. "Is that the reason people are so gung-ho for the new Harbor Club?"

Peg shook her head, passing a bowl of mint jelly my way. "Poor people on the club's waiting list may never get in. It's a problem. People pay millions for expensive properties and then discover it's a three-to-five-year wait to get into a beach club, impossible to join the country club, and they're surrounded by water and can't get their boats wet 'cause the yacht club's full."

"Will you join the Harbor Club, if it happens?"

"Probably not, unless the grandchildren want to have a little boat when they're here."

"Pretty expensive dinghy slip, Peg-o-my-heart. Initiation's ten thousand and yearly dues four. I think our grandkids will be perfectly happy on the pond."

"Such a fuddy-duddy." She waved at her husband, turning to me. "He's right, of course. We'll never join. What with the beach club, golf and tennis, woods and ponds, our kiddies have plenty to do."

"Do they come often?"

"Between our four children, that guest house is hopping from June to September. They each take three weeks."

"Lucky Milly caught us when she did," Bob said. "Ruth Bowen's havin' some big family reunion around Thanksgiving so she's rented it from Thanksgiving to New Year's. Don't know when I'll get in to take care of all the repairs Peg's been naggin' me about."

"Oh, fiddlesticks," Peg said, pointing a forkful of mashed potato in her husband's direction. "Those jobs would take you no more than a couple of hours if you put your mind to it."

"Don't halt progress on my account. I don't mind if you work on the house while I'm there."

"You'd mind if I tore up the bathroom. One of Peg's 'quickie jobs' is retilin' the bathroom and puttin' in new fixtures. Have to wait till Ruth's family vacates."

"So she's a good friend, Ms. Bowen?"

"Not exactly." Lips pursed, she gave him a look. "She's one of the old guard so she has her own circle. We see her at church and we serve on the Visiting Committee together. She's an incredible person, a real town treasure. Don't know where the town'd be without all her hard work."

"So I hear. Does she really put in a forty-hour week?"

"Most weeks, unless she's away. Goes to Florida for a few weeks every winter. And she visits relatives out of town from time to time."

"I assume the town pays her."

"Oh, no, all volunteer."

"But, I heard that she—"

"Try not to listen to gossip, dear. I know the Harps are your friends. Gosh, we love Milly and Karen, and Ron and his parents, Giffy and Jim. Do you know them?" I nodded. "I'm just mad about Giffy. Such a tower of strength this past year with poor Jim laid up. Anyway, as I was saying, people do get carried away. Ron was a lovely person, very smart and all, but he did like to hear himself talk."

"What will the town do when Ms. Bowen retires and no one's able to put in that kind of time?"

"Maybe that'll be when we hire this town manager people keep talking about. Ruth's still a sharp cookie. I expect she'll be around for a while. Still runs a business, you know. Looks after people's properties when they're away. Mostly the big summer places down near the point. Has about twenty homes, estates really, that she takes care of."

"Busy lady."

"Well, she does have help, Peg, remember? Patty and Ralph do a lot of the walk-throughs."

"The Boardmans?" He nodded as Peg rose to clear the plates. "I haven't met them. Are they friends of yours?"

He smiled, shaking his head. "They're what you'd call the younger crowd. Nice kids. Patty can be a bit brusque, but she's a great gal and Ralph's a peach and the best damn carpenter around. In fact, Peg probably told you he's coming by to put up the storm windows and repair a couple of windowsills while you're here. It's all outside work so he won't bother you."

"No problem. Happy to have him. He does do beautiful work. Your octagon room is gorgeous."

He nodded, looking up at his wife, who was now setting dishes of floating island in front of us. "Not my favorite dessert," she said, "but my boyfriend here loves it." She winked at me, patting his shoulder as she passed by. "Did I hear someone mention Ralph?"

Bob nodded, smiling indulgently. "Uh-oh, here we go. More ideas for spending money."

"Oh, hush now. I was meaning to mention one item to you. How about while he's here, having him build some shelves in the pantry? I've bought all those lovely new dishes for the cottage and there's no place to put them."

"Plenty of time for that in January when he won't be puttering around inside, bothering the tenants."

"I don't mind. Really, I don't. I'll be gone most days and, if I'm there, I'd enjoy the company. I spend almost zero time in the kitchen so he won't be in my way at all."

"See, Ricky doesn't mind."

"We'll see, Peg. We'll see."

I watched the interplay of husband and wife, and took up a spoonful of smooth, creamy floating island. "Yum, this is incredible."

"I rest my case," he said, nodding to her.

We had coffee in the study. After hearing about the break-in, Peg announced that they would have to hire a security guard, but calmed down once she heard Demaris's theory about kids and pranks. Nevertheless, as I put on my coat, she said, "With your bad leg, not to mention your harrowing experience last night, we will certainly see you safely home and check the premises."

As we neared the cottage, Skeeter tore off in the direction of the woods, Bob in pursuit, leaving Peg and me to walk arm in arm, Peg holding tight to mine. "Hope you don't mind, dear. I know I should be helping you, but I'm forever tripping over roots and rocks."

"Of course not."

"You're a sweet girl. Where did you ever get your name? Milly called you Dorothy, I believe, when she called to rent the cottage."

"It's a nickname. It was my little sister Annie's name for me when she was a baby and I guess it stuck. I never use Dorothy. I've found over the years in my manly line of work that 'Ricky Steele' attracts more clients than 'Dorothy Steele.' When people find out I'm a woman, they're usually sitting in my office so they tend to stay around, see what I can do."

"Milly said you're an artist and a writer, but private investigating? What a profession for a lady. Don't your parents worry?"

"My mother's gone and my father…He doesn't approve of any of my career choices, but he tolerates what I do. I've only been doing the investigating this past year and my work is mostly on the computer, in libraries and in musty old records rooms. I think he figures I can't get into too much trouble there."

"Families can be complicated, can't they?" We stood together at the cottage door, peering out into the night, waiting for the return of Bob and Skeeter. "Well, my dear, it was a pleasure. I'll wait here for Bob and that naughty Skeeter. You pop inside, make sure everything's okay."

The cottage was just as I left it so I returned to the stoop to wait with Peggy. Within minutes, Bob appeared, leading Skeeter along by his belt, which he had removed and was using as a leash. He took Peg's arm and waved as they disappeared into the darkness. I closed the door, happy at the prospect of a quiet evening.

I settled on the couch, cup of tea in hand, and called Karen. She sounded tired, eager to hang up. I said I'd be over in the morning to go through Ron's study and rang off. I then looked up Morse's phone number and dialed. Peter answered amid screams in the background. "Sorry, it's bath time," he shouted over the din. "That you, Ricky? Sure, hold on a sec. I'll see to the hellions and let Becca come to the phone."

Several minutes later, Rebecca's soft voice greeted me. "Ricky? Hi, sorry about the bedlam. We need to read a few dozen parenting books, I'm 'fraid. Peter says you wanted to talk to me."

"Yes, I wondered if you had any time this week. I know you're in the middle of a trial so I'm happy to come anywhere, anytime."

"Why don't we meet for coffee, say six thirty tomorrow morning, at the Lunch? Unless that's too early for you? That way I can head out to work from there. I'd invite you to dinner, but I'm spending every night preparing for the next day in court. If we need more time, maybe over the weekend if this thing settles?"

Thanking her, I rang off and closed my eyes, nodding off for a minute.

The phone ring startled me and I picked up, heart pounding. I was surprised to hear Jay Harp's silky voice. We talked about nothing in particular, but there was an edge to his voice I found unsettling. Finally, we said good-night and I headed to bed, my dreams once again peopled with marauding gremlins.

CHAPTER 20

My cell phone alarm chimed at 6:00 a.m. and I took a quick shower, skipping my bike ride in order to arrive at the Lunch to meet Rebecca Morse at 6:30. The place was hopping—fishermen, carpenters and tradesmen. No sign of Ruth Bowen and her minions, at least the minions whom I knew by sight. Rebecca was waiting at a booth in the far corner. Spying me, she waved.

After flirting with a bunch of fishermen seated near the door, Tessa sidled over. "What'll you have, ladies?"

Rebecca ordered a muffin and coffee. I asked for johnnycakes, sausage, and a large tea.

After observing Tessa's sashay to the kitchen, I turned to my companion. "She's a hot little number, isn't she?"

"Owner's niece. Great for business."

"I'll bet."

"So, what can I do for you? Karen told me her mom had hired you to look into Ron's affairs."

I nodded. "Thanks for seeing me. I know this is an insanely busy time for you. How you holding up?"

"Okay. Fortunately, work is a distraction right now."

"I was a little surprised you picked this place to talk."

"How so?"

"Well, it's not exactly private."

She shook her head, straightening up, adjusting the colorful scarf tied loosely at her neck. Hers was a wan, delicate beauty. In many respects, she and Karen resembled one another. Both were tall and slender with dark hair, stylishly cut. Each of them had expensive taste in clothes, which they wore well. Rebecca was a softer, earthier Karen, I decided, more grounded and safe. Much as I loved her, Karen was edgy, always seeming as if she might dart away at a moment's notice. "If a bunch of busybodies want to listen to our conversation, let 'em. It's all a matter of public record anyway. I certainly have no intention of hiding." As she spoke, her eyes scanned the room.

"Okay."

She brushed an imaginary crumb from the front of her pale yellow cashmere sweater, readjusting the scarf. "What exactly do you want to know?"

I leaned forward. "Do you think Ron's death was an accident?"

"Is that what this is about? Karen told me you were helping her sort through Ron's work, to help her decide what projects needed attending to."

"No." Now I was thoroughly confused. Will Ramsey had certainly known why Karen had hired me. Why not Rebecca? "I assumed you knew. Karen doesn't believe Ron's death was an accident."

"And she thinks it was related to something he was working on?"

I nodded.

"Ridiculous. This is small-town stuff. That's what people in small towns do, bicker and snipe at each other."

"What have you and Ron been working on lately?"

"Actually things have been kinda quiet the past month or so. Of course, the Harbor Club is an ongoing issue. And we're always watching Sedgie Montgomery. Other than that, not too much. We've been campaigning for the upcoming elections, vainly trying to get another Democrat or two on the council to support Laura Morrow. Have you met her?"

"Yes, she's fighting the good fight, isn't she?"

"You can say that again. It'd be terrific to defeat the big 'R,' but we're not looking for miracles. Ron and I had just started strategizing for next spring's financial town meeting. We were trying to quietly audit all the special accounts Ruth has set up, the ones that pay her 'salary.' Karrie might've told you about the group trying to build a new golf course, too? The land's all conservation trust property so they probably won't get far, but without Ron, who knows? We've been monitoring it closely."

"How much of what you monitor is actually illegal?"

She laughed. "That depends on who you talk to. These people are masters at circumventing almost any law they choose. We got 'em last year on the open meetings violation because it was clearly in violation of the charter. The rest of it, who knows? Our town solicitor is definitely on this side of shady, but he's very careful. There were a couple of other issues we were poking our noses into, but with Ron gone, I'll probably let them go."

"What kind of issues?"

Her eyes darted round the room before she met my gaze. "I'd rather not say. Not unless I'm sure. Another time, maybe."

"What can you tell me about the effigy business?"

"Ugly. We could have prosecuted, but Skip apologized publicly in the *Harbor Times* and by personal letter." She paused as Tessa set plates before us. "He also called on Ron and Karen and apologized in person, Chief Sisson right behind him."

"So, the chief made him do it?"

"The Town Council, actually. One time when our Ruthie did the right thing. Even if it was because she knew we were headed for the state attorney general."

She paused to slather jam on her English muffin. "Let's face it, the effigy was just a manifestation of the ongoing ugliness and pettiness around here. It wasn't any more malicious than what happens every day." She leaned forward, whispering now. "Stop in here at noon and listen to Patty Boardman for five minutes. She's unbelievable, the things she says and does. No one bats an eye. They all shrug and say, 'That's Patty.' Her cousin George Wilbur's sitting over there, so I better shut up. In case you haven't noticed, everyone's related to everyone in the Harbor."

We ate in silence for several minutes, my johnnycakes crisp and thin. Rebecca meticulously spread the jam to the edges of each muffin before taking a bite. Thus employed, her body relaxed, shoulders sagging, face casting off the mask that hid her pain.

"You and Ron were close, weren't you?"

Squaring her shoulders, she pursed her lips. "Yes."

"Do you mind my asking how close?"

"Excuse me?" She minded.

"Sorry, I didn't mean to pry. I had heard that you were high school sweethearts and I wondered if—"

"I loved him, if that's what you're asking, but as a friend, nothing more. We've known each other all our lives. Ron understood me and I, him. Our earlier relationship was in the past. We're both happily married and grateful for the time we'd spend together as friends. Now, if you'll excuse me, I've got to get going. The bridge traffic gets bad in another fifteen minutes and I have to be at the courthouse by 8:30 a.m."

Her demeanor had changed, warmth, ease and affability now replaced by cool efficiency. I wondered if it was my question, or if she was simply shifting into work mode. I suspected the former. As she reached for her purse, I took hold of her arm. "I've got this. Rebecca, I'm really sorry for your loss and for prying."

"Don't worry about it." I let go and she slid out of the booth, pulling on her jacket. "Peter and I will get you and Karrie out to dinner when things calm down at work."

"That'd be great. I really would like another chance to talk."

She sat back down on the edge of her seat, leaning toward me. "I lost my best friend last week. Honestly, I'd rather not talk about Ron or any of it for a while. I know this is Karen's way of dealing with her grief, but it's not mine. I'd rather grieve privately, in my own way. I'm sick of fighting. Let Ruth have her last few years of power, or let someone else take up the fight. I'm sick of it. Without Ron, it just doesn't have any meaning for me." With that, she rose, leaving a half-eaten muffin and a million unanswered questions.

As she crossed the room, Rebecca greeted people at practically every table, pausing to talk, patting backs, waving and exchanging chitchat as if she suddenly had all the time in the world. When she reached the entrance, the door opened and Ruth Bowen stepped in. The two women greeted each other like old friends.

Rising, I handed Tessa the check and a wad of crumpled bills. On my way out, I passed Ruth Bowen, now chatting with a group of fishermen.

I stepped around the group and into her line of vision. "Mrs. Bowen? Hi, Ricky Steele. We met at the Harps'."

"Yes, how are you? Heard you're out at Red Gate. Decided to have a vacation before heading home?"

"Something like that. Would you possibly have any time to speak with me today? Ten or fifteen minutes if you can spare them?"

"What's this about?"

"Just a few questions about town governance, policies, stuff like that."

"I shouldn't think a person like yourself would be interested in the civic affairs of a small town."

"Please, Mrs. Bowen, I won't take but a few minutes of your time."

"As you can see, I'm about to have my breakfast. Then I have several calls to make, but I should be back in the office by ten. Would that suit you?" Not waiting for my response, she turned back to her companions now seated behind us.

"I'll be there. Thanks." I spoke to her back, patrons staring as if I'd lost my marbles.

CHAPTER 21

It was only seven fifteen so I headed out to Nauset Point. My doctor claimed *controlled* forward motion was good for the knee to build up the muscles. I pulled windbreaker and gloves from the back of the jeep, pulled on my lightweight brace, and headed off at a brisk pace. It was a mile to Tripp's Beach, then another mile along the shore to the point.

The sun was out and the trees and bushes along the road blocked the wind as I neared the beach. At the crest of Bayberry Hill, I had my first glimpse of the ocean, a deep blue-green, punctuated by whitecaps and rippling swells. As I walked along the point road, the sea surrounded me on three sides, framed by huge shingled "cottages." No wonder the natives guarded it so zealously, I thought, making my way down the last stretch of road to the beach.

It was low tide, thirty feet of the rocky shore visible below the high tide mark. This left plenty of room for walking and exploring. I proceeded slowly, stopping every so often to rest and search the ground for shells and bits of sea glass. At the end of Tripp's, the sand ended and tumbling walls of boulders blocked the way. This was the hurricane barrier erected to protect the multimillion-dollar homes perched at the edge of the sea.

A year ago I would have scrambled over the rocks like a mountain goat, jumping from boulder to boulder. My sister, Annie, and I had spent summers climbing rocks such as these on the breakwater near our beloved summer cottage at Williams

Point, twenty miles down the coast. The cottage had been in my mother's family for generations. Two months after she died, Dad sold it.

No mountain goat today, I mused, searching for a way around. Fortunately the tide was low enough for me to skirt the boulders at the water's edge, my sneakers only a little soggy when I reached the other side. At last, I reached Nauset Point, a stretch of sand between me and Nauset Light. I plunked down on a large driftwood log and gazed out to sea, wondering about Rebecca Morse. What was she hiding? Why would she, who worked so closely with Ron, have such different perspectives than Karen? I didn't like to query Karen about this discrepancy, but maybe I could drop in and ask Will Ramsey after my trip to Town Hall.

I pulled myself up and headed for the road. Before long, I came to a parking lot, a sign at the entrance proclaiming it to be the "future site of the Harbor Yacht Club." Several dilapidated shacks stood at the edge of the network of docks crowding the tiny harbor, the only harbor for all Windy Harbor's private and commercial vessels. At the mouth of the harbor sat what remained of the Fisherman's Catch, the former restaurant's windows boarded, porch rotted and falling into the harbor. Across the road, another two-acre parking lot stretched to the edge of the sea, tufts of grass and weeds poking through nooks and crannies of crumbling asphalt. A second shiny sign declared this to be "the future site of the future Harbor Club Boatyard." I walked to the edge of the parking lot. Why did Ron and his cronies object to sprucing up what could be a beautiful spot?

I consulted my watch and discovered it was close to nine. Unsure of how long the walk back to the car would take, I began power walking, past houses, fields and golf club. Big mistake. After twenty yards, my knee throbbed and I felt sick to my stomach. After catching my breath, I proceeded more slowly. It was after nine thirty when the jeep came into view. I threw my gloves into the back seat, pulled off the brace and heaved myself in, grateful to be out of the wind and off my right leg.

Since I had plenty of time to get to the Town Hall, I cruised slowly back to the village center, taking a slight detour by Morse Greenhouses and Rebecca and

Peter Morse's home, a modern, shingled affair, designed by the same architect-in-training who had designed the Harps' house. I'd been in the Morses' home many times over the years. It was nice, but it didn't compare to the Harps'. Rebecca didn't have Karen's eye.

CHAPTER 22

I parked the jeep beside the white clapboard Town Hall at five minutes to ten and headed to the back suite of the building. Ruth Bowen's office was tucked away at the far end of a large room housing the desks of the town clerk, JoJo Kaufman, tax collector, Jim Baldwin, two secretaries, Sue and Lorraine, and Betty, the receptionist. Al Shortliff, the town moderator, also had a desk in one corner. Judging by the patina of dust blanketing its surface, it would appear that Moderator Shortliff had better places to spend his time.

Sue, Lorraine, Betty and JoJo were at their desks; the tax collector was not. Betty buzzed and her majesty emerged, waving me in. Amazing how far volunteerism can get you, I thought, nodding and smiling at the ladies as I wended my way around their desks to the inner sanctum. The office held three, four-drawer file cabinets, a desk and three chairs—a fake leather swivel chair behind the desk. Two orange molded plastic chairs for guests looked like rejects from the school down the street and I was tempted to peek under the seats to check for wads of bubble gum.

"Miss Steele, come in. Please sit. Looks like you need it with that limp of yours. A recent injury?"

I nodded. "It's Ricky."

I took the chair nearest her desk, then gazed at my surroundings. The paper-weight, pencil holder and other desk accessories were lined up precisely, the desk covered with a green felt blotter. One pen rested at the blotter's left edge, no doubt poised and ready in case Ruth was called upon to sign an important document. To the left of the blotter a wooden file box held several folders. A memo pad and small stack of Post-it notes sat next to the phone.

"Nice office. Spend much time here?"

"Miss Steele, this is a small town. If you've talked to anyone, you know that I do, indeed, spend quite a lot of time here conducting town business."

"It's a little unusual, isn't it? Your job, I mean. Most towns don't have council presidents who are able to put in forty-hour weeks."

She remained placid, serene. Questions from a nobody like me could never ruffle her feathers. "Is this what you wanted to talk with me about?"

"No. Actually, I'm here because I'm looking into the circumstances surrounding Ron Harp's death."

"What circumstances? It was an accident. Our very capable police have already looked into the matter quite thoroughly, I assure you."

"With all due respect, Mrs. Bowen, nothing I've heard so far suggests that the investigation was thorough, especially in what should have been treated as a suspicious death."

The feathers ruffled slightly. "Oh, and how would you know?"

"I often work with the police in my line of work and—"

"Now, hold on a minute, Miz Steele. No inexperienced Fall River private investigator is going to come waltzing into town telling our *experienced* police officers how to do their jobs. I don't know how things are done in the city, but here we don't hurl accusations around about things of which we know nothing. Here we let the trained professionals do their jobs. We don't second guess them. We don't interfere. And we certainly do not listen to amateurs who do." A fighting cock now, in full battle stance.

"Mrs. Bowen, I have no intention of interfering, but I've been hired to ask questions, which is my right as a citizen."

"I'd be very careful if I were you."

This interview was not going at all the way I'd planned. "Is that a threat?"

She leaned back, the swivel chair creaking. "I knew your parents, you know. Years ago, when I was a girl. Your father has remarried, I understand."

Normally I refuse to discuss my father, but if it kept her talking, why not? "Yes, a number of years ago. He and my stepmother love to travel. They're in Rome now."

"How nice for them."

"Where did you meet them?"

"Here, actually. They took a house one summer. It was shortly after they were married, I believe."

"Must've been. Dad never told me." Of course, my father never mentioned my mother or their life together. Ever. "Which house?"

"The old Bigalow place. Still belongs to the family, but Patty and Ralph Boardman have rented it for years. One of the few year round rental properties in town."

"Is that one of the properties you manage?"

She nodded.

"I hear the Boardmans help you out with your business."

"Is this what you came to discuss, my business, and my employees? Because if it is, I'm rather busy just now. Is there anything else you needed?"

"I'd like to take a look at Town Council records. I hear the meetings are videotaped nowadays. Before they began videotaping, you must've kept notes, minutes, that sort of thing, correct?"

She nodded stiffly, looking as if she'd swallowed a mouthful of cod liver oil. "Copies of the video recordings are at the library. People can check them out with a library card. All other records are kept here, in the archives. Were there particular meetings or topics that interested you? Our archivist, Sally Williams, could go through them with you."

"Thanks. That'd be great. Not sure exactly what I'm looking for, but I'll certainly contact Ms. Williams. Are the records available during regular Town Hall hours?"

"Most days, unless Sally's taking inventory or working on a project at the Historical Society. Her husband, Patrick, runs it."

I smiled, twiddling my purse strap round my finger. "I walked around the Point this morning. Quite a spot they've chosen for the Harbor Club. I'll bet those discussions would make interesting reading, or viewing." She gave an almost imperceptible shrug, but said nothing. "What's your opinion of that project? Do you think it's right for the town?"

She smiled indulgently. "I'm sure you're aware that as Town Council President I must keep my opinions neutral until we have all the facts and have rendered our decisions."

"And have you all the facts?"

"Not yet."

"But you must have some opinion you could share. I mean, does the town need another club? I should think most folks would welcome doing something with that incredible location. Sad to have such an eyesore in what could be a lovely spot for town residents to enjoy. I've heard that the town solicitor is pushing pretty hard for it. Isn't that a little tricky since he's also an investor?"

The feathers were fluttering, but she was preening like crazy, willing herself to remain calm. "I'd try not to listen to idle gossip, Miss Steele. Small towns are notorious for spreading rumors that invariably have no basis in fact."

"But he is an investor, is he not?"

"I am not in a position to comment on that. Now, if you don't mind, I have—"

"Mrs. Bowen, do you think Ron Harp was the victim of foul play?"

"No, I do not." She stiffened, hand on the phone, pencil in hand. "Now, if you'll excuse me, I have work to do."

"Well, thanks for your time. I'll give your regards to my father."

She blushed. "Oh, I...I'm sure he won't remember me. Why, it was sixty years ago, if it was a day." She fussed with the buttons of her sweater, pulling it round her as if she'd felt a draft.

"He's pretty good on faces. And surely he'll remember summering here."

"Yes, of course." Embarrassed by her display of coquetry, she placed her hands firmly in her lap.

Reaching the door, I paused, turning back. "I'll just pop in and see if Ms. Williams is in."

"She's not."

"Will she be back soon?"

"She and her husband are away. Not sure how long. Sue or Betty can tell you."

"Can I arrange to have a peek at those records anyway?"

"I suppose Betty or Sue could let you in, but not today. We're swamped."

"I'll call ahead, then, just to be sure."

"Yes. Goodbye."

She was already dialing as I said, "Thanks again" and stepped out.

CHAPTER 23

I headed for the cottage, intending to have a quick lunch and a nap before spending the remainder of the afternoon in Ron's study. When I pulled into the driveway, I found a battered green truck parked in front of the cottage. As I got out of the jeep, I spied a man on a ladder pulled up to the kitchen window.

Shielding my eyes, I went to the base of the ladder, peering up. "Hi, there."

"Hello." He hooked his hammer on the top rung and climbed down. "I'm the carpenter. Owners said you wouldn't mind."

"Yes, Mr. Boardman, right?" I extended my hand. "Ricky Steele." A hard callused hand gripped mine firmly.

Late thirties, early forties, I guessed, weathered face, sandy hair poking out from under a faded Red Sox cap. He wore work boots, dark brown work pants and a gray hooded sweatshirt, a patch of red-checkered flannel visible at the neck. Ralph Boardman was what you'd call ordinary, the kind of person who faded into the background, except for his remarkable dark blue eyes. Wrinkles etched his brow, no doubt from a life spent outdoors. He gave me a warm, mischievous grin. "Been hearin' 'bout you."

"All good things, I hope."

He chuckled, pushing his cap back to scratch his brow. "You sure got folks stirred up."

"About what?"

"Never had a private detective stayin' in town before."

"I'm pretty dull once you get to know me."

He grinned again, revealing a missing tooth at the side of his mouth. "Now, I don't believe that for a second. I expect it's your looks got the women riled up."

"What women?"

"Now, that'd be tellin'."

"Mr. Boardman—"

"Ralph."

"Ralph." I gave my best come-hither smile. "You can tell little old me, now, can't you?"

"Not if I want to sleep in my own bed tonight."

"You mean your wife's upset about me? We haven't even met."

"Not sayin' she is, not sayin' she isn't. Patty don't need to meet someone to know about 'em. Got plenty of sources. Harbor grapevine, doncha know. What's wrong with your leg there?"

"Torn ligaments. I'm waiting till the right time to operate. Who are your wife's sources, as you put it? Who's been gossiping about me?"

He laughed. "Forget I said anything. I was just kidding. You know, they get to talkin' down at the Lunch. Need somethin' to gab about over breakfast. Haven't had news like you for a while."

"What about Ron Harp's accident? Have people been talking and speculating about that?"

The smile faded, his gaze serious. "Now that was no joke. Real nice fella, too. My Patty wasn't too crazy about him, but I always liked Ronnie. Worked on their house when they built it. Wife had very definite ideas about the project, but he was real easy to get along with."

"What do you think about his death? Do you believe it was an accident?"

He pushed his cap back again, scratching his head. "If Cal and Skip say it was an accident, it was an accident. They're the best."

"Don't you think it's odd that someone would come along and take the bike?"

"Nope. Lots of kids ridin' around. Prob'ly grabbed it up fer a souvenir."

I paced back and forth, my cane stirring up clouds of dust as I poked it hard with every step. "I'm sorry, but I just don't believe that explanation."

"That's 'cause yer a foreigner. If you came from the Harbor, you'd know kids'll do anything. Kinda dull round here once Labor Day comes and goes. I was a foreigner before I married my Patty. It's taken me years to get the hang of things. Watch yourself so you don't trip and fall."

Ignoring his warning, I continued to pace, muttering to myself. "Hang of things or not, I believe Ron's accident deserved more attention."

"Funny patch of road, that. Been lots of bike accidents out that way. People skid comin' down the hill."

"Then why doesn't the town clear all that sand away?"

"They do. Comes right back with the next rain. That's whatcha call an alluvial plain. Couldn't stop it even if you wanted to. Just comes and comes and comes."

Tired and frustrated, I decided to change the subject. "Would you like a sandwich? I was just going to make myself one."

"Thanks, but I'm heading over to meet my buddies at the Lunch in half an hour. Wouldn't say no to a glass of water, though."

"Would you rather have coffee?"

"Water'd be fine."

When I returned, he was back at the top of the ladder. "Thanks, Miss Steele. Just set that over on the step. I'll get it in a minute. Gotta get something accomplished before I take my lunch break." So that was his strategy. Stay up on the ladder, thereby forestalling any further chitchat.

CHAPTER 24

When I arrived, Karen's car was gone. Rosalie, the housekeeper, answered the door. In her early seventies, petite and pencil-thin, flaxen-haired Rosalie had been with the Spenser family for as long as I could remember. Today she sported one of her signature ensembles—lime-green leggings, striped jersey, and pink platform sneakers.

"Hey, Rosalie, long time no see."

She grabbed me in a bear hug. "Why you limp? My poor little pumpkin."

Laughing, I returned her embrace. No one but Rosalie got away with calling me "pumpkin." I gave her the short version of my accident, immediately changing the subject at the conclusion by asking about Karen.

"She's out. Didn't say when she'd be back. She was gone when I arrived. Allie's at his Gramma's and I have my list. That's all I know."

I explained about needing to go through Ron's papers and she shrugged, "You go on in and I'll bring tea."

I had just oriented myself in the study when Rosalie appeared with a mug of Earl Grey and a plate of sugar cookies, set them on the desk, and moved to the hearth to grab a pile of newspapers. She bent over, straight-legged, years of yoga allowing her to twist and turn her body like a contortionist. Watching her, I was reminded of a strange, multicolored spider, lime green legs radiating from a bright, colorful middle. Bundle in hand, she slipped out, closing the door behind her.

I had just dug into a pile of folders and papers when Bobby Harp poked his head in. "Hey, Ricky, whatcha up to?"

"Bobby, hi." I set down the pile, swiveling in my chair to face him. "I have permission. Karen asked me to—"

"It's cool. Know all about it. Just stoppin' to get a few files related to the foundation. Jay called this morning and said he thought it'd be easier for me to find them than Karrie."

I started to rise.

"No, stay where you are. I know just where they are. Only be a sec." He reached over and pulled out a drawer on the right side of the desk. "Here we go." He waved two thick folders with a flourish, setting them on a table by the door. Leaning my cane against the wall, he grabbed the ladder-back chair I'd set it on and pulled nearer the desk. Straddling the chair, chin resting on his hands, he grinned, his ruddy face lined and wrinkled from a life outdoors. "How can I help?"

By leaving, I thought, forcing a smile. I'd never much cared for Bobby, although I couldn't exactly say why. He was always friendly, and handsome like his brothers. There was just something about him that grated on me. Like now, sitting there, grinning with perfect, white teeth, his powerful arms straining the fabric of faded blue work shirt, he reminded me of a hyena, moving in for the kill.

"I'm really not sure what I'm looking for. Just thought I'd poke around."

"Okay." He remained firmly rooted to his seat, hyena grin widening.

"Jay thought you might object to my looking into Ron's death. That it might cause trouble in town for you and your family."

"That's because Jay doesn't live in town. Big brother don't know shit about this place. Believe me, your snoopin' around's no skin off my back. But, then, I move with a different crowd than Karen and Ron. I'm friends with more of the townies than the skewks."

"The what?"

"Skewks. Term somebody came up with for summer folks, but it's grown to include the latest crop of 'newcomers.' You know, the IMPACT gang and all."

"So you weren't involved with IMPACT?"

He laughed a shrill hyena cackle, his boot tapping a steady beat on the bare wood floor. "I'm not a card-carrying member, if that's what you're asking. I get involved if it's an issue I care about. For instance, I've been helpin' out with the Harbor Club crap."

"So, you're not in favor of the Club?"

"Hell, no. Just a bunch of millionaires want to cut off the point so rest of the town can't use it."

"You mean the plan for public access?"

"The nonexistent plan for public access, you mean? You don't think the skewks wanna look out their fancy restaurant's ocean view windows and see a lot of redneck fishermen plunking in their lines?"

"Would you be in favor of it if public access was possible?"

He shrugged. "Maybe. I'm not in favor of any of these dickheads comin' in, but they're here so I guess we gotta put up with them."

"And I imagine they're good for business."

"Oh, yeah."

"So, who do you hang out with, anyway?"

"Younger crowd than Ron and Karrie." Grinning, he raised an eyebrow, daring me, as an "older person," to protest. I smiled, refusing to take the bait. "Patty and Ralph Boardman, the Cliffords, my fishing partner Gary Pauls and his wife Cynthia. They're a little too lowbrow for Ron and Karrie. And"—he leaned forward, whispering—"Patty and Karen don't get along. But she and Betsy are best friends. Grew up together, went all through school living practically right next door to each other."

"I met Ralph this morning. He's doing some work out at Red Gate."

"Ralph's a character, one of a kind. I'm never quite sure what to make of him, but like I said, Bets and Patty are best friends so we get along."

"I've heard a lot about Patty, but I haven't met her yet."

"Don't believe everything you hear. Patty tells it like it is, but she's good people."

"Where would I be likely to find her most days?"

"She's home a good bit, or maybe at my house or my parents'. She stays with Dad while my mom's out. She's been terrific with Dad."

"Bobby, what do you think about Ron? Do you think someone killed him?"

He stared at the floor for a minute or so before answering. "If you'd asked me a year ago I would have said, 'no way,' but now, hell, Ricky, I don't know. When Karrie told me she'd hired you, I told her she'd done the right thing. Maybe it was an accident, but I for one wanna know for sure."

"Do you trust the police?"

He laughed, less forced, more genuine. "That bunch of bozos. Don't quote me on that. 'Cept for Demaris, those morons couldn't investigate their way out of a paper bag. Most useless bunch of idiots you'll ever find. Whenever anything serious happens, they call in the state cops anyway. Like the murder last year. I'm sure Karrie told you about it. State police were involved within an hour after they found her. Not that the staties don't have their own problems too. Look how they bungled the mess last year."

"Tell me about that. I remember it was in the papers. An elderly woman, wasn't it?"

"Hattie Pauls, the old high school principal. Ninety years old, strangled in her bed. Nephew found her three days later."

"The case is still open, isn't it?"

"Yup. They've questioned almost everyone in town at one time or another. So many rumors been flyin' around, can't keep 'em all straight."

"You got a theory?"

He shook his head. "Hell if I know. Didn't look like a break-in so the cops figured it was someone she knew."

"What about the nephew?"

"Jack Pauls, her brother's kid? In his seventies himself. He and his wife had been away, cruise on the QE2. Been abroad six months. He'd just gotten back and was stopping in to say hey to auntie before headin' south. They live in Florida."

"Was he her only family?"

"Jack had a sister. She's in a retirement home in Vermont, I think. Jack's kids and grandkids are scattered around the country. None local that I know of. Hattie didn't grow up here. Came from Boston, straight outta college to teach first grade. Taught for a zillion years and eventually took over as principal of the elementary school, then later the high school. She retired twenty years ago with the last graduating class of Harbor High. Now the kids are bussed to the regional high school in North Point. Harbor School only goes to eighth grade."

"But she stayed after retirement instead of moving to be nearer her family?"

He shook his head, his foot tapping quieter now, less insistent. "Harbor and the school were Hattie's life. She was also active in the church. And she started painting after her retirement. Pretty good stuff, not that I know art from a hole in the wall."

"Any of her paintings still in town?"

"Bunch of people have 'em. She always sold well at the annual art show. Five or six hang in the library, couple in the Town Hall, and there's a beauty in the school, right inside the door. It's a painting of the town center, every bit as good as Norman Rockwell, if you ask me."

"What happened to her home?"

"Went to the nephew. He sold it almost immediately. Had a big garage sale. Don't know what he did with all the kitties, prob'ly euthanized."

"Kitties?"

"Hattie collected strays. Sometimes had close to thirty cats living with her. Had a handyman, did all her errands, and I think he took 'em to the vets for her, bought their food and such. The year before she died, she lost a lot of them kitties, but there were still a bunch, crawling round the body when they found her."

"How did she lose the others in the year before she died?"

"Disappeared. Found a couple dead in the yard. Not sure what happened. Could've been rabies or another animal. There's been a lot of problems with livestock round here the last few years. Could be coyotes, or maybe malicious two-legged predators."

"What kind of problems with livestock?"

"Dead sheep, chickens, couple of cows, a dog or two, Hattie's cats. Hard to tell with those cats 'cause sometimes they just disappeared."

"How did the other animals die?"

"Mostly their throats were slashed or they were run to the ground, then mauled. Bets and I keep a couple of sheep from time to time, but we said never again after last year. Had six and all but one were killed. Real hard on the kids, and Betsy. We've lost 'em before. Hot air balloons make 'em go crazy and jump fences and they're always impaling themselves or getting caught up and strangled, but this was different. To have 'em all go at once. Was probably a pack of wild dogs. Every so often a pack crops up. Rabies epidemic a few years ago wiped out the wild dog and cat population, but they're comin' back now."

"Would there be records about all these animal deaths?"

"Hank Mederois, our animal control officer, prob'ly has most of 'em, if they were reported. I know Karrie reported Jambalaya's death to Hank Rizzo. He's the animal control officer."

"Jambalaya?" I asked, referring to Karen's treasured white peacock given to her by a client. "With everything going on the past few days, I hadn't noticed he was missing."

"Died last spring. Now, his death was strange, if you ask me. Poor little bugger, looked like someone had wrung his neck. Surprising that they didn't hear him squawkin.' That bird made a huge ruckus if anyone so much as looked at him cross-eyed. But, like I said, lots of things could've happened. There's a lot of wild animals around here. Some people have even reported seeing mountain lions from time to time."

Mountain lions were pretty incredible, but I doubted they possessed the dexterity to strangle a peacock without leaving bite marks. Then again, what did

I know about mountain lions or peacocks? "So, who do you think might've had a reason to kill Ron?"

"Now, that's where I'm stumped. I know this town and these are good people. Sure, there are jerks like anyplace, but killers? I don't think so."

"What about the bike? Who would have taken it?"

"Well, if Ronnie was killed, maybe his killer took it? If not, could've been kids, I 'spose. Or, could've been Charlie Higgins." Higgins was a homeless man, a fixture in the Harbor for years. On my visits to Karen and Ron's over the years, I'd seen him walking the roads and ambling through town, talking to himself.

"Is he still living at Bailey's Ledge?"

He nodded. "Sure is, at the far end of East Beach. Charlie's always collecting shit, haulin' it back to his place. But I think it's pretty coincidental that Charlie just happened along right after Ron fell. And I'll bet if you ask Cal Ripler, the cops checked Charlie's place for the bike already."

I made a note to take a drive to Bailey's Ledge in the morning. "What about the people involved in the effigy business last year? That sounded nasty. Any chance Skip and his cronies might have taken their viciousness to the next level?"

He laughed. "Skip Burrows? I don't think so. That was all a big show to impress his bosses. Thought it'd put him in good with Cal and his cronies, you know, young, tough, rookie, razin' the village gadfly. Let's face it, Ricky, a lot of people around here hated my brother's guts. Ron was messin' with their crooked ways of doin' business. Cops just sit on their duffs and let Demaris do all the work.

"Town Council's got all kinds of perks lined up for themselves and Ronnie has the temerity to go askin' questions. Had the balls to question a bunch of their bogus 'line items' in the budget. At last year's financial town meeting, Al Shortliff nearly hopped down from his podium to come sit on Ronnie to keep him quiet till they passed the budget as a whole instead of considering each item, line by line. If it'd gone line by line, Miss Ruthie would have had some explaining to do 'bout her twenty thousand in contingency funds."

"But murder?"

Karen's voice called from somewhere in the house and the hyena reappeared, Bobby's body language shifting into defense mode. Why?

CHAPTER 25

"Do you think someone murdered your brother?"

Bobby rose, returning the chair to its place. "God, Ricky, what do I know? They hated his guts, that's for sure, but I'm not sure any of them has it in him to kill someone. This is small-town stuff, not high finance or espionage."

"What about the millions involved in the Harbor Club?"

He shrugged. "Now you're thinking about Sedgie and his crew. Another bunch of morons. They've got mega-cash tied up in it, but I doubt it's millions. Sedgie's prob'ly got ten grand, no more, and that's pocket change for him. Most investors put in around that, from what I've heard. It's a skewk project. Maybe a few old timers put in, for an investment. That was prob'ly Sedgie's doing. But he overestimated his powers of persuasion on this one, I'm 'fraid. Thought he could push it through quick and easy and it's not gonna happen. Ronnie wasn't the fly in the ointment there, though. Harbor Club's mostly Dick Chaffee's project, I think."

"Hi, you two." Karen popped her head in, shopping bags dangling from her wrist. "Mother took us shopping to cheer us up." She rolled her eyes. "More clothes neither of us needs."

"Where's my man?" Bobby circled the room, moving toward the door, peering over her shoulder. "Allie?"

"Mom took him home. He's happier there."

Bobby's face clouded over as he turned to grab his folders. "Gotta head out, ladies. See you, Rick." He pecked Karen's cheek on his way out and she stiffened, straightening her shoulders, keeping the hyena at bay.

"So?" She brought a chair to sit beside me. "Uncovered anything?"

"Haven't even started. Bobby's been here and we've been chatting. You never told me about Jambalaya."

"Poor baby, happened last June. I was away. Ron found her. He had Hank come out and take a look at her. Hank said it was coyotes, but Ron didn't believe him. Someone wrung her poor little neck. We buried her under the apple tree. At the time, Ronnie said he wanted to be buried next to her, but he changed his mind later on. His will specifies cremation. We made our wills last summer, before our trip to Chile.

"That reminds me. I'm picking up the urn, with his ashes, tomorrow. We're doing it Sunday and I'd really like you there, Ricky, please. It's just family. Jay'll be down, Ma and Pa Harp, Bobby and Betsy. I hope they don't bring their kids. I'm leaving Alex with Mother."

"Don't you think he'd want to say goodbye to his dad?"

"Ordinarily, I'd say yes, but he's been so traumatized, I think it's better if we say our goodbye in a quieter way. I'm keeping a tiny box of ashes and when he's feeling better, we'll bury those beside Jambalaya, just the two of us."

"Where are you scattering the ashes?"

"Bailey's Ledge."

"Oh?"

She nodded. "It was Ron's favorite spot in town. He spent lots of time there growing up. He was always dragging us out there for picnics, or to walk the bluffs. It's pretty, but I prefer the river, or Wiggins Wood—much better hiking and beautiful, quiet picnic spots. Bailey's is too open, too exposed for my taste, especially during the summer months. Anyway, that's where Ron wanted to be scattered, so we're going. Sunday afternoon, unless it's pouring rain. Then, I guess we'll postpone till the following weekend. Please say you'll come, Ricky."

"Of course, if you don't think I'd be intruding."

She reached over and squeezed my hands. "Hardly. You're family, especially since Jolie's not here. You're closer than a sister anyway."

"Where is Jolie?"

"Spain. She's been there for over a year. Works as a waitress, paints in her spare time. Loves it, but you know Jolie, never has a cent to her name. Mother offered to fly her back for the funeral, but I said not to bother. What was the point? She and Ron never got along anyway."

"I didn't know that."

"They're both stubborn and pig-headed. Never could be in the same room together for very long. There was a reason you were my maid-of-honor, my darling. Even though you're my oldest and dearest, I would have asked Jolie, as my sister, if Ron hadn't forbidden it. We almost didn't get married because of Jolie. Had a dreadful fight over her. I mean, what groom cares who is his bride's maid-of-honor? I didn't tell you about it?"

I shook my head.

"Funny, I thought I did. We do have a lot of catching up to do."

"What started the antagonism between Jolie and Ron?"

She laughed, tossing the bags by the door. "What didn't? You know what a sober sides Ron was. Dear and sweet, but not what you'd call easygoing. And Jolie loved to bait him. She was constantly needling. He'd say something, she'd disagree. It was constant. When we were living together, she was always on him about wanting to settle in Windy Harbor. That's when we were renting the Sampsons' place. We were happy at the Sampsons'." Her voice trailed off and she gazed out the window, dancing fingers of the late afternoon sun playing over her cheeks and forehead.

"Jolie came and stayed for a couple of months. By the time she left, she and Ron were at each other's throats constantly. That's really why he said no to having her as maid-of-honor. He was pissed. Claimed she trashed the house, used all our food and never replaced it. He was right, of course. My sister's a mooch. Always has been, always will be, I'm afraid. And Ron, the original Yankee, penny-pinching miser, would get furious when she didn't contribute."

"Has Jolie lived here since then?"

"Never. Didn't make too many friends with the locals either. Bobby can't stand her. One time she insulted Betsy's cooking when she thought no one but me was listening, and he really blew up. When she was living with us, she waitressed with Patty Boardman at the Fisherman, the summer before it closed. By the end of the summer, she and Patty weren't speaking."

"Why?"

"Something about tips and how they were divided up. I really don't know what happened. Jolie's a mooch, but I've never known her to be dishonest and I wouldn't put anything past Patty. 'Course, Ron and Bobby blamed Jolie. I didn't speak to Ron for over a week." She laughed, stretching, drawing her hair back from her face, massaging her temples. "It's a wonder we ever got married and even more a wonder that we stayed together as long as we did."

"Were you having troubles?"

"Nothing out of the ordinary, I suppose. These past few years the honeymoon was definitely over, but we'd fallen into an easy rhythm."

You travel. He stays home with the kid. Some rhythm, I thought, regarding her sadly. Things had certainly changed since our Maple Tree Club days when life had been simple —get dressed, have breakfast and head out to the porch. Everyone think of three things to do, pick one and we were off, occupied for the entire day. "When's the new nanny arriving?"

"Monday. Alex and I pick her up at the airport. You don't approve, do you?"

"It's not for me to say, Karrie. Besides, what do I know? I don't have kids. I haven't a clue what you have to deal with."

"I shouldn't have been a mother, Ricky. Allie and I have fun together for a couple of hours, when I have free time and can relax, but after that I need my space. I'm selfish."

"Me, too."

"Oh, Ricky, have I messed up your life completely?"

"Yup, my picture-perfect life is destroyed forever."

"No, I'm serious. Have you had to put your own work aside to do this?"

"You actually caught me at a good time. I brought work with me and I'm chipping away at it. The late-night gremlins set me back a little, but—"

"Oh, that's right. I'd forgotten about that. Did they find out who it was?"

"No, and your crackerjack police force is not inclined to."

"Pathetic, aren't they? Did they tell you anything?"

"Honestly? No."

"What about Ruth Bowen and her cronies?"

"Karen, do you really think they're murderers?"

"If Ron were here, he'd say, 'Yes, under the right circumstances.'"

"Well, he'd have to explain what those circumstances would be. All I've heard so far is a lot of small-town sniping. Even Rebecca thinks we're on a wild-goose chase and she probably has a better handle on Ron's projects than anyone."

"Well, she would, of course." Mouth set, she folded her arms across her chest.

"Want to tell me what that means?"

"No." Her eyes filled with tears.

"Karrie, you have to tell me what's going on. What's the problem with Rebecca?"

"Oh, you mean the woman who was screwing my husband?" She spit the words out, eyes dry, body rigid.

"You know this for certain?"

She laughed, a bitter, hollow laugh that made my blood run cold. What had happened to the warm, carefree friend of my youth? "They couldn't have been more obvious if they did it in our bed."

"How long?"

"A long time. Started when I was pregnant with Allie. How's that for sensitivity? I don't know why Ron married me in the first place when he was still madly in love with her."

"Did he know you knew?"

"Of course he knew. How do you think I managed to strike our little bargain? He did exactly what I told him to do because he knew if he didn't, I'd take the house, Alex, everything. The house was in my name, you know. Ron didn't like to have any assets on paper. Liked having people think all his wealth was tied up in the foundation. Except for a small portfolio, managed by someone in New York, everything else is in trust, for him and now for Alex. The trust officer gave him a small allowance every month, but that was it. We lived on my salary. Believe me, he had plenty stashed away, but he was a stingy old thing."

My head was spinning. I thought back to running the marathon with Ron and my incessant chatter, most of it about Karen and me, growing up in the neighborhood, our idyllic childhood until my mother's death. He had listened indulgently all the while probably daydreaming about Rebecca, soft, willowy Rebecca, who coddled him as Karen never would. "Does Peter know?"

"God, no. Mr. Straight Arrow, All-American would die if he found out. Of course, he knows they were an item in high school, but that's it."

Or maybe he had known, I thought, listening to my dearest friend, who sounded like a complete stranger. "They were very careful. They met at some motel near Newport, close to Rebecca's office. Isn't that pathetic? I never knew which one, didn't want to know. Only reason I know that much is because one time when I knew he was going to be with her, and I suspected they wouldn't be at her office, I insisted on a phone number. It was before we had cell phones. He hemmed and hawed, but finally gave it to me, and I called. It was a motel on Route 114, but, as I say, I don't remember the name."

"Karen, I don't believe this. Why did you stay?"

"For Alex's sake, I decided to make the best of it for a few years and see what happened. And I loved him, Ricky. In spite of everything, I was crazy in love with him right up until the end. You remember the night we met him? From that moment on, I knew there would never be anyone else for me. And in his way, he loved me, too. I just couldn't give him what he wanted. The sex was always great and we had fun together, especially when we traveled, but it was getting increasingly difficult to pry him away from the Harbor. He was always afraid of missing a committee meeting or a Town Council function. And I could have cared less about all his causes. I think that's really what drove him into Rebecca's arms, my apathy. She had the same fire in her eyes as he did. Peter's the same as me. He couldn't give a shit about all the battles. I don't know how he stands it, but he's so wrapped up in the greenhouse, he probably just tunes it out. Like I do."

Peter Morse was looking more and more like someone I needed to talk to. What a mess. "I don't know what to say, Karrie."

"Nothing to say. And don't look so glum. It's a new age, dearie. Modern marriages look different than our parents' did." Not my parents', I thought, shuffling papers. "I'll let you get back to work. Can I get you something? Tea? Soda? Water?" I shook my head. "Well then, call if you need me." She stooped, hugging me. "Thanks, Ricky. I'd be going crazy now if you hadn't stayed. It means everything to have you here."

"Happy to be here," I lied, giving her a thumbs-up as she left the room. What was I doing? Hearing more sordid details about friends' and acquaintances' lives than I ever wanted to know, that's what.

Methodically, I moved through each file drawer, then on to the shelves nearest the desk that contained a number of spiral-bound notebooks. I pulled one out and read, "Committee Notes: 1997." Flipping through the pages, I found Ron's notes from every Town Council meeting, every committee meeting, every financial town meeting. One account of a Town Council meeting ran eight pages, single-spaced. Incredible. The man should've been a secretary, I mused, imagining the huge case of writer's cramp I'd suffer if I scribbled on for eight pages.

Fortunately, unlike myself, Ron appeared to be a magna cum laude graduate of the Palmer handwriting program, his neat, looping cursive clear and legible. He must have gotten a gold seal every month, I thought, thinking back to the inferior blue seals I usually garnered for my scratchy, left-handed scrawl. Mrs. Horton, my witch of a first-grade teacher, had tried unsuccessfully to break me of my horrid left-handed writing habit. Luckily my mother had gotten wind of her tactics—tying my left arm at my back, knuckle rapping, and other torments—and had taken action. For this particular battle, she had even enlisted my father's aid, and Ralston Steele's formidable presence at the start of one school day had swiftly brought Mrs. Horton to heel. Although I was no longer forced to write with my right hand, I suffered in other ways for the remainder of the year, thanks to this well-meaning parental intervention. Mrs. Horton was a spiteful, vindictive soul, and a sneaky one at that.

With Ron's notebooks, I suspected I would have little need for the Town Hall archives, although these were notes filtered through one lens, and one lens only. The opposition might describe a somewhat different scenario. I sorted out the last five years, stacking them on the desk in a growing pile that I intended to take with me. Flipping through his date book, I found nothing much that I didn't already know. All town meetings were noted, board meetings for the Harp Foundation, doctor and dental appointments for him and Alex, and twice-weekly entries that simply said, "R." I wondered how Rebecca Morse noted these trysts in her date book. I doubted she'd let me take a peek.

After gathering my stack of folders, notebooks and papers, I hobbled to the kitchen, where I found Karen chopping tomatoes. "Stay for supper if you like. I'm making pasta with vegetables and a salad. Simple and boring, but I'd love the company."

"Thanks, but I think I'll pass. I've got a load of work to do and I'd like to start reading through these."

"Oh, Rick, what have I gotten you into?" She feigned dismay, at the same time looking relieved that I'd declined the invitation. We all needed time to ourselves, I decided, saying goodbye and heading out.

CHAPTER 26

As I passed the Crawleys' headed for the cottage, I spied Ralph Boardman, toolbox in hand, heading for the barn. His ladder leaned against the house and a red truck as battered and rusted as Ralph's was parked in my spot. I pulled onto the grass just as the cottage's screen door banged open. Patty, I presumed. Hands on hips, I watched Miss Bold and Brassy as she sauntered toward her husband, throwing me an off-handed wave.

I waved as Ralph came to stand beside his wife. He patted her shoulders, wide as a linebacker's, her arms rippling with muscle. Her cutoff jeans and tank top, at least two sizes too small, were stretched to the max across ample chest and rolling middle, every lump and bulge defined in sharp relief.

"Here's my Patty."

"Hello," I said, coming forward to shake her hand.

"Well, well, well, it's the famous private eye everyone's talking about," she said as her callused hand seized mine in a death grip. "Used your head. Hope you don't mind. No one locks their doors in the Harbor."

How neighborly, I thought, my hand limp and bruised, my jaw aching under the strain of maintaining my fake smile. "Anytime. You helping Ralph today?"

"No way, just lighting' a fire under his sorry ass. We're going out tonight and guaranteed we'd never make it unless I came by and gave him a goose." Although she was younger, husband and wife looked like siblings, same ruddy complexion, sandy hair. Patty's was long, tied back in a loose, scraggly ponytail.

"Nice to finally meet you," I said. "I've heard a lot about you."

She laughed, hands on hips. "All bad, I'm sure."

I shook my head. "Hardly. Although your husband tells me you usually speak your mind." I winked at Ralph. Big mistake. Patty's eyes flashed fire. My idiotic flirting had made another enemy.

"People around here aren't crazy about outsiders, especially snoopy ones," she said, leaning against her truck, arm draped inside the bed. For a second, I imagined she was reaching for a shotgun in order to blow off my head.

"Now, Pats, Ricky ain't doin' no harm." He moved as if to embrace her, but she pulled away. Now we'd both poked the bear.

"I'm looking into a suspicious death for an old friend. Actually, I'm surprised people aren't more curious about Ron Harp's death, given the bizarre circumstances. Wouldn't you want to know if your loved one had died like that?"

"Fallen off a bike, my Ralphie? Now, that's a laugh. Couldn't ride a bike 'less it had training wheels, could you, sugar? Now, come on, we gotta go."

"Patty, I wonder if I might have a word or two with you sometime when you're not in a rush?"

"About what?"

"I'm not sure exactly. Just trying to get some background on the town. You work for Ruth Bowen, don't you?"

"If you think I'll give you any dirt about our friends and neighbors, think again, lady. I got nothing to say to you or any other out-of-town snoop. Check with the police. They're handling this case."

"Not very thoroughly."

"If I were you, I'd be careful who I said shit like that to."

"Excuse me?"

She climbed into her truck. "Honey, I don't give a shit what you're doin' or who you're doin' it with. Don't gotta talk to you, and I'm not gonna. Sue me, what do I care?" She shoved the truck into gear and backed out in a cloud of dust.

Flirting with her husband in order to soften up Patty Boardman had definitely been the wrong approach. The phone's ring called me into the house and I ran to grab it, waving to Ralph as he backed out, considerably slower than his wife.

"Ricky? Myra Rollins here. Karrie tells me you're staying around for a few weeks. Dick and I are giving a small dinner party next Tuesday and wondered if you'd like to come. It's really a Democratic fundraiser, but also a good excuse to entertain. We planned it a long time ago with Ronnie and Karen. We thought about canceling, but then thought Ron would want us to go on, don't you think?"

"I'm sure of it."

"Great, then you'll come? Karen said she'd come if you would and we're trying to get her out of the house, if you know what I mean."

I accepted and rang off, wondering if I had suitable attire. In my hasty packing at home, I'd thrown only a few things in a bag, not paying attention to fashion. If need be I supposed I could go home and collect a few items, but then again, maybe Karen had something baggy, or a skirt with an elastic waist, that might do in a pinch. Most of her clothes were three or four sizes smaller than mine, but we were about the same height.

I spent several hours completing reports and wrapping up most of my current casework. Afterward, I turned my attention to Ron Harp, reviewing all of my notes, creating a time line that stretched back a couple of years. How to make sense of a series of random, apparently unrelated events—Hattie Pauls's death, cats missing, a peacock strangled and now Ron? I stared at the mess until finally, frustrated and hungry, I remembered dinner and the fact that I had nothing in my larder but a few snacks and cereal. Too tired to go grocery shopping, I grabbed my bag, deciding that dinner at the Hearthstone, a restaurant on the other side of town, sounded like a great idea. Before departing, I gathered every paper, notebook and file into two cartons, and loaded them into the jeep. I was not about to clean up after another round of "kid stuff."

Karen called the Hearthstone "blue-haired heaven" and she and Ronnie never set foot in the place. I suspected the reason was not disdain for the geriatric set, but fear of confrontation. The Hearthstone was a hangout for locals, and sure enough, the first person I spied was Alvin Shortliff in a booth right inside the door. Shortliff nodded as his companion, a younger man, turned to stare. Dressed in gray suit, salt-and-pepper hair meticulously lacquered down, green eyes studied me, or should I say, ogled. Snidley Whiplash came to mind. I was not at all surprised when he rose, coming over with hand outstretched. "Miss Steele, hello. Sedgie Montgomery."

"Oh, hi."

He gave me the once-over, eyes coming to rest on my cane. "Don't look much like a detective."

You were expecting Sam Spade? "Private investigator."

"Yes, well, same thing, isn't it? I hear you've been asking a lot of questions around town. You know, you really should be talking to me. As town solicitor, I usually field all inquiries such as yours." He leaned closer, eyes riveted on my chest.

"What kind of inquiries would those be?" I grabbed a menu, holding it in front of me like a shield.

He chuckled. "A coy detective. How charming."

"Truth is, I would like to talk to you, if you have some free time."

"Of course. Call my secretary Monday and have her set something up."

Thanking him, I turned, spotting the elder Harps seated at a table at the far end of the room. The hostess was still occupied so I strolled toward their table to say hello. "Oh, look, Papa," Giffy Harp exclaimed. "Look who's come to say hello."

In a wheelchair, his chin down, Jim Harp had difficulty setting his sights on me. Giffy rearranged what appeared to be a folded baby blanket under his chin, propping it up so he could look straight ahead. When our eyes met, he smiled. "Hello, Mr. Harp. So good to see you both." I bent down, patting his quivering hand.

"We're just finishing dessert. Papa loves the Indian pudding. Here, darling, your last bite. Otherwise, we'd ask you to join us, my dear. Are you here alone? Please sit for a few minutes, won't you? Have the waitress bring you a drink while I finish my coffee. Then I've got to get Papa home. Night nurse arrives at seven."

A short, compact woman, white hair, trim, athletic, Giffy wore "sensible, country clothes"—soft gray turtleneck sweater, gray flannel slacks and brown oxfords, and a bright scarf in blues, oranges and reds tied round her neck. Jim Harp, who at six-five had once towered over his petite wife, now sat dwarfed and shrunken in his customized electric wheelchair. He, too, wore gray flannels and a plaid sports shirt under a navy cashmere sweater, his hair combed and styled. Loving hands took care of Jim Harp.

Karen had often told me about her in-laws. Giffy had come from Pittsburgh, her wealth far exceeding her husband's considerable fortune. They had met when he was still in law school, and after several years working in New York, Jim had brought his young bride to live in the Harbor. People predicted Giffy wouldn't last six months before insisting they move back to the city. However, she had proved them wrong and thrived in her adopted home. She soon involved herself in every exclusive ladies' club in town, including the original garden club, and she was also active in the church, serving as deacon and chair of many committees over the years.

"Well, if I won't be intruding?"

"Heavens no. We love the company, don't we, Papa?"

"How have you been?"

"Well, last week was a setback. Papa was doin' pretty well till Ronnie. Ron was his favorite, you know. Parents say they don't have favorites, but we do. I've always babied Jay, fussing over him. Probably why he can't seem to stick with anything, relationships, careers, homes, poor dear. But, Ronnie was always Papa's boy. Fighting the good fight, you know. We're hoping Bobby will take up the reins, but I don't know. That boy's still a teenager at heart. Never had a care in the world. Frankly, I don't know how Betsy stands him. Oh, dear."

She gazed over at her husband, wiping a tear from his cheek. "Just mentioning Ron's name sets Papa to weeping. Me, too, if I don't watch out. Better get the check. Do you mind if we abandon you, my dear? He looks a little tired."

"Of course not. How can I help you? Can I walk you to the car?"

"No, dear, thank you. Willie from the kitchen comes out and gets Papa all settled in. I could do it, certainly do it night and day at home, but we take any help we can get, don't we, Papa?" As she patted his hand and waved to the waitress, I rose, saying good-night.

CHAPTER 27

The hostess was still nowhere in sight so I shuffled over to the tavern side and plunked myself on the bar stool nearest the kitchen. My stomach was growling. In fact, while talking to Giffy, I'd had to sit on my hands to keep from grabbing their leftover dinner rolls. The bartender took my order and soon returned with a draft beer, green salad, and warm loaf of bread. I dived into all three. My scallops arrived in record time along with a side order of mashed turnips and carrots.

I had just popped the last scallop into my mouth and was ordering Indian pudding a la mode when George Wilbur slid onto the bar stool next to me. "Miss Steele, isn't it?"

"Yes, hello. Mr. Wilbur, right?"

He nodded, shaking my hand. "Can I buy you a drink?"

"That's awfully kind. How about coffee?"

"Wanna make it Irish?"

"Why not."

"Saw you chatting with Jim and Giff. How they doin'?"

"Okay. Pretty fragile, as you can imagine."

"Can't. Can't imagine losing a child. Even a grown one. Worst thing can happen to a person. Parents aren't meant to outlive their children."

"Do you have kids?"

"Three and eight grandkids. All healthy, thank the Lord. They're what's keeping me alive now that my Franny's gone." George Wilbur reminded me of Hedgie the Hedgehog, a character from a favorite childhood storybook, his round and cuddly façade prickly to the touch.

"Do your children live around here?"

He nodded. "All but Kathy and her family. Husband's in the coast guard. They're stationed in Hawaii right now. Prob'ly be his last tour. Twenty years are up next year. You got a family?"

"Just me and my cat."

"Surprising, good-looking gal like yourself. Bet the mature bachelors round here have been giving you the eye."

I laughed. "They've been giving me the eye all right, but not because of my looks. They'd really rather I disappear, if you want to know the truth."

"Harbor folks are friendly, just give 'em time. Little distrustful of strangers 'tis all. Understandable given the last few years."

"Are you referring to Ms. Pauls?"

He nodded.

"But I was told that the police believed she was killed by someone she knew."

"Load of hogwash. Drifter killed Hattie, sure as I'm sitting here. There were a lot of guys around at that time, working on the house next door. There were a few local fellas doing the finish work, but mostly out-of-towners. Outfit from Fall River, bunch of rough customers, mostly Portuguese. Cops never really investigated that angle, but I can tell you, it's one of them fellas killed Hattie."

"But what possible motive would they have?"

"Those kinds of people don't need a motive, just kill for the heck of it."

Uh-oh, round and cuddly was a bit prickly, not to mention racist. "So, do you think it was strangers who killed Ron Harp?"

He smiled, prickles up. "You're a sly one, aren't you? Thought you'd catch me up. Ronnie's death was an accident. Fell off his bike, plain and simple, end of story. Hey, that pudding looks good." The bartender placed two tall Irish coffees with billowing towers of whipped cream in front of us. My bowl of warm Indian pudding soon followed, a generous scoop of vanilla ice cream already melting over the top.

"I could ask for an extra spoon?"

He shook his head. "Not 'sposed to be eating sweets. Bad for my cholesterol."

"Me, neither, but that seldom stops me."

"You enjoy it. I got my coffee."

"Have you lived here a long time?"

"My whole life. Was born in the house I live in. Never left it. Gonna die there, too. My Franny, God rest her soul, died there, and I will, too." Forearms rested on the bar, his hand curled round his coffee as he stared straight ahead.

"Looks like you have lots of good friends. That must help."

"Old friends, yes." The prickles rose again. "Went to school with Al over there. And, of course, Ruthie and I go way back. We're better pals now that her hubby and my Frannie are both gone."

"Were you in the same class at school?"

"All the way." He smiled, eyes sparkling. "Al and Ruthie were sweethearts for a time."

"Not you?"

He blushed. "Well, I might've been sweet on her, but she never knew I was alive. Al was more of a ladies' man, straight A student and all. I was kind of a plain, pokey little guy." I decided that I'd take George any day over Alvin Shortliff, who reminded me of Boris Karloff.

"For what it's worth, my eyes would be trained on you, not Al."

"Uh, oh, you flirtin' with me, young lady? Better watch out now."

I clinked my coffee cup against his. The Indian pudding was heaven, each spicy mouthful. The strong, bitter coffee liberally laced with whiskey was a perfect compliment, even if it would keep me up all night. We chatted about the Harbor, local landmarks he thought I should see, and what the weather was meant to be the next day. George deflecting any attempt to turn the conversation to Ron Harp's death. Finally, I gave up and sat back, enjoying his company. Older men were always such gentlemen. When we said goodnight, I promised to visit the Historical Society where George volunteered twice a week.

I drove home in a fog thanks to the beer and whiskey, only to find chaos in the cottage, again—every drawer, every box, every bin overturned. Stuff was thrown willy nilly and with only a few exceptions, none of it belonged to me. What in the hell was going on? I dialed 911, thankful beyond measure at my foresight in bringing my papers and files to dinner. When the dispatcher picked up, I requested Detective Demaris.

CHAPTER 28

As he stepped through the door, Demaris nearly tripped on an overturned kindling barrel, its contents strewn across the hearth. "Not this again. I've got a wicked headache," he said, kicking a piece of wood aside.

"Join the club. I don't even know why I bothered calling."

"I do. Missed me bad, didn't ya?"

"Ha!"

"Someone's mad at you, Ms. Steele."

"It's Ricky, and what makes you think they're pissed?"

"Weren't looking for anything, just making a mess. Doesn't look like they wrecked anything, except a some of your clothes. This sweater's been slashed up pretty good. Wonder what they used."

"This."

I handed him a small serrated knife I'd found on the bedroom floor. He stuck the knife in his jacket pocket, slowly walking through the room. Occasionally he paused, prodding something with his toe. He did the same thing in the kitchen and bedroom. Finally, he emerged from the bathroom—the only space untouched by the gremlins—running fingers through his thick, dark hair. His fingers left several strands sticking up, giving him the appearance of a young child just roused from sleep. "Okay. That's it then. Want me to send someone out to help you clean it up?"

"No, thanks. I'm going to bed. I'll straighten up in the morning."

"You know, this probably isn't the best place for you to stay right now."

"I will not be run out of town."

"I didn't mean for you to leave town, but a change of residence might not be a bad idea. This place is isolated and Peg and Bob are deaf as posts. So's their little rug rat."

"Skeeter? Guard dog extraordinaire?"

"Exactly. You can't even see this place from the main house. How about staying with your friend?"

"I'll be fine." He opened his mouth to protest, but then said nothing. "Do you have a couple of minutes?"

His furrowed brow and bloodshot eyes screamed no, but he plunked down on the couch. "Sure, what's up?"

"What can you tell me about Hattie Pauls's death?"

He studied me for a minute before answering in rapid staccato. "Strangulation. Killer used one of her scarves. Tied it round her neck, then lashed it to the bedpost and tightened it slowly. Poor woman suffered for a good ten minutes as the bastard slowly wrung the life out of her."

I shuddered. "Who had a reason to kill a ninety-year-old retired principal?"

"Who the hell knows. A disgruntled student? Someone she suspended back in the dark ages? Whoever it was left nothing—no fibers, no footprints, no fingerprints, no nothing. Must've worn gloves and been very careful."

"Did you work it?"

He shook his head. "Out of town. My first vacation in twenty years. A kind of post-divorce celebration."

"Where'd you go?"

"Caribbean, a cruise. Big waste of money. Ate too much, drank too much, read too many trashy novels and listened to a slew of middle-aged divorcees telling me their sob stories."

"Sounds idyllic. So, who was in charge of the investigation?"

"Ripler, but he didn't keep it long. The Chief quickly recognized they were over their heads and brought in the state police. Questioned practically everyone in town, all Hattie's neighbors. It was a real zoo."

"George Wilbur mentioned there were workmen next door."

"Georgie? Now, there's a reliable source. Don't believe three quarters of what Georgie tells you. Great old guy, but not the sharpest knife in the drawer. And lately, he's been more mixed up than usual. Don't know how much longer his kids'll let him live alone. That'll kill him, to move away from the Harbor, poor guy. Where'd you meet him, anyway?"

"Hearthstone. He bought me an after-dinner drink."

"Real ladies' man." He grinned, leaning back, arms behind his head. "Wish I'd been there."

"Is that an invitation?"

He sat up, eyeing me. "Sure, why not?"

"That exciting, eh?"

"You want a drink, I'll buy you a drink. You say when. My calendar's pretty free. I'm off tomorrow night."

"Sorry, I'm busy," I said, remembering my dinner date with Jay Harp. Another occasion that would require special clothes. I'd have to raid Karen's closet in the morning. "But how 'bout Sunday or Monday?"

"Sunday's better. Want me to pick you up here?"

"No, I'll meet you. Hearthstone?"

He shook his head. "The Riptide's better. Do you know it? Meet you there at seven thirty? Maybe we can even stretch that drink into dinner?"

"Count on it."

He rose, staring down at me for a long minute. "Well, then, that's it for me. I'll have Pete come by in the morning to check on you and the lock on the door. Go ahead, roll your eyes all you want, but this guy's pissed and he'll be back."

"How comforting. Good night, Detective."

"It's Roger or Rodge. All my drinking buddies call me Rodge." He was kind of cute in a middle-aged, pot-bellied, emotionally scarred way. Just my type.

As he closed the door, a feeling of loneliness crept up my spine, the bravado displayed for his benefit replaced by cold, jangling fear. While I doubted I'd be strangled in my bed, a sense of unease settled in my stomach, gnawing away at my insides. While my knee was getting stronger with each passing day, my reduced mobility made me feel vulnerable and weak. I dialed Karen's number, needing to hear a friendly voice.

"Hey, you, I'm glad you called. I'm sitting here all alone, feeling blue."

"Want me to come over?"

"No, that's okay. But Ricky, when you think about it, it's silly for you to stay at the Crawleys' when you can stay over here. We've got plenty of room. Even when the nanny arrives, we've still got the guest bedroom. I don't know why I listened to my mother about this."

"Because she was right. You need space, not a houseful of people." Truth be told, I was ready to move in that very second. "I'm fine here and you need peace and quiet. Besides, isn't Jay coming tomorrow night?"

"He can stay with his folks. He usually does. The brothers rarely sleep under the same roof."

"Oh?"

"No big deal. Ron was so fussy, all his routines and habits. And Jay's just the opposite. A fly-by-the-seat-of-his-pants kind of guy, never knows what he's doing next. Used to drive Ron crazy."

"Families are bizarre, aren't they?"

"Speaking of families, how's Annie? I can't believe I haven't even asked you about her."

"She's great. Still in California. We're all getting together at Dad and Rita's for Thanksgiving. That should be interesting. You know how I adore my stepmother."

"Her kids, too?" Rita, my stepmother has two kids, now young adults.

"Yup, they'll be there."

"Do they live with your dad?"

"No, they're with their own father in Chicago. He's remarried, great wife, loves the kids." My stepmother is not exactly the motherly type. She loves to travel and even grown kids tend to cramp her style.

"I'd love to see Annie. Let's get together next time she's here. Think you guys could break away for dinner one night over Thanksgiving?"

"Absolutely. It's a plan. Listen, Karen, while I have you on the phone, I got a call from Myra Rollins about Tuesday and I'm going to dinner with Jay tomorrow night—"

"Ooh la la!"

"Don't start. The thing is, I didn't bring many things with me and I wondered if you had any loose-fitting items that I could squeeze into. I know it's probably impossible, but—"

"I have just the thing. Actually, I have a few things that would fit you perfectly. Actually, one skirt is so big that if it fits you, you can have it. I wore it while I was pregnant."

"How flattering."

She laughed. It was good to hear her laugh, the old laugh of our childhood, not the forced, brittle tittering I'd heard this past week. "In the early months of pregnancy. Oh, Ricky, I almost forgot. I'm working at the pancake breakfast in the morning. Wanna come? It's at the Community Center. Another Democratic fundraiser. No one expects me there after what happened, but Ron would want me to go, so I'm making the effort. Wanna come work? It'd be fun and you could meet lots of people. Unless you think it might be too much with your leg and all."

I scanned the mess surrounding me. What the hell? It would keep a few more hours. "Sure, why not? I'll strap on my brace and be as nimble as ever. What time?"

"I'll be there at 6:00 a.m. Come later if you want, and bring an apron if you can find one in the cottage. Flippin' johnnycakes gets messy."

Assuring her that I'd be there promptly at six doing my best Betty Crocker imitation, I hung up. I started to lock up, then remembered the boxes of papers and Ron's notebooks in the jeep. The gremlins were probably in bed for the night, but just in case, I went out and locked the jeep. Before collapsing into bed, I set the alarm for 5:00 a.m. If I was going to be flipping, and presumably eating, large quantities of johnnycakes in the morning, I sure as hell needed a bike ride first.

CHAPTER 29

A biting wind whipped across the water as I rode around the pond in the semidarkness. A quick shower and I made it to the Community Center by 6:00 a.m. I hadn't found an apron in the cottage, so I tied a long, red-checked dish towel round my waist. Karen, in baggy jeans that had fit her snugly two months ago, wore a calf-length, blue-and-white-striped chef's apron, her arms full of pots and cooking utensils. "Hey, good morning." Arm in arm, we stepped into the maelstrom presided over by Dick Chaffee, who was barking orders like a general.

The whole crew was there—the Souzas, whom I hadn't seen since the funeral, Will and Val Ramsey, the Morses and Myra Rollins. Laura Morrow, the lone Democrat currently on the Town Council, was apparently out of town and unable to make the fundraiser. I had just enough time to nod hello to the crew before Dick said, "Steele, you go with Harp, back grill, start mixing. Cornmeal's on the counter."

"Pleasant, isn't he?" Myra said, flying by with a carton of eggs.

At least twelve of us were packed side by side in the large kitchen. Other volunteers bustled about in the dining area, setting up tables, preparing the buffet. Once Karen and I started mixing, I noticed nothing or no one for several hours. It seemed as though Dick was continually yelling, "Out of johnnycakes" so we worked at a feverish pace until almost nine, when the thinning crowd allowed us a little breathing room.

As the last diners trickled out, Dick announced that it was time for the volunteers to eat. We all loaded plates of eggs, bacon, sausages, and johnnycakes and sat at two of the long tables lined up in the main hall. Dick took his place at the head of the table. "Great job, people. Served two hundred thirty-four. Brought in almost six thousand dollars for the war chest." We all cheered, even me.

"How you coming along?" Val leaned forward, whispering conspiratorially. "With the investigation, I mean."

Ramona waved a sausage laden fork. "No need to whisper, Vallie. Everyone here knows what Ricky's doing."

Karen stiffened. I couldn't see Rebecca Morse, but she had certainly heard. Everyone had, thanks to Ramona, Megaphone Mouth. I smiled. "Probably not the time or place for this, ladies. Tell me about this place. Last time I was here, this was a boarded-up wreck."

"You can thank Dick and Myra for that," Ramona said. "They raised all the seed money, got a Board of Trustees started, and found Happy Whitaker. Happy runs the day-to-day, books all the special programs, exercise classes, whatever. You probably didn't see her, but she was taking tickets today. She had to leave early for her son's soccer game."

"Happy is the heart of this place," Dick said.

"Apt name," I said, slurping up a last bit of syrup with a sliver of johnnycake.

"And if Happy's the heart, Dick and Myra are the center's brain and soul, in that order." Ramona said.

Dick waved away the compliment, but looked pleased nonetheless. Myra had already risen and was in the kitchen doing dishes. "Do the Republicans use the center, too, or is this a Democratic stronghold?"

Dick laughed. "A strictly nonpartisan venture, I can assure you. The board is fifty-fifty and Ruth Bowen worked right along with us in the beginning. She was a real trooper."

Ramona sighed, rolling her eyes at me. "Joined right in, once she saw the political advantages." Alonzo shot her a warning look, which she ignored. "Ruth never does anything for anyone unless it benefits her."

"Thank you, Mona. What a nice compliment." Ruth Bowen stood in the doorway leading to the front hall reception area. "That was a great breakfast. Probably didn't see me in the crowd. Tripp is a Democrat, you know. He's here for the weekend and insisted we come. I was just showing him round the gallery upstairs. He hadn't seen the newest additions." Ramona stared, tight-lipped, as Tripp Bowen joined his mother. "Well, Trippie, we'd better go. Air's bit chilly in here. Thanks again."

The Bowens disappeared and for several minutes, no one spoke. Finally, Will Ramsey broke the silence. "Well, no one can say our breakfast didn't end with a bang." Laughing, we rose as one, clearing the tables. I noticed Rebecca and Karen avoided each other, both stiffening when they passed one another during the cleanup. Work over, Karen and I walked out with Peter Morse. Rebecca had flown out earlier to some kind of meeting.

"How you doing, Karrie?" he asked, his voice gentle, solicitous.

She turned, patting his arm. "Fine, thanks, Peter."

"I've been after Becca to have you two over for supper. Guess it'll have to be after the trial. Was supposed to have settled today, but you know how that goes. Anyway, see ya."

As Peter headed for his truck, Karen turned back to me. "What you up to today?"

"Got a couple of projects at the cottage, then I thought I'd try to catch up with Alvin Shortliff. Not sure if he has anything useful, but he's in cahoots with Ruth and the gang so something might jar loose. How 'bout you?"

"I'm on my way to the funeral home to get the ashes. Then I've got to get the nanny's room fixed up. It's a nightmare. Boxes, books, all kinds of crap. Been a junk room for so long, I'm not even sure what color the carpet is. But it's got to be done since I'm not giving her the guest room. Jay called after I talked to you last night and he's staying with his folks, so that's a relief."

"I saw Giffy and Jim at the Hearthstone last night."

"What were you doing there? I asked you to dinner and you said you were tired!"

Her mock outrage was delivered with a smile.

"I realized after I got home that I had nothing but Doritos and Cheerios. Besides, I thought I might hear something useful."

"Consorting with the enemy?"

"Something like that. Anyway, Giffy and Jim were just finishing up when I arrived. He's not doing very well, is he?"

"'Fraid not. He's been much worse since Ron's accident. For a while, the doctors thought he might regain the use of his legs, but it hasn't happened. And, now with Ron. He was Jim's favorite, you know, the golden boy."

"That's what Giffy said. How long ago was Jim's accident?"

"Nearly two years."

"Rotted steps or something, wasn't it?"

"More like the whole side of their porch gave way. All three of the boys had been trying to get him to have it repaired, but like Ron, Jim is a skinflint. Said it had another year left in it and refused to even discuss it. So, one morning he trotted out to get his paper and boom, the porch just gave way and down he went. You've been out there, right?"

"Years ago."

"The house sits on a huge rock. It's been hit by lightning a couple of times because of that. Anyway, Jim fell right on the rock, from a height of ten or twelve feet."

"Poor guy."

"Bobby and Ron were out there the next day. Had the porch torn off and a new one built within two weeks. Ralph Boardman helped them. He and Bobby are good friends. Ralph's a peach. I don't know how he stays sane, married to

Whip Woman. Only good thing about Patty is that she's been great with Jim. Helps Giffy so much."

"She was at the cottage when I got home yesterday, cracking the whip, as a matter of fact."

"Typical."

"Cheeky, isn't she? I caught her coming out of the cottage. Claims she was using the bathroom."

Karen's cheeks flushed. "Why, of all the nerve. That's it. You're moving in with me."

"We'll see next week. Ralph won't be back on the job till then, so I doubt I'll see Patty again."

"Look, I gotta run, Rick. The funeral home's waiting on me to pick up the ashes. I promised to be there by nine thirty and it's nearly ten. Catch up with you back at the house? How about lunch? Remember, you wanted to try on clothes?"

We agreed to meet at noon. Then I drove the jeep around the corner and parked in front of the Lunch. Unfortunately, Alvin Shortliff was nowhere in sight. I spied Tessa, the waitress, who waved, so I took a chance and asked her if she'd seen Mr. Shortliff.

"Not today, but they had that breakfast at the Community Center. Killed our morning business, but hey, it's for a good cause."

She came up close, whispering. "Don't tell anyone, but I'm a Democrat. I live in Island Park so they don't pay any attention to my party affiliation. Never know, though. Might hurt tips. Anyway, Al wasn't in this morning, but he'll be in at around eleven thirty. He always eats Saturday lunch here."

Thanking her, I headed out, stopping at the store for a paper and tea, which I took to the car. I drove out to the Point, where I spent a pleasant half hour reading the paper and sipping tea, forgetting about Ron Harp, Hattie Pauls, small-town politics and too many queer, unexplained accidents. I had just leaned back and closed my eyes when a tap at the window jarred me awake.

A uniformed police officer, sandy hair, crew cut, early twenties, stood glaring at me. I rolled down the window and read his name plate.

"Officer Burrows, how nice to meet you at last." I flashed my best smile, hoping to crack his stony façade.

"This is private property. No loitering, and no sleeping in cars. Town ordinance."

"Well, I wasn't sleeping, so you can rest easy. And I understood that this was a public right-of-way."

"For town residents."

"I'm a resident at the moment." I flashed him an even bigger smile.

"Permanent residents with a sticker."

"You mean renters can't—"

"That's enough, miss. Move along, now. If you're renting and want a sticker, apply at the police station."

"Don't you carry any in your cruiser?"

"Only issued on weekdays. You'll have to wait till Monday."

"I'll just do that. Will you be there?"

"That's enough." Arms akimbo, he tried to stare me down. "I heard about you, lady. Now move along."

"I hope you've been kept up to date about the crimes perpetrated at my residence by some of your citizens. I would hope the police are giving my breaking-and-entering case their full attention."

"Lady, I don't know what the hell you're talking about and I don't give a shit. Now start up this heap and get moving."

"I'm talking about the break-ins at my house, my rented house, at Red Gate, one of them as recent as last night." Stony silence. "I'm sure you've heard all about them. Just like I've heard all about you. You've been a naughty boy, Skip—effigies are nasty business. With the right judge, right courtroom, something like that might even be considered a hate crime."

That seemed to do the trick. All pretense of detached, military bearing dissolved into a fit of adolescent pique. Cheeks red, his eyes blazing, he took a step back.

For a second I imagined he might draw his pistol and shoot me dead. "I'm giving you thirty seconds to get moving. If you don't, I'm slapping you in handcuffs and bringing you in."

"You just do that." I opened the door, stepping out. I had a good five inches on the little shrimp. "I can see the headlines now. Harbor police officer arrests unarmed female sightseer enjoying the view. Go ahead, slap me in irons." I held out my wrists.

For a minute I thought he might cry, his look of disbelief giving way to fear and confusion. Finally, he turned his back, striding toward his waiting cruiser. "Go to hell."

"Can I quote you on that?" My list of enemies was growing by the minute.

CHAPTER 30

Before heading back to town to find Alvin Shortliff, I took a detour to Bailey's Ledge, hoping to find Charlie Higgins at home. I parked in an open field, the town's answer to a parking lot that served the Ledge and Town Landing. I rummaged around in the back of the jeep and pulled on a jacket against a chill, damp wind. A narrow dirt path wound along the cliff edge, making for a slow descent to the rocky beach below. Cane in front, bracing my every step, I passed through beach plums and wild roses that hugged the cliffs in gnarled, tangled profusion, thankful for the thorny handholds where the path was steepest. By the time my feet hit sand, I was drenched in sweat. The beach was deserted, jutting cliffs shielding the view on either side of me.

It had been years since I'd been at the Ledge, but my recollection was that the old beach shacks had been to the north. Choosing this direction meant I must either climb a wall of rocks and boulders, or wade in the icy water to get around to the next cove. I reluctantly chose the water, removing sneakers and socks, hiking up my jeans and stepping in, cold needles piercing my feet and ankles. Charlie Higgins had to have a better way, I thought, hoping he'd be at home to direct me on my return trip. He wasn't.

After drying my feet, I donned shoes and socks, my skin still clammy, sand between my toes. I sat down at the base of the rocks and slowly inched my way upward on my bottom, not trusting my knee on the vertical ascent. The shack was tucked into the cliff wall of the cove, its door wide open. The top hinge missing, the battered door was nearly vertical, swinging from side to side, flapping like the wing of a wounded vulture. Bits of junk were scattered everywhere in nooks and crannies of the cliff wall—old tires, a dinghy, bedposts, rusty mattress springs, chairs, a kitchen table covered with yellow linoleum, and piles of driftwood. A salvager's paradise until the next hurricane washed it all away. I climbed up to the doorway, peering in at a mess of overturned furniture, knickknacks, and boxes.

A mattress in the far corner had been torn open, its grimy cotton batting exposed. Chunks of batting were scattered around, suggesting the slasher had been searching for something. I looked for signs of habitation—clothes, food, personal items—but found nothing. I was about to begin a search for an easier route up the cliff when a spot of light caught my eye. Refracted from something near the ceiling, the tiny beam danced and skipped across the floor. Peering up, I saw nothing. I grabbed a chair and pulled it directly below a low-hanging rafter. Then I stepped on with my good leg, reaching up to pat along the dusty rafter, reassuring myself that black widow spiders and scorpions didn't live near the ocean. Finally, my hand touched metal and I brought down a stainless-steel canister. Old and dented in spots, a yellow grain of wheat painted across its middle, it looked to be one of a set of kitchen canisters, the kind used to store flour, sugar and tea.

Carrying my treasure outside where the light was better, I sat on a rock. Sheltered from the wind, I twisted the lid off and pulled out a wad of papers. In the bottom of the canister were a service metal I recognized as a Purple Heart, a set of dog tags, Charlie Higgins's driver's license that had expired ten years ago, a few buttons, coins, and a set of gold cuff links. I unfolded the papers and I realized I was looking at Charlie's idea of a safe deposit box. There was a handwritten will leaving everything to his sister, Maisy. There was also Charlie's birth certificate, military ID clipped to a letter confirming his honorable discharge, and several dog-eared black-and-white photographs.

One was a school picture, Harbor High School Class of 1956. Another was of four young men, soldiers, shoulder to shoulder, mugging for the camera. I recognized Charlie from his license photo. The last, a smaller snapshot, was of a young man and woman holding hands, Charlie and someone he loved, laughing, falling into one another as young lovers do. Who was she? Had there been a Mrs. Higgins years ago? There was something vaguely familiar about her, but she looked like every photo from that era, bobbed hair, pullover sweater, chiffon scarf round slender neck.

Carefully repacking the canister, I started inside, intending to return it to its hiding place. The image of the shredded mattress stopped me. Maisy Higgins lived in town, Maisy Grant now. Even if she didn't know where her brother was, surely she would want to hold on to his valuables for safekeeping.

After a few minutes searching, I discovered an overgrown path leading up the cliff behind the shack. Slowly, I climbed upward, hacking my way through brambles. By the time I reached the field, my wrists and hands were covered with scratches and my knee throbbed. I arrived just in time to see my car hoisted off the ground, the tow truck's motor whining against the weight.

"Wait!" I screamed, waving as I hobbled to intercept the driver. He stuck his head out of the cab. "What the hell, lady?" I recognized him as one of mechanics from Billy Mederois's garage.

Pain in my knee forgotten, I scooted around to the cab. "What are you doing?"

Giving me a look that said, "What's it look like, you moron?" he said, "This your car? I remember now. Thought this car looked familiar. Didn't we give you a tow last weekend?"

I nodded. "What's the problem?"

"Lady, I just take the calls. They say 'tow,' I tow."

"Who called you?"

"Cops."

"Who exactly?"

"Officer Burrows. Said it had to be done right away. Told me to drop what I was doin' and come straight out. Figured it was an emergency."

"Well, it isn't, so if you would kindly drop my car, I'll be on my way, no hard feelings."

"No can do."

"Excuse me?"

"Once the cops give us a job, we do it."

Red spots of fury danced in my eyes. "Look, this is ridiculous. I-I— Oh, what the hell. Where are you taking it?"

"Our station. We keep it till you pay up."

"Can I hitch a ride?"

"Sure. Hop in." He put the truck in Park and reached over, offering me his hand, which I gratefully accepted. It took all his strength and mine to heave me up and into the cab.

Mike Nugent, a grease monkey in his early twenties, happily told me his life story on the five-minute drive into town. High school dropout, drag car racer, married at sixteen, wife pregnant, baby girl, Carolyn, divorced at eighteen, her parents were raising the kid, ex-wife moved to Florida. Mike was living with his parents until he saved enough for his own place. Sees his daughter on Saturdays.

Using my best come-hither voice, not to mention a forty-dollar tip, I persuaded him to stop at the police station "on the way." For another twenty, he agreed to wait five minutes while I ran in to straighten things out.

Cal Ripler was the first person I saw. He was behind the desk, rummaging through a file cabinet, cigarette dangling from his lips. Dispensing with pleasantries, I said, "Where's Officer Burrows?"

He looked up, eyeing me slowly. "Out." He returned to his files as if I were invisible.

"Well, then you'll have to help me, won't you?"

"Listen, honey, I'd love to play cops and robbers with you, but I'm pretty busy today."

"You call me 'honey' one more time and I'll sue your ass. Now, will you get out there and tell Mike Nugent to release my car immediately?"

"What in the hell are you jabbering about?"

"My car. It's been towed, as if you didn't know."

"Lady, I've been in court all morning. I just got in. I don't need this shit right now."

"Well, then, fix it."

Shaking his head, he followed me outside, flicking his cigarette into the shrubbery lining the front walkway. As we approached, Mike hopped out of the truck.

"What's up, Mikie?"

"Skip called. Said to tow it."

"What the hell for?"

"Parked illegally. Bailey's Ledge."

Ripler shook his head. "Should've gotten a sticker, Miss Steele. No parking at the Ledge without a sticker."

"Bullshit. When was the last time you towed anyone?"

"Signs are posted everywhere."

"Well, I didn't see any."

"She's right, Cal. Signs are down. Must have been the last big storm. Saw one of 'em in the bushes."

Ripler bowed his head, pretending to be weighing the seriousness of the crime. "Hell, put her down, Mikie. We'll let her go this time. Give him fifty bucks, hon, Miss Steele, and you can be on your way."

"I will not." I wanted to slap his fat, smirking face.

"The fine's a hundred. I'm giving you a break. Take it or leave it. You got thirty seconds to decide. I got work to do."

I checked my watch and saw it was after twelve. Furious, I pulled two twenties and a ten from my wallet. "This is highway robbery and you damn well know it."

"Just keepin' our town safe," he said, turning away, heading inside.

"Just like you did for Hattie Pauls and Ron Harp?"

He turned on me, eyes spitting fire, face beet-red. "One more crack like that and I'll slap you in a cell. Now, get the hell outta here before I change my mind."

Hands on hips, chin out, I glared back at him. "What's the charge? Telling the truth?"

He shook his head. "Lady, you haven't got a clue, have you?"

So furious I was seeing stars, I nevertheless thanked Mike Nugent and heaved myself into the jeep. Mike waited to make sure it started up, then waved me out of the parking lot. I headed into town, counting to a hundred while taking deep, cleansing breaths.

CHAPTER 31

The Lunch was packed. I elbowed my way in the door, spotting Shortliff at a booth in the back with George Wilbur, Tippy Bingham and a younger woman I didn't recognize. George waved, and I headed over. He introduced me to Tippy, Alvin and the woman, Sally Williams, the town archivist. There wasn't room in the booth so George offered to move to a table with me. Williams rose. "You stay, Georgie. Come on, Ms. Steele, you and I can sit at the counter."

"I don't want to take you away from your friends."

"No problem. I heard you were looking for me, and this'll give us a chance to chat without George interrupting every other word."

Tessa took our orders—chowder and half a grilled cheese for her, chowder and a veggie pocket for me—then disappeared. "How you getting on?"

"Well, I just rescued my car from a tow truck and I'm ninety dollars poorer, if that tells you anything."

"Uh-oh, where'd you break down?"

"I didn't," I said, relating the events of the past few hours.

Sally shook her head. "I'm not surprised. Skip's a hothead. A lamb till you cross him. Then you'd better watch out."

"Is that what happened last year, when he made the effigy of Ron Harp?"

"No, that was showing off. Skip's a bit immature."

"Has his temper gotten him in trouble before?"

She shrugged. "Patrick and I have only lived in the Harbor a few years. Al Shortliff is my mom's second cousin. He called and told us the town needed an archivist, and someone to run the Macomber House and Historical Society. He knew Patrick was working for the historical society in Lenox. We lived in Amherst then. Both went to U. Mass. That's where we met. Anyway, Uncle Al—that's what we call him even though he's a cousin—he called and then Ruth. She was able to find me a job as well so everything worked out perfectly.

"But, to answer your question, I don't know much about Skip's past. All I know is the rumors about him being a hothead. I think he was a bit of a brawler in high school. Never took teasing very well."

And now he's a cop. Perfect. "Any trouble lately?"

"Not that I know of. Since the effigy business he's been a model citizen, officer and gentleman, helping out at the school, volunteering at the senior center. I think Chief Sisson read him the riot act. I understand that being a police officer is all Skip's ever wanted to do. And, his letter of apology seemed sincere. It was printed in the *Harbor Times*."

Our food arrived and we chatted about her work at the Town Hall and historical society. She had learned a lot about town history in three short years. When I asked about politics, she claimed she and her husband were "apolitical" and didn't follow town politics. "A member of the Town Council always volunteers to take notes at the meetings, so I never have to go." She leaned closer, grill cheese in hand, whispering. "I type 'em and file 'em, but Tippy usually writes them. History fascinates me. Squabbling doesn't."

"How convenient for you and him." If she noticed my sarcasm, Sally didn't show it.

"Town Council meetings are on book club night and Patrick and I hate to miss it. It's a special group, meets in Portsmouth. We read and discuss historical texts, mostly biographies, but sometimes we read primary source materials or historical narratives, too. We favor the colonial period. A couple of the younger members wanted to read Vietnam books this year, but the rest of us rebelled."

As I popped the last bite of my sandwich into my mouth, I remembered Charlie's canister stuffed in the bottom of my bag. "Sally, I have something I'd like you to look at." Rummaging around, I carefully extracted the photographs, keeping the canister concealed in the bag. I handed her all three.

For several minutes, she studied them, flipping from one to the other. Finally, she looked up. "Where did you find them?"

"I'd rather not say. Do you recognize anyone?"

"Well, yes. Charlie Higgins is in all three. Don't know his army buddies in the first one. But the school photo, that's Uncle Al, and Tippy. George is in front next to Ruth and …who is that woman? I can't remember. I've seen her before. And then, of course, this one is of—"

"Ruth Bowen and Charlie," I said, as she held up the picture of the couple. "Were they sweethearts, then?"

"Not that I know of. I expect she wouldn't want people to know either. Gee, they look cute though, don't they? That was when he had the whole world ahead of him, poor man."

"Do you know him well?"

"Not really. He comes into the historical society from time to time. Loves to talk. He's a bright guy, lots of wonderful memories about the Harbor. Occasionally Patrick lets him check out materials. Always returns them promptly."

"What kinds of materials?"

"Well, now, let me see. I think a while back he was after school records, things like that. We don't have much of that kind of thing, but there were a couple of boxes. Kind of a mishmash. One of the many projects we haven't gotten to yet. It's amazing what a town can accumulate in two hundred years."

"Did he ever talk to you or your husband about the materials he checked out?"

"No, at least not that I know of. Patrick's tried to persuade him to let him record some of his Harbor recollections as oral history, but Charlie always refuses. It's too bad, because when he gets going, he has a lot to say. It would be wonderful to preserve that."

"Has your husband taped many townspeople?"

"Oh, yes, over a hundred. They make fascinating listening. They're all at the Macomber House. You can check them out or listen to them there. It's an amazing collection."

"So this relationship is not common knowledge, I take it?" I held up the photo.

"No, but, as I say, I'm a newcomer. There's an awful lot I don't know and people don't bang down your door to tell you their secrets around here. Uncle Al might know. I'd wait and ask him in private, if I were you."

I nodded, returning the other photos to the canister, keeping the picture of the couple separate, tucked in the side pocket of my bag. Her companions were just finishing up as we paid our bill. Sally said that if I waited, her cousin would most likely be happy to talk with me. I didn't possess her confidence in Uncle Al's hospitality, but I ordered a tea to go from Tessa.

When Sally returned to say goodbye, I asked, "Did Ron Harp ever use your archives?"

"Yes, quite often, actually. Usually, it was to fill in his notes about town meetings. Funny you should ask though. Now that I think of it, he and Charlie both asked for the same materials at one point. I only remember it because Ron got there first and Charlie put up such a fuss when Patrick told him the things were checked out."

"Sally, do you remember which materials? It's important."

"Those school records, I think. I'm not certain, but Patrick would know. Give him a call or come by the historical society. This time of year we're open Tuesday through Saturday, ten to four."

I thanked her and she departed, stopping by the next table to whisper in her cousin Al's ear. A few minutes later, with nods and hat tipping, George and Tippy left and Shortliff came to slide into the booth opposite me. "Sal said you wanted a chat." When he smiled, his face brightened slightly, lessening the Boris Karloff resemblance.

"Yes, thanks. She's been filling me in on local history. Fascinating."

"That what you are, then, a history buff? Thought you were some kind of private investigator."

"Well, I enjoy history, but you're right. I'm also looking into Ron Harp's death. His family was concerned about the strange circumstances and the fact that his bike disappeared and all."

"Harbor police looked into it. Accident's what I heard."

"Is that what you think?"

He shrugged. "Always too bad when a young person dies unexpectedly."

"What did you think of Ron?"

"Nice kid. A bit of a troublemaker, but heck, town needs some excitement once in a while. Sometimes his bunch got out of hand. Like the business with the power plant. Would've brought in revenue for generations to come." He referred to the project that had spurred the creation of IMPACT. The state and a private contractor had spent three years negotiating with the town to purchase a hundred-acre parcel at the north end. The plan was to erect a coal-fired power plant sometime in the next ten years, a plant that would serve the energy needs of much of southeastern New England.

"While ruining pristine pastures, woods and fields. Not to mention the river and the millions of fish'd be dead in six months from water temperature fluctuations."

He shrugged. "Well, they got their way, didn't they? We've moved on."

"That's an interesting political observation. Who gets their way on whatever issue's at stake? Is that how you really see town affairs?"

"Depends."

"On?"

"On who I'm talking to."

"Where do you stand on the Harbor Club?"

"No offense, miss, but I'd have to know you a lot better to share my politics with you."

"You've lived in Windy Harbor your whole life, haven't you?"

"Yup."

"Went to school with Ruth Bowen, and your lunch buddies, right?"

He nodded, smiling. "Doesn't take a rocket scientist to figure that out."

"Do you always side with your friends on town issues?"

He shrugged. "Been friends for over sixty years, but I don't speak for anyone, on any issue."

"That's not what I asked."

"But that's all I've got to say." He smiled, retrieving his hat from the bench.

"Before you go, I wonder if you'd look at something?" I pulled the picture of Charlie and Ruth Bowen from my bag, holding it out to him.

He smiled, taking it from me. "Well, now, that's something. Where did you ever get this?"

"How long were they together?"

Another shrug. "Just friends, as I remember it."

"Looks like more than friends to me."

He laughed, handing me the photo. "You're asking the wrong person, miss. What's an old bachelor like me know about affairs of the heart?"

"But you know your friends."

Another shrug.

"What about Charlie Higgins? Are you still friends with him?"

"Charlie and me were never close. He was a jock. I've always been a four-eyed bookworm."

"So none of his old schoolmates have tried to help him these last few years?"

"Charlie doesn't need help. He's doin' just fine on his own."

"Oh, really? Where is that, anyway? I went down to his shack on Bailey's Ledge. He sure isn't living there. And from the look of it, someone's trashed the place."

For a second, he looked surprised. Then the expression of bland neutrality returned. "Darned if I know. Haven't laid eyes on Charlie for six months. Listen, miss, I've got an appointment so gotta run. Nice talkin' to you. Good luck with your snooping."

I flashed my best smile. "Thanks so much, Mr. Shortliff. You've been very helpful."

"I hope not," he said, winking as he turned away and strode out the door.

It was nearly one, so I dropped two dollars on the table and headed for Karen's and my wardrobe fix. If she didn't have anything for me I was going to be a sorry sight when Jay Harp picked me up for dinner.

CHAPTER 32

Karen met me at the door, rubbing her hands. "Where have you been? I thought we were having lunch."

"Oh, Karrie, I'm sorry." I filled her in on my lunch meetings with Shortliff and Sally Williams.

"Never mind, then. I forgive you. Come on, I've got everything laid out on the bed."

I'd forgotten how much she loved clothes. Loved to shop for them, try them on, talk about them, give advice. "Hold your horses, girl. Let me use the bathroom. Too many cups of tea with Alvin, George and the gang have caught up with me."

"Well, hurry up. I've got to go in about half an hour."

I filled her in on my morning's activities, while she whisked one outfit after another in front of me. Some I tried on. Others were rejected mostly because I couldn't have gotten them over my big toe. Finally, after much fussing and fuming, I selected two outfits—a black sleeveless dress with matching jacket, and a pair of gray linen slacks with an elastic waist, which Karen insisted I keep since they were "miles too big." These we paired with a long silk blouse and what Karen called a "big shirt," a flowing cashmere sweater in a soft mauve. She then flew around, accessorizing both outfits—a string of pearls and matching earrings for the dress, and a soft floral scarf and silver tea drop earrings for the other. As she selected each item, Karen arranged the ensemble on the bed.

Finally, she stood back, surveying the array. "Now, have we forgotten anything? Oh, my God, shoes. What are we going to do about them?" Karen's feet were the only part of her that was bigger than me—she wore tens, and I wore seven and a half.

"Well, we could fish my flats out of your trash barrel, wash 'em up and give 'em a quick coat of shoe polish."

"Very funny." She was frowning, concentrating on this unforeseen dilemma.

"How far's the nearest shoe store?"

"Half an hour, but that's Dartmouth and there's nothing there. You have to go to Providence or Newport."

"I'll wear tennis shoes. It'll be dark. No one'll notice."

"Don't be ridiculous. Now, hush and let me think. Myra—no, she wears a ten. Betsy? Forget it, she wouldn't have anything suitable. Ramona's a possibility, but her shoe collection is pitiful. Hmmm, let me see. Val! She's an eight, I think. She may be a little frumpy, but I'm pretty sure she has a pair of decent black shoes. Let me give her a call."

"Now, wait a second, Karrie. Val Ramsey was witness to me ruining my own nice shoes. Why would she want to let me borrow hers?"

"Because I'm going to tell her Mother will buy her a new pair if you wreck 'em, that's why." She gave me a sweet smile, grabbed the phone and dialed. Val was at home and said she'd be happy to lend the shoes. Triumphant, Karen rang off, declaring the shoes would go nicely with both outfits, "thank goodness."

Everything on hangers, she slipped clear plastic laundry bags over the entire batch. "Sorry, dearie pie. I've gotta run," she said, bussing my cheek. "Imagine, Ruth Bowen and Charlie Higgins, sweethearts. Now, wouldn't that make a great headline for the *Harbor Times*? And wouldn't Ron have loved it? Ta- ta! Have fun on your hot date."

She was in her car, the motor running, before I could think of a snappy reply. Hot date, indeed. And what if Ron had discovered Ruth Bowen's teenage romance? Would it have mattered? Would Ruth have killed to keep it quiet? She certainly couldn't have done it alone. I recalled Trippie Bowen at his mother's side, steering her around the Harps' living room. Where had he been last Sunday morning? I wondered, gently laying my new wardrobe across the back seat.

The Ramseys lived at the north end of town not far from the conservancy land saved from the power plant project. Like the Harps, Will and Val had designed and built their home, albeit on a more modest scale and budget. The tiny, two-story bow house sat on a grassy knoll, surrounded by thick woods. Will had cleared several hundred yards out from the house in all directions, but it was clearly a constant battle between man and nature. Man appeared to be losing along the property's east end, the wild roses and scrub maples already thirty feet high clawing over what appeared to be a new fence.

I knocked on the door, the sound unleashing a chorus of barks and screams from the rear of the house. Through the glass front door, I spied Val in the hallway accompanied by a scrambling ball of fur and several small people. "Ricky, hi, come in." As she opened the door, she held back the menagerie, a white ball of fur yipping and barking for all he was worth.

"Tigger, stop it."

No effect.

"All right, out you go. Come on back, Ricky. Kids, this is Ms. Steele. Ricky, this is Martha and Willie. Can you say hi?"

I wasn't sure if she was talking to me or the kids, but I bent down, holding out my hands to the girl first. Dark-haired like her father, she stared at me with dreamy eyes the color of the sea. "Hi. You're a big girl. How old are you?" She held up three fingers.

"She'll be four next month, though, won't you, darlin'? She's her momma's best helper, aren't you? Now take Willie into the playroom, will you, sweetie?" Martha grabbed hold of her brother's hand none too gently and led him toward the kitchen. "That'll last about three minutes," she whispered, "so we'd better get you outfitted. Come on. I have a couple of pairs that might work. I don't expect with your knee that you'd be wanting heels, right?"

She led me through to the dining room, where she had placed three shoe boxes. A woman who kept her shoes like new in the boxes had no business lending them to the likes of me and I told her so. "Don't be silly. Besides, I never wear them anyway. And…" she winked, "if Milly's gonna replace them, what do I care?"

After inspecting all three, I chose a simple pair of flats, slipping them on. They fit perfectly. The other two pairs, heavy buckles, shiny tops, were definitely not my style. "Thanks, Val. This pair should work fine."

"Excellent." She snapped them into a shoe box with such efficiency that I half expected her to bag them and give me a receipt. "How 'bout a cup of tea or coffee?"

"Tea'd be great, if it's not too much trouble."

We sat in a sunny breakfast room sipping lemon mist tea, the children's voices muffled in the background. We talked about Will's business and she related the saga of building the house. "We couldn't have done it without Ron and Karen. I actually went home for a while. I was so sick after Martha's birth. Depressed, really, and I needed to be home with Momma. Karen helped Will pick all the paint colors, the tiles, linoleum, countertops. I don't know what would have happened if she hadn't stepped in. Will's color blind, poor dear. We'd have had pink countertops and lime-green linoleum, I expect."

"How long have you lived in the Harbor?"

"This is our twelfth year. We rented for the first few years while Will built the business. Then, when we decided to start a family, we wanted our own place." A scream from the other room signaled the end of brother-sister harmony. Martha ran past us on her way to the stairs. "You can have him now! I'm going to play dolls."

"Oh, dear. Hold on and let me see." She returned with a sobbing Willie, thumb in mouth, dark curls matted with sweat. "Were you acting like a terrible two again, sweetie pie?" She smoothed hair, planting a kiss on his damp brow. He responded by burrowing down under her blouse. I thought he was hiding until he hiked the blouse higher and Val's left breast appeared, clutched in his chubby hands. She smiled at me, leaning back as soft sucking sounds told me his mouth had found its mark.

"If only all problems could be solved as easily," I said, sipping my tea, watching the look of contentment wash over Val's face.

"Where were we? Oh, yes, talking about Karen and Ron—they are the dearest friends. This town has lost a real hero in Ronnie. Any news? Have you found out anything about the accident?"

"Not much except the fact that your top-notch police force ruled it an accident. Period, end of story."

"Oh, please. Cal Ripler couldn't investigate his way out of a paper bag. What a pompous ass that man is."

"Val, do you know anything about the animals that have been killed? I know about Karen's peacock, but I've heard there've been other animals that have died over the last few years under mysterious circumstances."

"It is odd, isn't it. Ow, Willie, that hurt!" She sat up, breaking suction, pulling her breast away, smiling sheepishly. "He bites." Willie emerged from under the blouse, mouth rimmed with milk, a drunken look on his cherubic face.

"The person to ask would be Hank Mederois, the animal control officer, but he's murder to get a hold of. Tigger was missing for two days and we couldn't reach Hank. Finally, Will went to the station and demanded Cal send someone out looking for Tigger. It's not as if they have anything better to do over at that stupid police station."

"Did they find him?"

"No. Turned out he'd been out with Charlie Higgins. Charlie, the old fool, was feeding him bits of fish and canned beans. Tigger had diarrhea for two weeks after he got home."

I told her about my trip to Bailey's Ledge and the discovery of Charlie Higgins's treasures. Like Alvin Shortliff, Val hadn't seen Charlie in a while, but she suggested I take the canister to his sister. "Maisy'll know where he is. She's a sweetheart. And, goodness knows, she's tried to get help for her brother. It's pathetic, isn't it, what happens to people?"

I nodded, watching Willie disappear under her right breast, emerging triumphant several seconds later, his mouth clamped firmly over his mother's distended breast. I winced inwardly, assuring myself that if I had ever had children, I would have weaned them before they had teeth. "Did you know Ruth Bowen had a thing with Charlie years ago?"

"No."

"Yup, I've got the photographic evidence."

"Wouldn't she have a pickle if that got out. Couple of years ago she tried to get Charlie committed. Tried to tear down his shack and get his family to commit him to the state home. Maisy refused. I don't think the state home would've taken him anyway. Charlie's not crazy, just different. Anyway, it was a bitchy thing for Ruth to do. Ruth and that ridiculous excuse of a town solicitor."

"Montgomery? What'd he care?"

"I think he was just following orders, but who knows? Maybe some of the investors in the Harbor Club were behind it. That's one of Charlie's favorite hangouts, the old Fisherman's Restaurant. Sits out on the deck on sunny days, or he goes out fishing on the breakwater."

I felt a chill creeping up my spine, remembering condition of the shack, shredded mattress, furniture scattered everywhere. Where was Charlie Higgins and what did he know about Ron Harp's death? I rose, setting my tea cup by the kitchen sink. "I better go. Thanks for the shoes. I'll take good care of them."

Reaching down, she broke the suction between breast and mouth, settling the now sleeping Willie on the window bench beside her. Angelic in slumber, a drool of milk snaked down his rosy cheek as he mercifully slept on. Tiptoeing out of the room, she accompanied me to the door, still adjusting and readjusting things under her blouse.

I considered swinging by Maisy Grant's home, but checking my watch, I decided it would have to wait until morning. I had to shower, change and reinvent myself, all before seven o'clock. No problem. I had two hours.

CHAPTER 33

Jay Harp was late, thank goodness, since I was still blow-drying my hair when I spied the lights of his B.M.W. in the driveway. I heard the door creak open, his feet stamping on the inside door mat, and decided he was feeling a little too much at home. "Be right out," I called, throwing down the dryer and flying to the mirror. "There's wine in the fridge. Pour yourself a glass if you'd like."

I heard him open and close the fridge door. I thought I heard him mutter, "I'll wait," as he crossed into the living room to sit down. A wine snob. That figured. Kendall-Jackson not good enough for him. Humph.

On the best of days, my shoulder-length hair is a tangled snarl of brown curls—"burnt umber," my last boyfriend had called it-- although the salt and pepper conversion was definitely in progress. Periodically, I consider streaking, dying or highlighting it, but then I remember the *m*-word—*maintenance.* My hairdresser calls me a "wash and go person" and she's right, except on the rare occasions, like now, when I try to look special. I brushed and fussed, sweeping it back from my face with tortoise shell clips. Then, deciding I looked like Donna Reed, I yanked out the clips, gave one pass with the brush, applied a few swipes of mascara and turned my back to the mirror. I slipped into Val's shoes, grabbed the black jacket and made my entrance as best I could while leaning on a cane.

Gorgeous in dark blue suit, Jay had the good grace to whistle, standing as I emerged. "Wow, you look sensational."

"I'll bet you say that to all the girls." I waved my hand and snatched up my bag. It did not go with my outfit, but too bad. I wasn't leaving it, or Charlie's treasure can, at home for the neighborhood gremlins.

His hand found the small of my back, sending shivers up my spine, and I quickened my pace, flitting ahead to the jeep.

"We're going in that thing?"

"No, just locking up."

Satisfied that all was secure, I hopped into his B.M.W. and we were off. On the way to the restaurant I told him about the break-ins.

"That's it. I'm going straight to the police station in the morning to lodge a formal complaint. And Ricky, Demaris is right. It's not safe for you to stay here alone." I made no comment, deciding to wait and see how the evening went.

We drove thirty minutes to the Regatta, a restaurant housed in an antique red colonial, the building's façade lit with thousands of tiny white lights in trees. The maître d' greeted us warmly, falling all over "Mr. Harp."

At his insistence, we started with Bombay Sapphire martinis, so I was already a little fuzzy by the time our escargots arrived. Since we both had decided on rack of lamb, the "house specialty," Jay ordered an excellent Saint-Emilion, which we sipped while sharing the snails, pungent and earthy, loaded with butter and garlic.

Feeling downright tipsy and light-headed, I gulped water and nursed my glass of wine. After slurping up the last of the garlic sauce with bread, I excused myself and headed for the ladies' room.

I stared at my disheveled reflection in the mirror, and whispered, "Get a hold of yourself, Steele." I splashed water on my cheeks, ran a brush through my hair, paced the room several times, and sucked on a Life Saver. Finally, unable to stall any longer, I returned to the table, where I found him grinning like the Cheshire cat.

"You look very pleased with yourself."

He laughed. "Why shouldn't I? I'm with a beautiful woman, at my favorite restaurant, about to have a fabulous meal. Now, relax. I'm not going to take advantage of you just cause you can't hold your gin."

"Ha, ha," I sniffed, lifting my wineglass. "Take care that someone doesn't take advantage of you, Mr. Harp."

"Is that a promise?"

A change of subject was definitely in order. "How's everything at your parents'?"

"Great. Mom said they saw you the other night. You know, she's crazy about you. Always said one of us should have married you—daughter of the great Ralston Steele and all."

"Don't start." The mention of my father sent my head to throbbing. "Karen was telling me about your dad's accident."

"Ruined their life. Really clipped Mom's wings. She loves to travel, but they haven't been able to go anywhere since it happened. Except that stupid Canadian cruise. He didn't come out of the stateroom the whole time except to eat. Spent all day and night watching movies."

"When you live in a paradise like this, why travel?"

"Mom hates the Harbor. If something happens to him, she'll be out of here like a shot."

"To where?"

"Boston, probably. She has friends there. She'll probably keep the Naples place. She likes that well enough, but she's sick of the Harbor."

"But she's into everything —garden club, church, the whole bit."

"Just 'cause she's in them doesn't mean she likes them. You know what, let's not talk about parents tonight, okay? You clearly don't wanna discuss your dad, and I don't either. Spoils the mood, if you know what I mean."

"Fine. Let's talk about you."

"Let's not. That sad, sordid tale would definitely spoil our dinner. Let's talk about you. Have you accepted that Ron's death was an accident?"

I shrugged. "Who knows at this point? Your town is full of intrigue and ghosts, I'll say that for it. What do you know about Charlie Higgins?"

"Charlie? How'd you get hooked up with him?"

"I haven't hooked up with him. That's the trouble," I said, filling him in on my day's activities before pulling out Higgins's photographs, handing them to him one by one.

He whistled, shaking his head. "So old Charlie's kept this one of him and Ruth all these years."

"Did Ron know Charlie well?"

"Never heard him mention him. Charlie wasn't his type. Too flaky. Ron didn't suffer fools very well. Charlie's also older, our parents' generation, really. Only thing they might've had in common was history. Ron was a history buff. So was Charlie."

"Did your dad know him growing up? He came here summers, didn't he?"

"Yes, but I've never heard Dad talk about Charlie either. Even in those days townies and summer folks didn't mix. Skewks, they call summer people now. Awful name, isn't it?"

"Why would Ruth Bowen care if people knew about her and Charlie? I mean, it was thirty years ago and he was a decorated war hero."

"Who says she does? Care, I mean?"

Everyone, I thought, smiling, as the waiter set our dinner in front of us. The lamb was succulent, juicy and sweet, served with grilled baby vegetables and risotto. As we ate, we chatted about recent movies we'd seen and books we'd read. It felt good to talk about normal, everyday things instead of dwelling on the sordid little secrets of Windy Harbor. Just as we had years ago, Jay and I found we had a lot in common, and we fell into easy conversation that carried us through dessert to our after dinner brandies in the restaurant's lounge.

He insisted on paying the check and we walked arm in arm to the car. As I settled into the B.M.W.'s soft leather seats, I sighed. "I feel wonderful."

"Me, too." He reached over and took my hand, his touch gentle, caressing.

I pulled my hand away, pretending to fuss with my bag, knowing with absolute certainty how the evening would end. As we swayed arm in arm up the cottage's steps, I closed my eyes. "You look. I can't face another mess."

He took my key and opened the door. "All clear." With that, he swept me into his arms and carried me into the house. I started to protest, but it felt so good to be off my feet, letting someone else carry the load. Then his lips found mine and I was a goner. I'd forgotten what a good kisser Jay Harp was. A good kisser and lots of other things besides.

I woke to a kiss on my nose, lips tracing a shivering path down my neck. I moaned, realizing that it had been almost a year since I'd spent the night with a man. Morning breath, I thought, before Jay Harp erased all coherent thought from my mind. Our lovemaking left me warm and relaxed.

"Good morning, gorgeous," he said at last.

"Hmmm, it is a good morning, isn't it?" I turned away so as not to knock him out with my breath.

"Come here, Ricky Steele. I'm not done with you yet."

"Oh, yes, you are," I said, pulling a blanket around me as I rose on my good leg, gingerly testing the other before deciding that I needed a prop. "I've got things to do and you've got to get going. Karrie's expecting you, isn't she?" I wended my way to the bathroom, leaning on a chair, pushing it along in front of me.

"Hey, I could've helped you… Come on, Rick. You don't have to be anywhere till noon. We've got plenty of time. Come back to bed."

Tempting, I thought, smiling over my shoulder as I closed the door behind me. However, I was a professional with a job to do, and I was determined to find Charlie Higgins before another day went by.

We ate breakfast, making love on the kitchen table as soon as the plates were cleared. From there, he followed me to the shower, where our raucous behavior and my death grip on the soap dish nearly pulled it out of the wall. The man had incredible stamina, that was for damn sure, and it was amazing how my knee stood up to certain types of activities.

Once out of the shower, I reasserted myself, keeping him at bay with outstretched cane as I dressed. At some point, he appeared with a small gym bag, from which he pulled a change of clothes and running shoes. "You were sure of yourself, weren't you?" I said, eyeing the bag.

"Always keep it in the trunk, for emergencies. Not this kind. Other things."

"Uh-huh."

"What about tonight? I can stay and leave early in the morning?"

"Sorry, can't. Got a date."

"With who?"

"Jealous?"

"You bet I am." He crossed the room, drawing me into his arms. "Who is he? I'll kill him."

"Watch yourself. He's a cop."

"Not one of Harbor's finest?"

"Roger Demaris, actually."

"Well, what do you know? Should I be worried?"

"About what?"

"A rival. This was incredible… I mean, I want.. I'd like to see you again, Ricky. Soon."

I kissed him long and deep before pulling away to grab my bag. "Lock the door on your way out, Tiger. And call me sometime." Truth was, I didn't trust myself to stay a second longer. If I stayed I might do or say something I regretted and I wasn't ready to tell Jay Harp how I really felt about him. I'd done that the last time and he'd run out the door back to Sheila, the fiancée, faster than I could say "toodle-loo."

CHAPTER 34

Through Val Ramsay, I learned that Maisy Grant lived about a mile up river from the Point in an A-frame her in-laws had built thirty years ago as a weekend getaway. She taught second grade in Portsmouth and her two kids, a son and a daughter, were both away at college. Her husband, Andy, worked at Island Shellfish, a seafood processing plant in Brook Haven. Val told me the Grants house "always reeks of low tide" from Andy's clothes, boots and person. Nothing Maisy tried—lemons, ammonia, disinfectants, air freshener sprays or chlorine bleach—made a difference.

As I approached their lane, the A-frame was hard to miss. Its roof pointed up like a middle finger in a neighborhood of modest capes and shingled cottages. The yard was neat as a pin, not a blade of grass out of place, a sharp, sad contrast to her brother's domicile. I knocked and waited for almost five minutes. She finally appeared in a well-worn pink chenille robe, white bath towel tied round her head. "Sorry, you caught me in the shower. Can I help you?"

"Mrs. Grant?"

"Yes? Do I know you?"

"No, and I'm really sorry to barge in on you like this on a Sunday morning."

"Are you selling something, because if you are—"

"No, my name's Ricky Steele. I'm a private investigator here about Charlie. I have something of his that I think he'll want. Is he here?" I slipped my card through a crack in the door. She took it, squinting as she studied it.

"You'd better come in." She stepped aside, allowing me to pass. "Have a seat. I'll be out in a minute."

I took a seat on a sofa covered in dark green corduroy. The fabric's wide wales were only a distant memory in most places. The room spanned the length of the house with a bay window at the opposite end, which afforded a sweeping view of the river. The Grants' dining room table was placed in front of the window. The sunny spot reminded me of my own breakfast nook at home, where I drank tea every morning, gazing out at "my river." A pang of homesickness hit me as I imagined Beaky sitting on the table, watching the sea, pining away for me.

I didn't smell low tide, but cinnamon and vanilla from scented candles lit on several of the tables and the mantel above the woodstove. I spied knickknacks and several framed photographs between the candles and rose to take a quick peek. Charlie Higgins was not in any of the pictures.

Shortly after I sat down again, Maisy reappeared, now dressed in jeans and a yellow turtleneck, damp ringlets of red hair now framing a heart-shaped face. For a woman in her late sixties, Maisy Grant looked terrific. I was dying to ask for her antiaging secrets so I could rush to the nearest drugstore and buy a truckload, but I bit my tongue.

"Can I get you something? Coffee? A soda? Water?"

"Thanks, but I'll only stay a minute."

"It's no bother, really. The coffee's hot. I just made a fresh pot."

"That'd be great. Milk and two sugars, please."

She returned several minutes later with two huge mugs, handing one to me. She took a seat at the far end of the couch. "You're here about Charlie, then?"

"Yes. Is he living with you?"

She shook her head. "No, I wanted to have him, but Andy said no, and if I want to stay married, I have to respect his wishes. He's put up with a lot over the years."

"Do you know where he is?"

She sipped her coffee, staring out the window. "What is it that you have of Charlie's?"

I dumped the contents of the canister on the table and told her about my trip to Bailey's Ledge and the condition of the cottage. "I'd feel better if I handed the canister to Charlie since it appears to hold his most valued possessions."

"You're right about that." Tears rimmed her blue-gray eyes. "Poor Charlie didn't have much, but his memories were precious to him. His Purple Heart… he was wounded in Korea, saved a fellow marine. They were good buddies and they stayed in touch through the years. Charlie's always had a hard time, and goodness knows he used to drink too much, but at least he managed to hold a job. Then Carl died about ten years ago. That was it. Charlie just gave up. That's when he started living out at the Ledge. We tried to help him, but he would have none of it. He spends the summer, fall and spring on the Ledge and then moves to Providence when it gets cold. Goes from shelter to shelter. I think he stays mostly at Amos House, but I'm not certain. We tried to have him here one winter and Andy nearly divorced me."

"So, you think he's moved to Providence already?"

"Well, I'd have said it was a little early. He usually goes up in late November, right after Thanksgiving, but his arthritis has been bothering him lately. We have lunch once a month and he told me he'd been aching at night, having trouble sleeping."

"Did he see a doctor?"

She smiled ruefully. "You don't know my brother. Hates doctors with a passion. Wouldn't go near one if he was on his deathbed."

"Why is that?"

"Not many people around town know this, but Charlie was engaged to be married once, to a woman he met soon after he got out of school. She was a student of his."

"Charlie was a teacher?"

She smiled again, this time a warm, comfortable smile. "I keep forgetting you don't know him. After the service, Charlie went to school. First undergraduate, then graduate school, most of it paid by the GI Bill. He actually completed all his coursework for a doctorate in history, but never quite got around to the dissertation, so he's what you called A…something."

"ABD."

"That's right—all but dissertation. Anyway, that was Charlie. He went to work at the community college. Rachel was one of his students. She was in her early twenties, a single mom, pretty little thing. She and Charlie began dating. He was head over heels in love with her and they were planning to get married. Then she contracted equine encephalitis from a mosquito bite. Dead in four days. Charlie was devastated. Blamed the doctors for misdiagnosing her. By the time they decided it was encephalitis it was too late. Course, it was nobody's fault. Encephalitis is often fatal, but no one could convince Charlie of that. He went through an awful time, lost his teaching job, alienated all his old friends except Carl."

"So, what kind of work did he do after that?"

"Worked on fishing boats, construction crews, mostly manual labor. A few times over the years he's taught an adjunct course or two at U Mass. Dartmouth, but he never wanted to go back full-time."

"So, aside from Amos House, is there anywhere he hangs out in Providence where I might be able to find him?"

She shook her head. "Hard to say, but knowing Charlie, I'd guess he spends a lot of his days in the library."

We spent a few more minutes looking through the contents of the canister, discussing each item before I repacked Charlie's treasure and closed the lid. Then I remembered the photographs, tucked in my bag. She had seen copies of the school photo many times and identified Carl Reinhart as one of the marines. Finally, she picked up the photo of Charlie and Ruth Bowen. "Well, I'll be. I'd forgotten all about their little fling. Talk about a mismatched pair."

"Was it serious?"

"For about a minute. It was kind of funny, you know? They went around together for a couple of weeks one fall. Early in the school year, it was. Charlie never talked much about it and then Ruth was gone. When she got back, it wasn't a month before graduation and Charlie had enlisted."

"Where did Ruth go?"

"Her father had a job transfer. Temporary assignment in the Midwest somewhere. He sold insurance, for Prudential, I think."

"No sparks when she got back?"

"Nothing. It was one of those goofy things that just happened, you know? When friends fall into romance and then realize it's a mistake. Charlie had a close group of friends, male and female. More than I ever had. Ruth was one of them. George Wilbur, Al Shortliff, Tippy, Ruth, there were a bunch of 'em. Then there was Ruth's best friend, what was her name? Mary Conway, that's it. Mary moved away, Seattle, I think. She and Al were an item for a while. Of course, there was Franny Wilbur, George's wife. She was Franny McNichols then. What a character."

"He's a character, too," I said, smiling at the recollection of round, prickly little George, Irish whiskey in hand.

"You've sure gotten around in a short time. More coffee?"

"Thanks, but I've taken up enough of your time. Time for me to head out."

"Will you keep looking for Charlie?"

"Count on it. If you don't mind, I'd like to hold on to these a few more days. If I don't find him before I leave the Harbor, I'll get everything back to you. Is that okay?"

She nodded, following me to the door. As I stepped over the threshold, she grasped my arm. "If you find him, tell him we love him, please?" For a second, the anguish of a lifetime played across Maisy Grant's features and she looked every bit her age.

I squeezed her hand. "I sure will." As I pulled out of the drive, I looked back to find her still in the doorway.

CHAPTER 35

The scattering of Ron's ashes was set for three. With several hours to kill, I gathered up Ron's folders and notebooks and headed for the Bayside Tea Room. A fussy little place two towns upriver, it was quieter and more private than the Lunch. I sat in the corner near the window and ordered tea and a blueberry scone, then spread out my materials to sift and sort.

As I munched my warm, flaky scone, I read through Ron's chronicles, a rehashing and interpretation of every significant town political event. I marveled at his meticulous organization and unwavering dedication. One thing the town gadfly had in common with Ruth Bowen—the countless hours he put in on the town's behalf. Unlike his nemesis, however, Ron Harp received no compensation for his time. There was no "contingency fund" set aside to pay him for the thousands of hours he put in.

After each meeting account, notes, related newspaper articles and other documents were catalogued and clipped. As I read, I noticed some notes and documents were duplicates, copies he had made to keep his filing system going. The same issues arose again and again, his elaborate cross-referencing system staggering. The copier and scanner in his study must have been humming 24/7, I mused, reading an entry about the Button's Marsh development.

Will had told me that Ron and Becca's efforts had halted this project. I wondered whether its proposer, a Kit Reston from Wellesley, Massachusetts, was still around, waiting in the wings for a chance to try again. Perhaps Reston, tired of waiting, had taken matters into his own hands? With Ron Harp out of the way, Rebecca Morse might be less inclined to carry on the fight. I had forgotten to ask Becca about Button's Marsh and made a mental note to call her even though I suspected she'd tell me to get lost.

One notebook bulged with documents, papers and scribbled notes pertaining to the Harbor Club project. I skimmed those, but found nothing new except a partial list of investors next to which Ron had written, "known investors, more to come." The usual suspects were there—Thomas Bigalow, alias Tippy, Alvin Shortliff, Sedgewick Montgomery—who would name their child Sedgewick?—and a bunch of names I didn't recognize. I was surprised to see Peg and Robert Crawley, but then, who knew how much they'd put in and how long ago? Might've been before they'd gotten into the club and were now no longer interested.

Finally, I came to a folder marked "History and Misc." This held a bunch of newspaper clippings, notes and papers, mostly pertaining to town history. There were a number of letters to the editor of the *Harbor Times*. Most were written by Ron with a couple by Will Ramsey, two from Dick Chaffee on wetlands issues and one from Rebecca Morse protesting the new golf course project. Another thing I'd forgotten to ask her about, I thought, feeling incompetent and disorganized in the face of the "Ron Harp filing system."

As I read through the letters, I marveled at the way people's voices came through in their writing—Ron's impatient, humorless and often strident rhetoric, Rebecca's disdainful whine, Will's folksy common sense drawl. Even Dick Chaffee's pompous oratory rang out from the graying pages.

"Excuse me." The waitress' voice startled me and I jumped, nearly spilling my tea. "Sorry, this was on the floor. Must've dropped from your papers." She handed me a copy of what looked like a page from a daily planner. At the top, I was surprised to read the date, "September, 1955." I nodded thanks and she disappeared.

The page was filled with text, handwritten in looping, beautiful cursive. Definitely Palmer Method Gold Star material, I thought, taking a sip of tea and reading:

Two teachers out sick. Substitutes unavailable so, once again, I covered English literature. Thank goodness it was Mr. Bickley. The science classes are impossible. Day ended with one of my saddest duties—suspending the Simmonds girl. Poor dear, such potential. Why do they do these things to themselves? Family church goers, parents seem responsible. What could have gone wrong? Too much freedom, I expect. Letting them run wild. In my day our parents knew where we were every minute. I expect she'll be back next spring in time for graduation, poor dear.

There was a space, then an entry dated the following day that read,

Not unexpected visit from the Simmonds this morning. They've circled the wagons, made up a ruse. He's feigning some kind of business thing. I've agreed to play along for the girl's sake. Poor Ruth will be spared any embarrassment now. I hope for all their sakes that she's learned her lesson.

The diary went on about school affairs until the end of the page. The diarist's name was not in evidence, but I had no doubt I was reading the ramblings of Principal Hattie Pauls. While I didn't know Ruth Bowen's maiden name, I felt certain the student Pauls had suspended was none other than the current Town Council President. And I had a pretty good idea of the reason behind the suspension. Attached to the diary excerpts was Ron's handwritten note, "Charlie Higgins also inquiring about this. Why?"

Why, indeed, I thought, certain I'd stumbled across the very papers Charlie had been so agitated to discover were missing from Historical Society records.

Chapter 36

Noticing the time, I gathered my things and paid the check. If I hurried, I had just enough time to stop by the fire station. A quick phone call and I discovered both the E.M.T., Pat Reid, and his volunteer assistant, Aggie Bruner, were on duty for the entire day. The desk clerk directed me to the "lounge," where five men and a woman sat, two of the men in front of the television, one reading and two playing cards. With the exception of the bookworm, all were in civilian clothes. The woman appeared to be cleaning up. The men ignored me, but she nodded. "Can we help you?"

"I'm looking for Aggie Bruner and Pat Reid."

"You found me. Hey, Pat, you're wanted." She gestured to one of the two television watchers. He rose and joined us, plopping down beside Aggie on a turquoise Naugahyde couch.

"I'm Ricky Steele, the—"

"The gimpy dick that's been snoopin' around. We heard about you."

She blushed to the roots of her strawberry blond hair, crinkling up her freckled nose. "Don't pay attention to him, Miss Steele. He's a redneck. What can we do for you?"

"I understand you took Ron Harp to the hospital."

"Sure did. Pat and me got there soon as we could, but he was in bad shape, poor guy."

"What can you tell me about the scene? Where was he exactly?"

"These sound like questions you should be asking the police. What'd Cal say?" he said.

I gave him my best smile. "Lieutenant Ripler has been very helpful. In fact, he suggested I might like to talk with you two, to get a medical perspective."

"Pat's the best person to answer that. I just help out, do what he tells me," she said.

"Mr. Reid, I'd be really grateful for anything you could tell me."

He sat silent for a minute while Aggie and I waited. Finally, he mumbled, "Was unconscious when we got there. Cal and Skip had moved him onto the grass, put some kind of towel round his head, trying to stop the bleeding. One look and I knew he was gone."

"There was so much blood, you see." Aggie folded and unfolded her hands, her eyes darting from her partner to me.

"What about the bike? Where was it?"

He shrugged. "Hell, lady, we were too busy to check out the bike. I mean, Christ, the guy was dying."

"It was on the grass," she said softly. "All twisted and bent."

"What do you remember about it? Can you think which parts were bent?"

She closed her eyes. "Well, now, let's see. From what I remember, the handlebars were okay, and maybe the seat and back wheel, but the front wheel was really a mess, spokes missing, nearly bent in half."

"That's strange, isn't it?"

"Not if he hit a rock," Pat said. "Had to be goin' real fast and it was one of those lightweight, European racing jobs. Pieces of shit, if you ask me, but like I said, Aggie and me were busy, strapping him in, getting him into the ambulance, so we didn't have time to bother with the bike."

"Did the police tell you how they'd found him?"

"No."

"Now, Pat, remember, Cal said he was on the rocks, kinda all twisted up with his bike."

Aggie's description was rewarded with a glare from her partner.

"Pat asked them why they'd moved him. We were concerned about his neck, you see, and that's when Cal told him."

"Did you notice anything else? Branches, sticks, anything that might have caught up in the wheel?"

"Look, Miss Steele, that's all we remember, okay? Aggie's got work to do and I'm sure the rest of this information is stuff you can get from Cal. Harp was dead when we reached St. Anne's. Never regained consciousness. That's all we know."

"Just one more question. Did it look like an accident to you?"

She opened her mouth to speak, but he beat her to it. "Cal says it was an accident, it was an accident."

"That's not what I asked."

"You ever seen a person who's fallen off a bike at high speed? Just as dangerous as a motorcycle. Harp had to have been be going forty or fifty. That's some serious speed when you hit the ground. Poor bastard never had a chance. Now, if you'll excuse me, I gotta get going. Aggie, too."

"Pat's right," she said, rising. "I do have a lot to do. This was only my second bicycle accident. The first was kids playing in the playground lot, just a couple of scraped knees. Pat knows better than I do what can happen. He's worked some really serious accidents. Nice to meet you, Miss Steele."

"Same here," I said, kicking myself for not interviewing Aggie Bruner alone. Now that Pat had told her what she'd seen, I doubted I'd get anything more from her.

Chapter 37

Giffy and Jim Harp lived at Whitman Bluffs, a private association of homes overlooking the ocean. This stretch of bluffs lay just north of Nauset Point and the lighthouse at the southern edge of Barney's Ledge. The Ledge had been the Harp brothers' playground, their childhood spent there climbing the rocks, building forts, and fishing for bass off the breakwater. Giffy called their house her fourth child. Over the years, she and Jim had completely remodeled the hundred-year-old cape and added several shingled wings.

After greeting Giffy in the kitchen, I headed for the living room, where I was relieved to find everyone dressed comfortably for the outing on the Ledge. I had changed into a pair of my own slacks and a slate-blue sweater, but had thrown Karen's scarf round my neck to dress up my drab ensemble. My hair was uncooperative, as usual, so I reined it in with clips and avoided mirrors, fearful that if I caught my reflection I would want to crawl into a cave and never come out. Jay was in gray flannels and a navy sweater. My libido shot skyward the minute I laid eyes on him and I was half tempted to call Demaris and cancel our dinner date. I caught his eye and smiled. He nodded, giving me a queer look I couldn't decipher.

At that moment, Karen came up behind me and grabbed my arm. "Thank goodness you're here. I was afraid you weren't coming."

"I told you I was."

"But I thought you might be on the case," she whispered conspiratorially. "Any new developments?"

"A few. I'll tell you later. Who's that woman talking to Betsy and Giffy?"

"Oh, that's Marty. I can't believe she came. She and Jay are practically broken up. She has no business here. No one invited her and she didn't know Ron at all. She's such a pushy bitch. Big-time attorney in Jay's firm. She's the reason for Jay's divorce. Twenty years younger than him, of course. Avoid her at all costs."

Well, well, things never change, I thought, now understanding the reason for his queer look. I followed Karen to the buffet table. We filled plates with Giffy's grilled chicken, wild baby greens and garlic bread. Then, given the circumstances, I decided a drink was in order. I set my plate next to Karen's in the living room and returned to the sideboard for two glasses of chardonnay.

As I reached for the glasses, he intervened, practically snatching the bottle from my hands. "Here, allow me." He filled both glasses, handing them to me.

"Thanks," I said, refusing to meet his eyes.

He grabbed my arm and wine to sloshed on the floor. "Ricky, wait."

"You're lucky this isn't red wine."

"I didn't know she would be here."

"Jay, relax. It's fine. We're adults. You have a life. Don't apologize."

"We're not together." His hand still gripped my arm, eyes pleading.

"Great. Now, will you please unhand me?"

"You're angry."

"No, just feeling a little awkward."

"Well, don't. There's nothing to worry about."

"Who's worried?"

"Hon, who's this?" She was taller than me, almost five-eleven, straight, dark shoulder-length hair, dark eyes, slim, stylishly dressed in black pants and a red sweater that hugged her figure in all the right places. Catlike, she pressed against him, pointy breasts digging into his arm.

Face registering defeat, he let go of my arm. "Ricky Steele, Marty Becker."

"Are you a cousin I haven't met?" Her hand was draped over his shoulder now, caressing, kneading. The same shoulder I'd been nibbling six hours earlier.

"Ricky's a family friend. A close family friend."

I extended my hand. "Hi. I grew up with Karen."

She gave me a quick dead fish before returning her hand to Jay's shoulder. "How nice for Karrie to have you here. Must be such a comfort. Ready to eat, hon?"

Jay's neck and cheeks reddened and I softened, deciding to put him out of his misery. "Nice to meet you, Ms. Becker." As I turned away, I thought I heard him say, "Stop it." When I sat down, Karen leaned over, whispering, "What's wrong with Jay? He looks like he's going to be sick."

"Poor guy," I said, sitting beside her on the floor, our plates on the coffee table in front of us.

"You vixen! Something happened last night, didn't it?" Her eyes shone. "Tell!"

"Not here, not now."

"I knew it. The minute he said he was taking you to dinner, I knew something was up."

At that moment, Betsy mercifully intervened. "Mind if I join you two gossips?" She took a seat beside me on the couch. Setting her plate down, she leaned across me, whispering to Karen. "What's the Wicked Witch of the East doing here? I thought they broke up."

"You know Jay," Karen said, waving her fork toward the pair in the dining room. "Always been a pushover. Has a unique talent for attracting bitchy women, with one possible exception." She winked at me and I was tempted to lean over and dump my plate on her head.

"That's right. You guys had a fling at the wedding, didn't you? Why don't you get together, Ricky? That'd be great."

I wanted to crawl under the table and never come out. "Ladies, can we change the subject, please? Betsy, where are your kids?"

"They're with Patty and Ralph. I thought about bringing them, but Bobby and I thought it might be better just grown-ups. Gives us a few hours' peace. Besides, they don't understand and it'd just be a game to them."

"Ralph's working on the Crawleys' cottage."

"So I heard."

"Nice guy. I met Patty, too. She came by Friday to hurry him along."

"That sounds like Patty. Always on the go."

"So I hear. She works with Ruth Bowen, doesn't she?"

"Sometimes, when Ruth gets busy. Now, wait a minute—you're not trying to pump me for information, are you? Patty's my dearest friend. She and Karrie don't see eye to eye, but—"

"That's ancient history, Bets." Karen said, rolling her eyes at me behind her sister-in-law's back.

"Anyway, she's a sweetheart, once you get to know her. She's been great with Papa Harp. Comes by nearly every day to check on him. Helps Mama with getting him around. Patty's really strong. She can lift Papa much easier than any of us. She started training as an O.T., then got pregnant with Ben, her oldest. Ralph's been terrific with Ben. Loves him just like his own two."

"Oh, so this is a second marriage for Patty?"

"Not exactly. She met Ralph when she was pregnant. She's never said who the father is." She leaned close to my ear. "My guess is, she doesn't know. Patty went through a bit of a wild phase. Ralph was the best thing ever happened to her. He's a real sweetie pie."

"He seems like a great guy."

"Did you know Patty's a painter? A darn good one, too, isn't she, Karrie? Now, admit it, even if you don't like her, she's a great artist."

"Great might be a bit of an overstatement. Competent, certainly. And she sells well. Her landscapes of the Harbor area sell like hotcakes during the summer. You know the type- fields, ocean, stone walls, cows. Patty specializes in cows, doesn't she, Bets?"

Betsy laughed, waving a dismissive hand at her sister-in-law. "Don't listen to her, Ricky. Patty's a wonderful artist. Just check out her paintings. They're everywhere around town, at the store, community center, in the Lunch."

I smiled, sipping the last of my wine, deciding that this was a conversation I would stay out of.

It was close to four, the sunlight fading, when Bobby Harp announced, "It's time, folks."

Chapter 38

Most of us walked while Giffy and Jim met us in the car. I stood beside Karen, huddled together against the wind, now whipping across the fields from the sea. Karen clutched the urn to her breast, staring straight ahead as Jay and Bobby helped their father out of the car and into his wheelchair. On the verge of tears, Karen mumbled more to herself than to us. "It's all going to fly back and hit us in the face. Poor Jim won't even be able to get out of the way."

I pointed to the right. "If we walk to the far end of field, we'll be far enough out on the point so the ashes will blow out over the water."

Still talking to herself, Karen trembled and shook, the ceramic urn tapping against the buttons of her jacket. "We should have left Jim at home. I should have done this myself. I could have walked out onto the jetty."

Jay approached, Marty glued to his side, her hand in his pocket. "I think if we stay at the edge, we'll be fine."

The group assembled at last, all eyes turned to Karen.

I stood on Karen's right, Jay and Marty beside me, Giffy and Jim just behind us. Bobby and Betsy moved to stand at Karen's left. "Karrie?" he said, arm circling her shoulders. "Did Ron say anything specific about this?"

She was crying now, numb with cold and seemingly unaware of her brother-in-law's attentions, which I suspected would ordinarily be unwelcome. "No. Just that this was the place."

"Well, then, sweetie, why don't you go first. Then we'll all have a turn. Does that sound good?"

"Ricky, come with me, please?" I nodded and we stepped closer to the edge.

She pried the urn's lid off, handing it to me as she clutched the urn. Scooping a handful of ashes, she inched forward, her arm locked onto mine, pulling me with her. As we reached the edge, I turned to see if Giffy needed help with Jim, so I was not looking down as Karen lifted her fistful of ashes. When I turned back, she was screaming, the urn dropped from her grasp, dashed to bits as it made its descent to the rocks below. Like a volcanic winter, Ron's remains drifted all round us as we struggled to understand what had happened. Finally, the ashes settled and we peered downward, spying the body in the tide pool, his arms akimbo, scarecrow legs bobbing. Bobby stepped to his parents' side. "It's Charlie Higgins, poor bastard."

Jay and Giffy wheeled Jim Harp back to the car. Betsy and Karen accompanied them while Marty dialed the police on her cell phone. Bobby scrambled down to the beach using the overgrown path nearest the shack. I followed, holding on to his collar for dear life. By the looks of it, he'd been in the water for several days, but he certainly hadn't been there when I explored the shack since I'd passed right by the pool.

Charlie Higgins, or what was left of him, was not a pretty sight. His eye sockets were empty, skin swollen and bluish-yellow, there was an angry gash across his forehead. Bobby bent over, studying the gash. "Must've fallen and hit his head. Drunk, most likely."

"His sister told me he stopped drinking a few years ago."

"Well, she would. Maisy Higgins has always had blinders on about her brother."

I was just stooping down for a closer look when Cal Ripler yelled above. "Get away from the body, now, both of you! Step away and get your fannies up here."

I groaned, stepping back. Where was Roger Demaris when you needed him? We kept our fannies right on the spot, waiting until Cal, Skip and two others slipped and tumbled their way down the path in their shiny black police shoes. Red-faced and out of breath, Cal slipped several times, clawing at the brambles to keep his footing, all the while cursing under his breath. Finally on level ground, he brushed himself off, glaring at me. "Didn't you hear me? I said to get outta here. This is a police investigation."

Bobby stepped between us. "Now, hold on, Cal. No need to get so excited. Ricky's with us. Have a little respect, will ya? We were scattering Ronnie's ashes when we found him."

Ripler took a step backward. "Okay, you found him. Now, we're here and we need room. So, Bobby, if you'd kindly take her up with you, I'd appreciate it."

Defiant and angry, I faced him. "I'd like to stay, if you don't mind. I'll keep out of the way."

"Well, I do mind and you can't. Eddie, take her up to the car, would you? And radio for more people. Where the hell's rescue?"

The officer made a move toward me and I stepped back, holding out my hand. "I have a right to stay and I shall. Don't worry. I won't be in the way."

Face scarlet, eyes flashing fire, Ripler looked ready to implode.

Bobby took my arm. "Let's go, Ricky. Let 'em do their job. We should check on Karrie and the others."

The mention of Karrie broke the standoff. I took hold of his hand, leaning into him as we wended our way up the path behind the shack.

Chapter 39

When we reached the Harps, Karen was curled in a fetal position on the couch, wrapped in a blanket, sobbing softly.

I slid next to her, arm cradling her shoulders. "Hey, you."

"I've called Milly," Giffy said, appearing at the door in an apron. "Soon as I get Jim settled, I'll bring her some tea."

Marty had disappeared and Jay was on the phone. Betsy had gone to collect the children, fearing they would hear about the body. Karen slumped against me, murmuring, "Ron, Ron, Ron, he must be so cold. The water's so cold."

"Karrie, listen to me." I took her shoulders, forcing her to meet my eyes. "It was Charlie Higgins, not Ron. Old Charlie, remember him? He lived in the shack on the beach?" She stared at me blankly, shaking her head.

"Here, give her this." Jay handed me a snifter of brandy and I put it to Karen's lips. She took a big gulp, choking, but it seemed to perk her up.

"Charlie?"

I hugged her, hoping she knew what she was saying. "Yes, sweetie. It was Charlie."

We sat huddled together, Jay keeping vigil in a chair opposite us. Finally, our eyes met. "Where's Marty?"

"Went back to Boston, to her place, not mine."

"No need to explain."

"Yes, there is, Ricky. I—"

"Not now," I said, mouthing the words.

"I'm swamped the beginning of the week, but I'm coming back Wednesday night through the weekend. I'd—"

"Oh, my poor baby!" Milly Spenser burst into the room, arms flailing. "Here, Dorothy, let me have her." She yanked me off the couch, plopping down beside her daughter. "Here, honey, take these." She laid two red capsules in Karen's palm, bringing the snifter to her lips. The rest of us invisible, Milly cooed and fussed over Karen, rearranging the blanket, smoothing hair from her face, patting her shoulder. Finally, she announced she was taking Karen home. Alex had apparently been left with her housekeeper. She insisted that daughter and grandson would be spending the night with her and sent Bobby to "see to things" at Karen's house.

Jay had vanished soon after Milly's appearance so I wandered back to the kitchen, where I found Giffy feeding Jim his dinner. We hugged and I said goodbye, telling her to call if she needed me. Jay caught up with me in the driveway, his arms reaching out.

"Ricky, don't go like this. Not after last night. I need you. I want—"

I wanted nothing more than to melt into his arms, but my arms shot out to keep him at bay. "Not now. Not tonight. We can talk when you get back. I'm not up to this right now. Okay?"

He tried to kiss me, but I stepped back. "Please, don't." I climbed into the jeep, afraid to look back. I am not, I repeated to myself, I am not going to get hurt again.

CHAPTER 40

I got lost twice on my way to the Riptide. Given the afternoon's events, I wasn't sure Demaris would show up, but there he was, in a back booth, clean shaven, wearing beige corduroy slacks and a moss-colored V-neck sweater.

"You look like hell."

Throwing my bag in ahead of me, I slid into the booth opposite him. "Really know how to flatter a gal, don't you? Guess you haven't heard."

"Just came from the station. Shame about Higgins. Man never hurt a fly."

"Got himself killed, so he must've irked someone."

"Ripler's callin' it an accident."

"Oh, I see. Charlie hit himself in the head, lay around for a couple of days, then dragged himself to the tide pool to die?"

"Could've fallen."

"That's bullshit and you know it."

He laughed. "Yup, and everybody else does this time."

"Then you don't believe Ron's death was an accident."

"Now, hold on. I didn't say that." He smiled up at the waitress, then back at me. "What'll you have?"

"Merlot, thanks." Demaris was drinking seltzer. "None for you?"

"Not tonight."

I nodded. "Any news about Charlie?"

"You know I can't say."

"He was hit in the head, wasn't he?"

"Appears that way, unless he fell."

I rolled my eyes.

"You a forensic pathologist now?" he said.

"No, but I know Charlie Higgins was murdered and I think I know why."

"Oh, and why's that?"

"Why should I tell when you won't?"

"Because you're a private citizen and I'm an officer of the law."

"Private detective, thank you."

"Not on this case."

Frustrated, I threw up my hands. "Oh, forget it. Be quiet and I'll tell you. I've gotta tell someone."

"Who's flattering who now?"

He was cute when he smiled. I leaned across the table, lowering my voice. "Did you know that Ruth Bowen had a teenage pregnancy?"

"You're kidding."

"I'm not absolutely certain—"

"There you go!"

"But I'm pretty sure."

He rolled his eyes. "

Ninety-nine percent sure. What else could it be?"

I related my activities over the past few days, telling one small lie and leaving out the events of the previous evening and my overnight with Jay Harp. The lie concerned the canister, which I told him I had given to Maisy Grant. And I surely would, as soon as I spoke to Ruth Bowen in the morning. I concluded with, "Who else could it have been? Simmonds is Ruth's maiden name and she was the right age in 1955."

"Maybe it was something else. Maybe she was caught cheating, or skipping school."

"Oh, please, haven't you been listening? All that stuff in the diary about God-fearing and keeping a close eye on her. Little Ruthie was knocked up and I know who the father was."

"You're pushin' it, Steele. An old photograph, from who knows when, doesn't prove a thing."

"Maisy said they had a thing, before Ruth went away."

"Where'd the family go, anyway? Did you bother to find that out?"

"Not yet."

"Well, then, you won't get far with your theory. If Ruth went away pregnant, she had to have given birth somewhere."

"Hmmm, who could I ask about that?"

"Be very careful."

"I just know it's related to Ron's death. Hattie Pauls, Ron, and now Charlie. Somehow, they're all connected."

"Well, if you're gonna tell me Ruth Bowen's been runnin' around killing people to cover up a youthful indiscretion, I don't think I'll stay to dinner."

"It could be any of them, don't you see? They're circled around her like the knights of the round table. Oh, they're friendly enough—that George is a real cutie-pie—but I think the lot of them would do anything to protect the Queen Bee. That cave woman Patty Boardman would, too."

"Where'd that come from?"

I shrugged. "Someone was talking about how strong she is. And, who knows what she'd do to protect her boss and whatever those two are in cahoots about."

He laughed. "Cahoots? You've been watching too many bad detective movies. Let's order. I'm starved."

He ordered meat loaf, extra gravy. I ordered crab cakes, with sweet potato pancakes on the side. I hadn't exercised in two days. At this rate I'd be a blimp by the time I got home. In between his questions about my life beyond Windy Harbor, I continued to needle and he to deflect. Our food arrived and we ate in companionable silence for several minutes. Finally, I pushed my plate away, staring at him. "What do you know about the Button's Marsh project?"

He set down his bite of meatloaf dripping with thick, dark gravy. "You do get around, don't you?"

"Ron was working on a lot of things. I'm just trying to follow his leads."

"Button's Marsh is old news. From what I hear, Harp and the Morse woman won that one, didn't they?"

"Maybe. Did you ever meet the developer, Kit Reston?"

"Yup." He was grinning ear to ear now.

"What? You know something about him, don't you?"

"Maybe."

"Who is he? What's he like?"

"Couldn't say. Only met the man once."

"Where? When?"

"Town Hall, when he came to make his pitch to the Town Council. Nice enough guy, one those young lions from the big city."

Demaris was hard to read and right now I couldn't tell if he was teasing, blowing me off, or making a genuine observation. "What are you talking about?"

"It wasn't him so much as who he knew, who he was livin' with at the time. Ultimately, I think that hurt his case more than anything else with the old timers. Harbor's still a conservative place. Gays are tolerated, but that doesn't mean people want to do business with them."

"You mean to tell me the project was defeated because Kit Reston is gay?"

"No, I said it was a factor. Lost our Ruth some credibility, too."

"Why in the world would Reston's sexuality have anything to do with Button's Marsh or Ruth Bowen?"

"Because, my dear Ms. Steele, at the time Kit Reston and Tripp Bowen were domestic partners. They've since broken up, I understand. Maybe the strain of the project falling through, but back then they were quite the item. People were always spotting them around town, holding hands, making out. Nearly killed his mother. Almost cost her reelection that year."

"How long had they been together before Reston proposed the development?"

"Dunno. Trippie and I aren't exactly pals."

"I wonder," I gazed into space, making a mental note to find out more about Mr. Reston.

We both ordered desserts and for a few minutes we forgot all about murder, mayhem and ancient over warm blueberry cobbler a la mode. At nine thirty, I limped out of the Riptide, my knee stiff, the top button of my slacks undone. Demaris suggested we do it again the next night, same time, same place, and I accepted. Let Jay Harp have some competition, I thought smugly. Roger Demaris was fun, and a hell of a lot safer.

Chapter 41

After my dinner with Demaris I had flopped into bed, sleeping the dreamless sleep of the overtired, but my week of overindulging had caught up with me. After rising late Monday morning, I slowly pedaled my way around the lake, wondering if I'd make it home. As I emerged from the woods, I spied Ralph Boardman already at work. Perfect. He was high on his ladder working on the bathroom window, which had no shade or curtain under the frilly two-inch lace valance.

"Morning." I squinted, shielding my eyes, my head pounding rat-a-tat along with his hammer.

He tipped his hat. "Morning. Nice day for a bike ride. Been around the lake? Beautiful country."

"Sure is. Don't forget, I'm buying lunch today. After I shower, I'll come out and take your order."

"Righto." He smiled, returning his attention to the rotted sill.

Draping a sheet over the bathroom curtain rod, I showered and dressed in privacy. After breakfast, I pulled out the phone book and looked up the number of Levitt and Montgomery, Attorneys at Law. A woman answered, aghast at my request for an appointment on such short notice.

"I only need a few minutes and he told me to call. Is he in yet? Could you tell him who's calling and ask if he has a couple of minutes anywhere today? I'm happy to meet him wherever it's convenient for him." She put me on hold and I waited over five minutes. I was just about to hang up when Mr. Important Himself came on.

"Miss Steele, you're up bright and early. I always keep my first hour free for emergencies. Can you be here in ten minutes?"

I assured him I could, jotted down directions, and headed out. On the way to the jeep, I called up to Ralph for lunch order.

Levitt and Montgomery occupied three floors of a yellow Victorian on Main Road just west of the town center. The receptionist, whose voice I recognized from the phone, motioned me in. "Last office on your right. He's expecting you." I tried not to stare as I passed by, but it had been years since I'd seen a foot-high beehive hairdo, not since Miss LaFleur's, one of my seventh grade teachers.

Sedgie rose, coming from behind massive mahogany desk to shake my hand. "Sit, please. Coffee?"

"Thanks, that'd be great. Milk and two sugars, if you have it."

He buzzed the receptionist, who appeared within seconds. "Two coffees, Ceil. Ricky likes hers just like I do. Thanks." Ceil closed the door and Sedgie returned to his seat behind the desk instead of taking the seat beside me. "So, what can I do for you, Miss Steele?"

I went through my usual spiel about doing a favor for an old friend, ending with, "So if there's anything you can tell me about the projects Ron was researching, I'd be really grateful."

"Well, you probably know, Harp and I weren't exactly buddies, so I'm not sure what he was working on. Can't see how I could help you there. He was a farmer, wasn't he? I know he grew some exotic vegetables, sometimes sold them at the farmer's cooperative. Always at the Town Council meetings, taking notes and such. Occasionally, he'd speak his mind."

"Wasn't too popular with some members of the Council, I understand."

"Not sure where you're from, but small towns are notorious for their gossip, and most of it's hogwash. Don't believe everything you hear, that's my advice." How many times had I heard that since coming to Windy Harbor? Snidley Whiplash grinned, and I imagined him tweaking a long, shiny black mustache.

"People tell me you have a lot tied up in the Harbor Club."

"And?"

"And, you've been lobbying the Town Council pretty hard to grant the development permits. Isn't that a bit of a conflict of interest?"

Fire glinted in his dark eyes for an instant. "Now, that's just what I mean. Don't know who you've been talking to, but you got it all wrong. First off, I favor the club. Sure I do. Be a tremendous town improvement project. I'll always champion and try to lend my support to projects that will benefit the town. Second, I don't have a cent in that project."

"But your wife does?"

"Says who?"

"Says anyone who's looked at the list of investors, which is a matter of public record."

"Alice is her own woman. Like most women, she does what she pleases. I couldn't influence how she spends her money if I tried. It's her money."

"Still, I would think you would stay out of the—"

"What I choose to do is frankly none of your business." He looked up as the door opened. "Thanks, Ceil. Set 'em there." He grabbed his cup, stirring his coffee, taking a moment to compose himself.

"What about the Town Council? Isn't Ruth Bowen's role a little out of whack? Most Council Presidents around the state don't put in the time she does."

"And, we're damn lucky to have her."

"But, is it right?"

"Who the hell knows?"

"She's parlayed a volunteer job into a paid, forty-hour week. Don't you find that problematic?"

"No, and I don't know what the hell this has to do with Ron Harp's death."

"Perhaps nothing, except he was a thorn in her side."

"If you're suggesting Ruth Bowen had anything to do with Harp's death, you're crazier than he was."

"Oh? Why would you say Ron was crazy?"

"Trust fund brat. Never did an honest day's work in his life. All he ever did was nose into other people's affairs, causing trouble. And what for?"

"Did you know he had a law degree?"

"No, I didn't."

"I expect that may have had something to do with his concerns. As a citizen, he saw questionable things happening, perhaps illegal things, and—"

"Look, I don't know what you're talking about, but I have an appointment in five minutes."

I set my coffee mug on the desk. "Thanks for your time."

He leaned back in his deep leather swivel chair, arms akimbo behind his head. "Don't mention it. And, Miss Steele, I'd be very careful if I were you. Ruth Bowen is loved and respected here. People do not, I repeat, do not take kindly to unfounded accusations. If you want to know the truth, I was getting very close to slapping a lawsuit on Harp for his harassment of Ruth Bowen. Wouldn't want to find yourself in the middle of a lawsuit, would you?"

"Is that a threat?"

He laughed. "Darling, if I threaten you, you'll know it."

How comforting, I thought, closing the door behind me.

CHAPTER 42

It was nearly ten so I headed for Town Hall, figuring the breakfast meetings at the Lunch were over. JoJo informed me that Ruth Bowen was upstairs in a meeting, but was expected back momentarily. I told her I'd wait, stepping into the hallway, where I meandered along, reading the bulletin board notices and clippings. The bulletin boards were evenly spaced along the corridor, broken up by office doorways and a variety of paintings, all landscapes of local scenes—the church, beach, ocean, fields. A closer inspection found two excellent watercolors by Hattie Pauls, depicting seascapes, one of Nauset Point, the other a stretch of coastline I didn't recognize.

Farther down the hall were five paintings by Patty, rough, primitive works that suggested artistic limitations rather than aesthetic decision-making. Two were of rolling pastures, black-and-white cows grazing in the foreground. While they were the right color, Patty's looked more like tapirs with their narrow heads and snouty noses. As I studied them, the Ogden Nash poem came to mind. "The cow is of the bovine ilk. One end is moo, the other milk." Patty's cows were definitely not of the "bovine ilk."

A seascape by Patty was positioned opposite a very decent painting of the identical view by K. Harp. I wondered if Patty was aware of how sad and pathetic her piece looked in comparison to Karen's. Where Karen's watercolor reflected the beauty and power of the landscape, Patty's rendition tore it down, chopped it up, the end result cheap and tawdry. Patty's final piece was her best, an open field surrounded by stone walls and trees depicted in the subtle browns, umbers and golds of fall. If she had stopped there, she'd have had a decent landscape, but alas, she did not. Dotting the field were Patty's rendering of the spiraled bales of hay that dotted the town's open fields after mowing season. A beautiful sight on a sunny day, the swirling bales were one of the area's most charming sights. In Patty's hands, they looked like giant blobs of manure, or maybe mud bombs dropped by Martian invaders.

I was peering closer, imagining I could see paint-by-number lines on Patty's seascape, when Ruth Bowen appeared out of nowhere. "Miss Steele, JoJo said you wanted to see me?" I nodded. "I have five minutes. Come on back."

Once seated in her office, I felt uncomfortable. What right did I have to nose into her past, which, among other things, must be quite painful? Then I remembered that Ron was dead, possibly because he'd discovered something about the Town Council President's past. "Why do you tell everyone you've spent your whole life in Windy Harbor, when it's not true?"

Regarding me as if I had three heads, she said, "Whatever are you talking about?"

"You moved, during high school."

She blanched momentarily, then straightened in her chair, guffawing. "Oh, that. Well, yes, technically we were away for about a year."

"Why?"

"Frankly, it's none of your business, but if you've been talking to someone—George Wilbur, I suppose—he no doubt told you my father was in the insurance business. The Chicago office needed him for a project so we went with him."

"What kind of project?"

"How would I know? It was over fifty years ago, for goodness' sake. What teenager pays attention to her father's business dealings?"

"So he uprooted his family for that short period of time?"

"It was just my mother and me. I'm an only child."

"Where'd you live?"

"Is this what you came to see me about?"

"No, just curious. You must've missed your school. Did you enroll out there?"

"Miss Steele, really. I haven't time for this today. Now, if you'll excuse me, I—"

"Any news on Charlie Higgins?"

"You know I can't comment on that."

"I'm not asking for the lurid details, just what you'd tell the public. Was he murdered?"

"Listen, Miss Steele. As you can imagine, I am very busy this morning. I really must insist that—"

"You were classmates, weren't you? You and Charlie, George, Alvin, the whole lot of you."

She nodded.

"Don't you care about what happened to Charlie? You've spent your whole life together. Didn't you even try to help him?"

She was furious, but fighting hard to control it. "You haven't the faintest idea what you're talking about. And, what's more, it's none of your business."

White-knuckled hands gripped her desk. I stepped closer and pulled the photograph of Ruth and Charlie from my bag, setting it in front of her. For a second, her eyes softened, but only for a second. "Where did you get this?"

"It was with his things. Maisy identified it." A little white lie never hurt anyone.

"We were friends, that's all. Friends enjoying a day at the beach. Georgie took it. We were playing to the camera."

"You look like more than friends."

"Well, you're wrong. Now, if you'll excuse me, I have work to do." She began shuffling papers and files.

"Just one more thing. I wonder if you've ever seen this." I handed her the page from Hattie's diary. Setting papers aside, she snatched reading glasses hanging from a chain round her neck and perched them on the end of her nose. As she read on, a red flush crept up her neck. Finally, she looked up, her face a cold mask of fury. "What in the hell is this supposed to be?"

"I believe it's a page from Hattie Pauls's diary, or log, or whatever she called the journal she kept at school."

"Rubbish. Was this with Charlie's things? Probably something he wrote. The man was crazy, you know."

"That's not what I've heard. And, besides, Charlie didn't have this. Ron Harp did. It's a copy. Must've come from the Historical Society's archives."

She laughed, her tone haughty and dismissive. "Well, now the truth comes out. That man was so spiteful and deceitful, if you found it in his things, my guess is he made it up to slander me."

"It's a matter of public record."

"Oh, and have you located the original?"

"No, but I will, unless it's mysteriously vanished, just like Ron Harp's bicycle."

Arms folded over her chest now, she leaned back. "Find it and we'll talk. But Miss Steele, unless you do, I'd be very, very careful."

"I don't scare easily, Mrs. Bowen. And if this entry's missing from the historical society's papers, I won't keep quiet."

"Please leave. Now."

Rising, I leaned over the desk, keeping my voice low. "You want to know what I think? I think you got pregnant and that Charlie Higgins was the father. You were suspended from school and Daddy pretended to get a transfer for nine or ten months so you could go off and have the baby somewhere else. Am I right?"

"Get out!"

"Then—what did you call him—spiteful and deceitful Ron Harp discovered your secret. Did he ask you to step down from the Town Council, go away quietly or he'd make the story public? Couldn't have that, could you? So you killed him, or had him killed."

A fighting cock in full battle plumage, she rose from her chair. "If you're not out of this building in three minutes, I'm calling the police."

I stepped out of the office, wincing as the door slammed behind me. JoJo and the others, mouths agape, averted their eyes, pretending to work as I passed by and exited the building.

Before leaving the town center, I stopped in to see Will Ramsey. He was at his computer when Lotty Mendoza ushered me in, but swiveled round, hopping up to greet me. "Ricky, how nice. How are you? I heard about yesterday. Must have been terrible for poor Karrie. How is she?"

"She stayed with Milly last night, so probably not so hot. I'm going by to see her in a minute."

"Well, sit for a minute. Want coffee or something?"

"No, thanks. I just had a question about the Button Marsh business. Were you aware that the developer, Kit Reston, was living with Tripp Bowen? That Tripp was gay and Kit his partner?"

"This is a small town."

"Is that why Ruth Bowen caved in on that project?"

"I told you, I wasn't involved with that one, just Ron and Becca, and maybe Dick Chaffee because of the wetlands and because the project was happening in his backyard. Town governance issues are the ones I usually stick my nose into. I just don't have the time Ron does, or did, so I picked my battles carefully."

"I heard that Kit and Tripp were seen all round town, arm in arm, during that period."

"That part's no secret. I mean, everyone knows Trippie's gay, brings his boyfriends home to meet Mummy quite often, especially in the summer."

"Well, thanks, Will. I won't take up any more of your time. I've just been kicked out of Town Hall so I think I'd better hightail it in case Ruth's posted snipers at the windows."

"That's a public building. She has no authority to kick you out."

"It's okay. My fault. I pissed her off."

"Should I ask?"

"Probably not. I'm still gathering the facts. I'll fill you in later." On my way out, I found Lotty Mendoza in the hall outside Will's office, running a dust mop across the bookshelves lining the walls. I'd have bet a dinner at the Regatta that she'd been listening at the keyhole.

Chapter 43

When I pulled into the driveway, Karen was weeding her perennial beds and Alex was in the side yard, chasing chickens. Face flushed, eyes sparkling, she stood and stretched as I approached. "Hey, you." In baggy pants and a sweatshirt, leather gloves on her hands, she looked almost healthy.

"How you doing?"

"Better. I don't know what hit me out there, Ricky. It was like such a shock to see him, you know? And I never did see Ron after the accident. Bobby identified him and Ron's will specified immediate cremation with "absolutely no calling hours or viewing of the body." He hated that kind of thing. But it was a mistake for me not to go and see him one last time when I had the chance."

"Neither way is easy," I said, recalling the hours Annie and I had sat beside our mother's closed coffin as the calling hours dragged on and on.

"So sad about poor Charlie. He was a sweet man. A bit odd, of course, but he had a good heart. We'll miss seeing him around town. He was always so nice to Alex when we'd see him walking. Had a couple of magic tricks. When Alex was younger, nobody could get him giggling quicker than Charlie. Ron didn't much care for him, but I thought he was a sweetheart, poor man. Who would do something like that?"

I shrugged, sitting beside her on a cement garden bench. "I think they're connected—Charlie's death and Ron's."

"Then you

do believe Ron was killed?"

I nodded. "Who? Have you found something?"

"I've found lots of somethings. Trick is to figure out which ones are important. At the moment, they're all in a muddle. I think everything's connected to a past that Ruth Bowen and Charlie Higgins shared. I'm convinced of it."

"But how?"

"Dunno, but I'm going to spend some time on my computer this afternoon. See what I can dig up." Alex greeted me, a chicken in each hand, held upside down by their feet.

Karen sighed, setting down her trowel. "Alex, is that necessary?"

I followed her toward the side yard, where Alex had now disappeared into the wood-shingled chicken coop. "Where's the nanny? I thought she was coming today."

"Mother's gone to collect her. I couldn't face the drive. Alex, it's filthy in there. Come out, please!" Several chickens flew out, but no Alex. "Alex, do you hear me?" She stooped down, peering into the doorway, hand resting on a ramp littered with chicken droppings. "Oh, Lord, come on," she said to me. "We'll have to lift up the back."

The rear wall of the coop was hinged, I assumed to facilitate cleaning or the retrieval of the occasional dead chicken. We each took a side, lifting the wall to reveal Alex, sitting next to a nest of eggs, every one of them broken and oozing.

She sighed. "Just what I need this morning."

I held out my hand, which he took as Karen reached in and pulled out the soggy, dripping nest, throwing it into the compost pile. "I'm getting rid of these chickens. I swear, they're all going to the processor as soon as Bobby can help me round them up."

She was muttering to herself, Alex and me invisible bystanders. Or, I should say, I was a bystander. Alex had stalked off without a word.

Much as I wanted to help, I decided that this domestic drama was best left to the principal players and an army of competent therapists. I promised Karen I'd call and made my way to the jeep.

It was nearly noon, so I stopped by Harbor Deli and ordered sandwiches for Ralph and me. While I waited, I flipped through the latest issue of *Harbor Times.* There was no mention of Charlie Higgins. However, the police report had an account of Ron's accident. "Ron Harp, 33, died October 10, approximately 10:00 a.m., in a bicycle mishap, Willow Road, Windy Harbor. Police ruled it an accident." Reading on, I found a report of "Malicious mischief October 13, approximately 9:00 p.m., at 404 Main Road, rental cottage owned by Robert and Margaret Crawley." There was no mention of the tenant.

CHAPTER 44

When I got to the cottage, I spied Ralph at ground level, sawing a board for what looked to be a replacement sill. A stack of storm windows were lined up along the fence beside him.

"You're making progress."

"Yup. Should finish up by end of tomorrow. My Patty's comin' later today to clean the windows for me."

"That's nice of her."

He nodded, pushing his hat back, scratching his head. "Gotta finish up here P.D.Q. and get over to a project I was s'posed to start today. Thought I could squeeze in Bob and Peg's no problem, but the owner's gettin' testy. With Patty's help I should be done here tomorrow, Wednesday at the latest." Unhitching his tool belt, he came to sit beside me at the picnic table. "Thanks, this was real nice of you, Miss Steele," he said, unwrapping his Reuben.

"Ricky."

"Thanks, Ricky. How's the snoopin' going?"

"Slow."

"Too bad about Charlie. Heard you were out on the Ledge when they found him."

I nodded. "Did you know him well?"

He shrugged, taking a bite of his sandwich, then wiping mustard from his chin. "As well as anyone, I guess. Kind of a loner, Charlie was. Real private, but a nice fella. Patty didn't much care for him. He was always givin' her and the Beach Commission fits. And that shack of his was regarded as a bit of an eyesore, but Charlie was okay in my book. Worked on a couple of jobs with me before he ran off the rails, so to speak."

"What kind of jobs?"

"Carpentry. He was a decent finish carpenter and a hard worker when he wasn't drinkin'. We worked out at the Sampson place together. Lemme see, might've even worked here a couple of times."

"The Sampsons live out by Hattie Pauls's old house, don't they?"

"Yup. Funny you should mention Hattie. Me and Charlie was workin' next door round the time she died. Police grilled everyone in the crew for weeks after that. Where were we that day, what'd we know about her?"

"And, did you know her?"

"Not well. Saw her around town from time to time. Seemed like a nice enough lady."

"Did Charlie ever talk about her?"

"Just in passing. Don't forget, she was his old principal, down at the high school. Lot of folks in town remembered her that way."

"Fondly?"

"'Cuse me?"

"I mean, do you think people who remembered Hattie as a principal remember her fondly?"

He grinned, giving me a look. "Do you remember your high school principal 'fondly,' as you put it?"

An involuntary shudder passed through me as a vision of Muriel Petty, my boarding school headmistress, flashed before my eyes. "Hmmm, no comment."

"Well, thanks for this." He rose and tossed his sandwich wrappings in a trash barrel. "Was real kind of you."

"My pleasure."

I left him bent over his sawhorse and headed into the house for a few hours' work. After a brief nap punctuated by muffled hammering, I settled on the couch with my computer and a cup of tea for a little online work. It was time to consult the Mormons, I thought, clicking into to their massive genealogy website. I punched in my request and began searching for babies born to a Ruth Simmonds in 1956 in the Chicago area. Her romance with Charlie Higgins had begun and ended in September 1955, so counting nine months ahead put me at May 1956. According to Maisy Grant, Ruth had returned to Windy Harbor in time for her June graduation. Just to be safe, I widened the search to encompass January through June 1956. Figuring it would be morning before I heard back, I clicked off and spent the remainder of the afternoon catching up on my "real job."

A call to Janice, my assistant, precipitated a ten-minute diatribe about the mountains of work piled up, angry clients' calls and underappreciated employees. I apologized profusely and hung up before she could threaten to quit. I then called Bud Dixon, my regular insurance client. Bud's an old friend whose office had been next to mine until he moved into ritzier quarters downtown.

As always, Bud was sympathetic, but firm. He gave me a deadline and said he'd give the jobs to Dickie Greenleaf, one of my competitors, if I hadn't wrapped things up by then. Bud knew me well. Mentioning Dickie was like waving a red flag in front of a bull. The work would be done if it killed me. Let Dickie horn in? Not on my watch!

I spent about an hour, doing whatever I could on a couple of jobs—calls, online searches, notes. Then, feeling restless, I headed out for a hobbling walk. Instead of the woods, I walked out the driveway and onto Main Road, where I headed east toward the ocean. When I returned just after five, Ralph was gone.

CHAPTER 45

I had arranged to meet Demaris at seven, which gave me plenty of time to spread out my notes. The theory about Ruth Bowen's teenage pregnancy was probably just that, a theory, brought on by my overactive imagination. Maybe her father had been transferred. I might be able to find that out through a search of insurance company files. And, what if she had been pregnant and given birth? Was it a secret worth killing for? Despite the accusations I'd hurled at Ruth Bowen, I seriously doubted Ron would have blackmailed her had he learned the truth. He hated her and wanted her gone, but blackmail was not his style. Besides, Ruth had a gay son who flaunted his sexuality for all the town to see. What did she care if people found out about a teenage pregnancy over fifty years ago?

More than likely, Ron's murder had nothing to do with Ruth Bowen. The Harbor Club certainly had plenty at stake. The specter of gaining or losing millions made for a powerful motive. What about the Button's Marsh development? Had it really been stopped or had Tripp Bowen's ex-lover simply gone underground temporarily, waiting till all the opponents were out of the way before once again bringing his proposal before the Town Council? I had meant to ask Ruth how to get in touch with Tripp, but after our morning's conversation, I doubted I'd ever be granted another audience with the Queen Bee.

And, what about all the other funny money changing hands around town? My disorganization hit me in the face as I realized I had forgotten all about Carl

Acevedo, the rumored-to-be-shady building inspector, erstwhile pig farmer and second cousin to Ruth Bowen. Recalling Will and Ramona Souza's discussion about a disgruntled property owner, I grabbed the phonebook, located Alonzo Souza and dialed. Ramona answered and invited me to stop by for coffee in the morning. Feeling a little more organized albeit still clueless, I schlepped all my materials to the jeep, showered, changed and checked the time. Six fifteen. If I hurried, I had time to stop by the pig farm on my way to meet Roger Demaris.

CHAPTER 46

I was aware of Carl Acevedo's place long before I reached the driveway. The stench wafted for several miles on the wind. I spied a rusty, dented mailbox with black letters spelling *A-C-E-V-E*. Adorning the front of the mailbox was a pink dancing pig in blue tutu and yellow ballet slippers. I turned onto the driveway, wondering how long I could hold my breath.

The jeep bumped down the bumpy dirt road. Rocky mounds punctuated bare, open fields on either side. Hundreds of sea gulls scavenged in the fields and circled above me. Passing through a small stand of trees, I reached a clearing. The Acevedo complex spread out before me—four trailers, a couple of sheds and a dilapidated barn. Interspersed between the buildings were all manner of rusting farm equipment—tractors, plows, garden mowers, scythes and a backhoe. No pigs in sight, but I could sure smell them.

I parked the jeep beside the barn and stepped out, my knee stiff after my walk. I limped toward a lime-green trailer with a plastic picket fence around one side and a partial deck that led to the front door. Several pumpkins were lined up on the deck, which was furnished with broken lawn chairs and a picnic table with three legs propped against the deck rail. No one answered my knock, so I turned and headed for trailer number two, a faded shade of puke orange.

I hadn't gone far when he called from behind me. "Hey, who the hell are you?"

I turned to find a vision I assumed to be Carl Acevedo, scratching his bald head while also adjusting his soiled wife beater tee shirt. Attempts to pull the undershirt over a sizable beer belly proved futile so he crossed tattooed arms over the whole mess.

"Ricky Steele. Mr. Acevedo?"

"You from State?"

By that, I assumed he meant the state of Rhode Island. I shook my head. "No, I'm just visiting in the Harbor and I heard you kept pigs. I've always loved pigs."

"Why?"

"Well, for one thing, they're so intelligent." Who was I kidding? At this moment I knew one thing—pigs were more intelligent than me. What did I think I was doing barging in on a man who lived out in the middle of nowhere? Did I have a death wish? I sure as hell wasn't going to question him about shady building inspection practices.

"Listen, lady, I don't know what you're on, but I don't give tours. 'Sides, with that bum leg you're liable to trip and fall and I'm not about to pay no lawsuit."

"Of course not. I shouldn't have bothered you. I'm trespassing. Please forgive me. I'll just be on my way." As I hobbled backward toward the jeep, I kept one eye peeled for junk, the other for a loaded shotgun.

"Now, hold on." He grinned, revealing a mouth with many teeth missing. "You really wanna see the pigs?"

"I'd love to, if it's not too much trouble."

"Lemme get a jacket. Be right back."

He returned a minute later and led me around to the back of the barn where a low, narrow corral stretched for several hundred yards into the woods. As we neared the pen, I heard snuffling, snorting, grunting. Despite the smell and snorting cacophony, I was still unprepared for the sight that greeted us. Hundreds of mud-encrusted mounds were everywhere—lying, standing, rolling, and eating from long wooden troughs. I'm always amazed at how big pigs grow to be and these were no exception. Not the cute little critters of children's picture books, these were giants, some the size of small elephants, or at least they looked that way from my vantage point.

"Come on," he said, heading for the barn's side door. Just inside, an enormous sow lay on her side, a dozen tiny piglets fighting for space to suckle pendulous teats. "Don't usually get a litter this late in the season, but the boar got at her. Want to hold one?"

I smiled, fighting to keep from gagging. He lifted an adorable, pinkish mud ball from the fray. I took the wriggling bundle, wet nose rooting at my jacket and bright eyes staring up at me. "Cute little fellow, isn't he?" And, he was, just like baby piglet Wilbur in E. B. White's *Charlotte's Web*, drawn so beautifully by the brilliant Garth Williams.

"Don't stay cute long." He made a soft clucking sound taking the piglet from me. Little legs went a mile a minute as he was lowered back it into the pen.

"How long do you keep them?"

"Six, nine months, sometimes a little over a year. Some out there are much older. They get away from me sometimes."

"Do you do the slaughtering?"

"Nope. Place in Northport. Comes and picks 'em up, butchers 'em and I distribute. Mostly local customers, a few supermarkets."

"Is this your full-time job? Do you also work in town?"

He stared at me. I gave him my most innocent *silly little ole me* smile. "Building inspector, but probably not for much longer with all this trouble. They've been threatening to take the job away on account of my pigs."

"That doesn't seem right. Does the council support you?"

He shrugged. "Pigs are a lot of work." Clearly, he was not going to chat about his building inspector duties.

I played along. "Do you have help?"

"Nope. Unless you count my wife's no-account nephews. They're supposed to help with the feeding and cleaning out of the pens, but they're friggin' useless." He hadn't needed to point that out. One whiff, not to mention one gander at the piles of manure everywhere, told me that cleanup was a rare occurrence. "Pigs are actually very clean, you know. Most of the smell's not them. It's the clams."

"Excuse me?"

He nodded. "Come on, I'll show you." He led me to the far side of the barn, gesturing towards a white mountain almost as tall as the barn. "Clamshells. I had a whole scheme goin'. Was gonna get clamshells delivered, let pigs lick 'em clean, then crush the shells, dry 'em out and sell 'em as driveways. Trouble is, the pigs didn't like 'em and didn't do a very good job cleanin' 'em, so, as you can see, they stink." He was right about that. The stench on this side of the barn was so strong it made my eyes water. "So, now I'm stuck and the State's all over me."

Suddenly aware of the growing darkness, I peered at my watch. Five minutes to seven, shit. "Mr. Acevedo, thanks for showing me your pigs. I lost track of time and I've got to meet someone." I was trying to talk without breathing, which made my words come out in breathless gasps.

"No problem, anytime. Smell bother you?"

"Just a little." I smiled, hoping I could get back to the jeep and out of the area without vomiting.

"You get used to it. I hardly notice it at all no more."

I nodded, thanking him again and trying to keep from breathing as I sidled, crablike, towards my car.

Chapter 47

It was nearly seven twenty when I stepped into the Riptide, fearing Demaris might have given up on me. He hadn't. I found him at the bar, a seltzer water and half-eaten bowl of popcorn beside him. "You're late."

"I'm sorry."

"I forgive you. Wanna get a table?" I nodded, and he beckoned to the hostess who held up her 'just a minute' finger.

Once we settled into a booth, me with a glass of pinot grigio, Demaris another seltzer, he said, "So? What was so important that you had to keep an officer of the law waiting?"

As I related the details of my visit to Acevedo's pig farm, he whistled, waving a hand in front of his nose. "Thought I smelled something when you walked in."

"Ha, ha. What have you heard? Any news on Charlie?"

"Cause of death, blunt force trauma, inconsistent with a fall."

"I knew it! What else?"

"Nothing else. Now, stop panting and look at the menu. What the hell were you doing out at Carl's anyway?"

"What do you know about his building inspections? Any complaints?"

His eyes narrowed. "What kind of complaints? Is this because you've just found out whose cousin he is?"

"No, but she's involved."

"Involved in what? Listen, Ruth Bowen may be a little overbearing, and she likes things done her way, but she's not dishonest."

"Unless you count the way she compensates herself."

"Now, that's never been proven. You've been listening to Ron Harp and his buddies too long. There's two sides to that story and neither are completely true. Ron had his own set of blinders, same as she does."

"Maybe, but he didn't have a deep, dark secret he was protecting." He looked away, pretending to search for the waitress.

I leaned across the table, grabbing his hand. "You know something, don't you? What did you learn? Is it about the baby?"

"Why, Ms. Steele, I didn't know you cared."

"Tell, me please! I've got an online search in progress, but no response yet."

He stared back at me for several second before sitting back and reclaiming his hand. "Baby boy, born April 2, 1956, Cedar Hills Presbyterian, right outside of Chicago. Mother, Ruth Simmonds, age 17, father, unknown. They were living in Cedar Hills, old man Simmonds' office was in downtown Chicago."

"How did you—?"

He waved his hand.

"Never mind. I knew it, Roger, this is what she's been hiding, what Charlie knew and Ron, too."

"So, Bowen arranges a bike accident for Harp, clubs Charlie over the head, and drags him all the way down the Ledge to dump him in the surf?"

"He wasn't killed at the shack?"

"Nope."

"I know she didn't do it, but one of her minions might have."

He shook his head. "Most of 'em are a little long in the tooth for that kind of shenanigans."

"Shenanigans?"

He laughed. "And, following your logic, she'd have had to let them in on her secret. Doesn't seem likely, does it?"

"I don't know. Let me think."

"You do that, Ms. Private Eye. Me, I've been waiting a long time and I'm ordering dinner."

By mutual agreement, we put Windy Harbor secrets aside and spent the meal sharing tales of our sad, miserable love lives. Demaris was clearly interested, even if ten to fifteen years my junior. Between my wild night of passion with Jay Harp, and the sad-eyed, craggy Roger, my love life had gone from nonexistent to spinning out of control.

Truth be told, someone like Roger was much safer. I'd never had much luck with pretty boys, especially the ones with bitchy ex-girlfriends waiting in the wings, but unfortunately I wasn't interested in Roger Demaris. As he walked me to my car, I was pretty sure that had I asked him home, he'd have come. I didn't.

He said goodnight, then turned away, headed to his car.

CHAPTER 48

Ramona had coffee and a warm cheese Danish ready when I arrived. She was alone, kids packed off to school, Alonzo nowhere in sight. I accepted the coffee and Danish with a smile.

She grilled me about "the case" and I gave her a sketchy update, omitting anything related to Ruth Bowen's past or the canister I'd found at Charlie Higgins's shack. I concluded with a description of my visit to Acevedo's pig farm.

"Wow, you actually went there? You're brave. A couple of years ago I wanted to take the kids to see the pigs and Alonzo blew up and forbid me to set foot on his property."

"Why?"

"Because Carl Acevedo is not a nice man."

I remembered Carl's soft gaze as he set the frisky piglet down. The image didn't match, but then again, that was pigs. He had certainly "clammed" right up when I mentioned his other job.

Ramona caught me smiling at my mental pun. "What?"

"Nothing. Just thinking about the pigs. They were awfully cute. But, Ramona, what I really wanted to ask you about is Carl's inspections. Will said you heard about a complaint from a homeowner last year?"

"Yes, Betty Atwood. She and her husband are new in town, been here two or three years now. Early on they were doing some remodeling and called Carl to come and inspect a project in progress. He said the work didn't conform to code. Told them they needed plumbing and electrical work before he'd approve them going forward. When the Atwoods called their contractor, he said his people were swamped and couldn't get to it for at least a month. Carl told them if the work wasn't done immediately, they'd have to wait till spring. That would have held them up for six months.

"Anyway, Carl said he could get people there the next day to take care of it. And, he did. Paul Warren and Zippy Kaufman, the electrician and plumber he called, came out and fixed the "problem," charging the Atwoods three thousand dollars, payable up front for their work."

"And they didn't fight it?"

"They were desperate and didn't want to wait six months."

"What did their contractor say?"

"He was disgusted, but he told them they'd better do it if they wanted to get on with the project. Don't forget, he works in this town, too. Carl could hold up permits for all of his jobs."

"And does he do that when someone pisses him off?"

She shrugged. "Rebecca and Ron were looking into that last year so she'd know more. From what I've heard, it's the new people Carl preys upon. Folks who have lived here for awhile don't seem to have a problem. We haven't, for instance, but then, I grew up here. Alonzo didn't, but I guess if you've got one native in the family they don't hassle you. Ron and Karen didn't have problems, or Peter and Becca. And I don't imagine they'd dare try anything with Myra and Dick, them both being lawyers. Alonzo doesn't like me to talk about it. Says it's none of my business, but it's a shame, isn't it? People being preyed upon that way. I wouldn't be at all surprised to hear that Ruth Bowen gets kickbacks from Carl and the contractors involved."

"Do you have any proof of this?"

"No, but I don't trust that woman as far as I can see her."

We talked a while longer and I said my goodbyes, thanking her for the coffee, which was already doing strange things to my insides.

CHAPTER 49

The Souzas' modest cape was right on East Road, not a half mile from the police station, so I decided to swing by, hoping to catch Hank Mendoza, the elusive animal control officer. Miraculously, he was in, sitting in his office two doors down from Ripler's. As a part-timer, he shared the office with two officers, and all three names were on the plaque by the door.

He rose to shake my hand, his calm, languid movements designed not to startle. "What can I do for you?"

Tall and thin, with an unruly mop of dark curly hair, Mendoza appeared to be in his early thirties. Somehow, he didn't go with his wife, Lotty, Will's receptionist. One could never account for affairs of the heart, I mused, taking the seat he offered. We were alone, his office mates nowhere in sight.

"I'm Ricky Steele. I'm visiting in town and I'm—"

"I know what you're doing."

"Well, good. Then you know I don't believe Ron Harp's death was an accident."

He stared back at me, noncommittal. "And?"

"And Charlie Higgins was murdered, not to mention Hattie Pauls last year."

"Maybe you hadn't heard, Miz Steele. I'm the Animal Control Officer. I don't do people."

"That's exactly what I want to talk to you about. Animals, all the animals that have died under mysterious circumstances over the last few years."

"Lady, this is the country. Animals are always dying under mysterious circumstances. We've got coyotes, foxes, bald eagles, maybe even a mountain lion. Something's always getting carried off, mauled or maimed around here. And if that's not happenin' we got the skewks riding around in friggin' hot air balloons. Scares the shit outta the livestock. We got pigs and sheep jumping fences, impaled or gored on fence rails, horses having heart attacks, dogs clawing through screens. Every hour animals meet their makers out here."

"I'm interested in animals that may have been helped toward their Maker by people. Like Hattie Pauls's cats or Karen Harp's Jambalaya."

"Hattie's cats were most likely killed by coyotes or disease. Never had 'em vaccinated. And that stupid peacock probably strangled himself on a vine."

"What about Bobby Harp's sheep?"

"Could've been anything. Sheep are real hard to keep alive. They get sick at the drop of a hat."

"All six of them?"

He shrugged.

"You must keep records."

"On every last one." He pulled a tall black ledger from the bookshelf behind his desk. "This is the last two years. Knock yourself out."

"Can I borrow this?"

"Lady, this isn't a lending library. You got twenty minutes. I'm going down to feed our tenants. Got six strays and two litters of kittens, if you're interested in adopting a pet."

"Thanks, but one cat's all I can handle."

"Just so you know, when I come back up, I gotta get out on the road."

Nodding, I took up a pencil and notepad and started wading through pages and pages of notations—"dog dead on Nob Road, cat frozen, Briggs Pond, cows struck by lightning." The list went on and on, recording death after death, along with countless reports of missing pets and livestock. When I came to the previous winter, I was surprised to read, "dead Corgi, belonging to Mr. and Mrs. James

Harp, 14 Beach Road, found on the beach. Probable cause—coyotes." I continued, my eyes growing bleary as the clock ticked on.

I had just come to another interesting entry dated July 22, this past summer. "Dead, Dumpling, a two-year-old Vietnamese pot-bellied pig belonging to Ruth Bowen of 67 Main Road. Probable cause—coyotes." Windy Harbor's coyotes were a busy bunch, indeed.

"All set." It wasn't a question. Mederois grabbed his jacket and held out his hand for the ledger.

"What about Mrs. Bowen's pig? What happened to him?"

"Dunno."

"Excuse me?"

"She called it in. I just recorded that it happened. Never saw Dumpling, poor old fella. She buried him on the property. Someone helped her, Ralph Boardman, I think."

"You were acquainted with Dumpling, then?"

He laughed, returning the ledger to its place. "Everyone knew Dumpling. He was always running off, up the road, into town, into people's gardens. He was a cute little fella, but not very popular with the garden club set. You ask me, one of them bumped him off after he dug up her prize peonies."

"Anyone in particular?"

"I'm only kidding, but if you want a suspect, I'd talk to Peg Crawley. She came in last spring ranting and raving about her precious delphiniums and a bunch of other things. Dumpling apparently had himself a good ole time in her flower beds before Ruth managed to get a leash on him and haul him home."

"She lives that close to Red Gate?"

"Two driveways down, other side of Main Road. But, hell, distance never stopped Dumpling. He used to roam all over town. We even found him in the Hearthstone dumpster one night."

"Sounds like a colorful character," I said, rising and thanking him for his time. I exited the police station quickly, having no desire to run into Roger Demaris and his sad, puppy dog eyes.

CHAPTER 50

Mindy Church was a library assistant two days a week. The first time I had spoken to her had been a Thursday and I hoped Tuesday was her other day to work. I found her in the stacks, reshelving books, the rolling cart beside her almost empty. Dressed in heather-green slacks and a matching wool sweater, her look screamed middle-aged preppy—trim, understated, expensive. She recognized me and lowered her glasses from the bridge of her nose, allowing them to hang loose from a beaded chain around her neck. "Miss Steele, hello. You're back."

"How was your trip?"

"Hectic." She rolled the cart against the far wall. "Follow me. We can talk back here." She led the way into a study, couch along one wall, table with four chairs in the center. There were four large paintings lining the walls, landscapes of local scenes. Oils, quite skillfully done and certainly not by Patty. Noticing my gaze, she said, "Those are our Hattie Pauls'. Beautiful, aren't they? We were lucky to get them."

"I was admiring her watercolors in the Town Hall. Pretty good for a school-marm." I took the chair opposite her.

Folding her hands on the table, she met my eyes. "You want to ask me about finding Ron Harp, don't you?"

"Yes."

"I was glad I was busy last week. I wasn't ready to talk about it. Of course, I spoke to Cal. Had to. Getting away helped. I feel better now. So, what exactly do you want to know?"

"I'd be grateful if you could retrace your steps that morning. Tell me exactly what you saw, heard. Where he was? The position of the bike, anything you remember."

She nodded. "Well, I was on my way home, so I was traveling on the opposite side of the road. As I approached, he was in the shadows, lying just off the road. The bicycle was beside him, half in the road. I stopped just past the spot and ran back. There was quite a lot of blood from his head wound. He was unconscious but still breathing. His left foot was tangled under the bike so I pulled it away. Afterward I thought I probably shouldn't have touched him, but he looked so uncomfortable.

"I ran back to my car, beeped the horn, then grabbed a towel and ran back. I tried to stop the blood, but there was so much. Poor man was bleeding to death right before my eyes and I couldn't do a thing. Cliff came to his front door during the time I was ministering to him and I screamed to him to call Rescue."

"So, you didn't leave to get Mr. Wright?" I asked, remembering Cal Ripler's account.

"Oh, no, I didn't like to leave Ronnie alone. Cliff came right away. He called Rescue and then ran over. By the time he got there, Ron had stopped breathing. Rescue came soon after. They worked on him a bit, then took him away. I went to sit on Cliff's porch for a little while to collect myself, then I drove home.

"Didn't the police question you?"

"Lieutenant Ripler and Officer Burrows came over a few hours later to take a statement. I understand they did the same thing with Cliff. He lives alone since his wife Mary passed away three years ago."

"Do you have a theory about what happened? What I mean is, based on his injuries, could you tell what happened?"

"Well, it's hard to say. Naturally, I was upset. I was focusing so much on his head and helping him. It looked as if he'd hit his head on a rock. There was a horrid gash, right above his temple, and he was lying across a pile of rocks. Have you been by there? There are piles of stones from the old culvert just sitting there on the shoulder. Probably one of Harbor Public Works's many unfinished projects. That's a town road, not state, so it takes forever for them to get around to fixing it."

"Was there just the one gash?"

She nodded. "At least, as far as I could see. He was on his side when I found him, but in untangling his leg, he rolled over onto his back. There might have been a cut on the back of his head but I don't think so. He appeared to have gone over the handlebars, as if the bike had flipped him head over heels."

"Why do you say that?"

"Well, the bike was facing the opposite direction and it was quite mangled up. If he'd just fallen over, to the side or something, I would have expected that he and his bicycle would be facing the same way. I remember thinking it was odd because there were papers everywhere, so he was obviously returning from town. Must have taken the scenic route, don't you think?"

"How so?"

"Well, it's more direct to take Sadley, but he took the wider circle. He was an experienced long-distance cyclist. You'd see him everywhere around town so him taking the long route wasn't unusual."

"Can you tell me anything about the bicycle? Was it badly damaged?"

"Truthfully, except for its direction, I didn't pay much attention to it. Cliff pulled it out of the way. Perhaps he noticed something? I do have a mental image of it being twisted, but he was, Ron, I mean, he was so twisted, too."

"Did you know him well?"

"Not socially, but he was a regular library patron, so I saw him here. Quiet, kept to himself, not much of a chatter, at least when he was here."

"Where would I find Cliff Wright during the day?"

"Town dump, if he's on duty. He's semiretired, but puts in a couple of days at the recycling center."

I thanked her and handed her my card, on the back of which I had scrawled the cottage's phone number. "Mindy, please call if you remember anything else. No matter how insignificant it seems."

CHAPTER 51

From the library, I headed to the dump, following Mindy's directions. This was not Cliff Wright's day to work, but the man on duty suggested I try his house.

As I headed for Willow, my stomach growled and I noticed the time. One fifteen. I stopped at the deli for a bagel and hot tea. I inhaled the bagel, but was still sipping the tea when I pulled up beside Wright's raised ranch. A painted ceramic deer guarded the lawn. As I headed for the front porch, I heard a voice from the backyard so I walked around the house, where I found Wright by the garage swearing and cussing as he wrestled with a tangle of garden hose.

"That reminds me of home. I've been meaning to get one of those hose carts for three years now."

Straightening up, he stared, expression bland. "You selling something?"

"No." I quickly explained who I was.

"Oh, the lady dick. I've been hearin' about you. Not too popular, are ya?"

"Alas, I seem to have that effect on people."

I smiled, wondering who he'd been talking to. I had so many fans in Windy Harbor.

"Better come in," he said, dropping the hose and heading for the back door.

I followed him into the house. Wright was in his sixties, maybe seventy, his step quick if a bit unsteady. About my height, he was heavy-set, balding. His flannel shirt and work pants were well-worn, and did not appear to have seen the inside of a washing machine for many moons.

He patted the kitchen table's yellow linoleum surface. "Sit. Want a beer?"

"Thanks, that'd be great." It was a little early for me, but anything to make a friend. He pulled two Budweisers from the fridge, uncapped them and set one in front of me.

"Cheers." He clinked his bottle to mine and took a long swallow. I followed suit. "So, you're here about Ron Harp, I'm guessin'."

I nodded and asked him to tell me what he could about the accident.

He gave a very similar description to Mindy Church's. "Rough break for a young guy like that."

I nodded. "Mindy said you pulled the bike away from him. Is that right?"

"Yup."

"What can you tell me about it? Was it badly damaged?"

"Wrecked. Frame bent, wheels mangled."

"Didn't that seem odd to you?"

"I'm no expert on bicycle accidents, but it looked like he flipped over. Probably hit a patch of sand, put on the brakes too hard and over he went. No helmet, that's what made the difference. Always wore a helmet, too. We'd see him all over, always had a helmet until that day."

"His dog chewed it up and he hadn't had a chance to replace it."

"Should've taken the car."

"Tell me about the wheels. What do you mean, mangled?"

"Bent and twisted, one of those newfangled jobs. Not like the old Schwinns we had as kids. Crumpled right up, spokes dangling out."

"Didn't you think that much damage was strange?"

"Not if he hit a rock going forty miles an hour. Cyclists really move down this hill, getting up steam for the big hill ahead. If he hit sand, then rocks, that'd do it."

Or, if someone threw something in the spokes, I thought. "You didn't notice any sticks nearby?"

"Nope. There were newspapers scattered all over the place, but we weren't payin' much attention to anything but him."

We chatted a few more minutes. No, he hadn't known Ron well. Hadn't seen anyone take the bike. Had gone to the police station to make a statement and when he got home it was gone. Had been watching television when he heard Mindy's horn. Hadn't noticed Ron going into town nor had he heard more than a couple of cars and trucks that morning. "But," he said, as I rose to go, "don't go by me. I'm getting a little deaf and once the set's on, I don't hear much of anything from the road."

I thanked him and departed, cursing Cal Ripler for his sloppiness. I was certain Ron's bike had a story to tell, which, of course, was why it had been taken away, perhaps by Ron's killer?

CHAPTER 52

I spent an hour at the cottage, making calls and researching online for the two jobs Bud Dixon had threatened to take away. Irritable and bleary-eyed, I finally decided a walk might clear my head. I waved to Ralph on my way out. At this rate, I doubted he'd finish the job before nightfall. Just as I reached the end of the driveway, Patty's truck roared by me. She saw me, but made no attempt to slow down or wave, her tires churning up clouds of dust.

When I returned forty-five minutes later, Ralph was on the ladder, Patty below barking orders. They had already put up all but four of the storm windows. "Fast work," I called. "Can I help?"

She grabbed the next window. "We've got it." Moving around the house, she waited impatiently as her husband collapsed the stepladder. "For Christ's sake, Ralphie, just leave it open."

"Now, Pat, don't get all huffy just 'cause we got an audience."

He winked at me, passing by, moving as slowly as he dared. He was deliberately trying to irritate her. Having no wish to be in the middle of a marital spat, I beat a hasty retreat into the house.

When I came out dressed for the Chaffees' cocktail party, they were cleaning up, the sawhorses and tools all packed away in his truck. Ralph paused when he spied me. "Hey, don't you look nice." The compliment prompted an icy glare from his wife.

"Thank you. I'm off to a Democratic fundraiser so I want to look my best."

"Chaffees, right?" she said, her tone friendly.

I nodded. "You going?"

She snorted. "Yea, right."

"You both Republicans?"

"I am. Ralph doesn't vote."

"Oh? Why not?"

"Doesn't approve of politics, do you, hon?" The woman was amazing. One minute she was throwing daggers at us. the next, it was "hon" and even a smile for me.

Ralph shrugged, shoving a large metal tool kit into the truck bed. "Don't take sides, don't lose friends." It could have been my imagination, but I thought he looked angry.

"Well, fortunately some of us do or no telling what this place would've turned into."

"What are you afraid of?"

"You one of them. You'd never understand."

"One of who?"

"The skewks."

"Try me."

"Have you ever been in the store in the height of the season? Heard skewks askin' for caviar and whatever else they eat? Ever heard 'em chewin' out Bonnie or Rita 'cause their friggin' *Wall Street Journal* is late? Ever gone into the fish market or Morse's Greenhouse and heard them ordering people around? It's disgusting."

"There's a simple solution. Ignore them."

"Not with the money they throw around. Oh, people do tell 'em off, believe me. I sure don't take any shit from the shitty assholes at the beach."

"Patty runs a snack bar at Sandy Point."

"So I heard. That's not far from the Ledge, right? Heard you thought Charlie Higgins was bad for business."

She gave her husband a sharp look. "Had no ill will toward Charlie. Folks that say otherwise don't know what in the hell they're talking about."

"If you ask me, which you haven't, I'd say you're guilty of the same kind of snobbery of which you accuse the skewks. You've even made up an insulting name for them. How charitable is that?"

"You don't have a clue."

"Where I live, summer people and year-rounders get along just fine. I'm in the Grove. My house and my neighbors' houses are modest little bungalows, but there are some huge houses nearby. Doesn't matter. We're all friendly."

"Well, la-di-da. What're you, the little rich girl slummin' in the Grove? How many years will you stick it out before runnin' home to daddy?"

"Excuse me?"

"Don't try and play the 'just one of the little people' game with me, hon. I know who you are. I'm not as gullible as my husband either. Come on, Ralph, let's get outta here."

Ralph shrugged, giving me a quick smile. "See you around, I guess."

I hadn't time to reply before she had yanked him toward the trucks.

CHAPTER 53

The Chaffees lived at the Bluffs, an exclusive enclave of million-dollar homes on the fringes of a multimillion-dollar neighborhood. I pulled up the clamshell drive and parked on the grass, just as the Morses drew up beside me. From the look of things, they'd been fighting, their expressions stony, both staring straight ahead. When they spied me, smiling masks slipped on.

"Hey, Ricky, nice night for the Democrats," Peter said, attempting to slide his arm round Rebecca's waist.

She stepped away. "Hi, Ricky, nice to see you. How's it going?"

"Great. How's the trial?"

"Settled this morning, thank God. I've barely seen my children the past month."

"Or your husband."

He grinned, giving her a pleading 'I'm sorry look,' which she ignored.

"Thank God, you're here," she said, taking hold of my arm. "I hate to walk into these things alone."

Life was strange. A few days ago, Rebecca couldn't wait to get away from me and now, a little marital spat and we were best friends. Peter trailed along behind, stopping near the back door to greet a couple I didn't recognize. Rebecca and I proceeded in without him.

The Chaffees' fifteen-year-old post-and-beam home was a showplace for Myra's collection of Native American art. Navaho rugs hung from walls and pottery and artifacts were everywhere, in glass cases, on tables, mantles and shelves. Myra's brother, a sculptor, specialized in enormous metal pieces and his fanciful sculptures dotted the lawn as well as the interior of the house. An eight-foot, wrought iron and ceramic archer, Orion perhaps, stood in the front foyer. We found Karen and Jay standing in Orion's shadow. I hugged her, avoided looking at him and fumbled with my coat.

"Allow me." Strong hands slipped the coat from my shoulders then he moved to assist Rebecca with hers.

"Jay, so nice to see you."

I watched as Rebecca hugged and kissed him, wondering if she was thinking about Ron, wishing she was embracing her lover instead of his brother.

Karen nodded at Rebecca and turned to me. "We tried to call. We were going to swing by and pick you up, but no one answered."

Jay slid between us, endeavoring to catch my eye. "We did, that's the truth. Soon as I got in."

"What happened to working all week?"

"I was able to rearrange my schedule. Have to go back Friday, but I wanted to be here for Karrie."

Rebecca drifted away and Karen waved, distracted by someone in the living room. He leaned closer and whispered, "So, you have me for three days. Your own private love slave."

Love slave, my eye! I sniffed and turned away to greet our hostess, Myra Rollins, resplendent in teal-green slacks and a shimmering top.

"Ricky, so glad you came. Bar's in the kitchen. Dick'll fix you anything you'd like."

I beat a hasty retreat and found Dick in the pantry, chatting with a woman I didn't know—big hips, narrow waist, long, straight blond hair, horn-rimmed glasses. She was dressed in a flowing denim skirt and a light pink turtleneck, a necklace of silver seashells round her neck.

"Laura, great," he said, spying me. "Look who's here. You haven't met our resident P.I., have you? Ricky Steele, Laura Morrow."

Laura Morrow shook my hand, her grip firm. "Hello. I've heard a lot about you. You're a childhood friend of Karrie's?"

"Since our playpen days. Nice to meet you. I hear you're fighting the good fight."

She laughed, giving Dick a look. "Something like that. It's not that bad most of the time, if you don't mind continual insults, character attacks and never getting your own way."

Dick handed us both ridiculously large goblets of white wine and we wandered into the living room. "This your second year?"

She nodded.

"Were you involved in IMPACT?"

"Oh, yes, but I've had to cut back since getting elected. Mustn't take sides. Gotta remain impartial. As if that ever happens in this town."

"How well did you know Ron?"

"Pretty well. My husband, Steve and I have been here for ten years. He's the one over by the fire, gesturing wildly. He's either talking about fishing or Ruth Bowen. Those are the only subjects that really get him that fired up."

"He looks familiar."

"Did you grow up in Fall River?" I nodded. "So did he. At least from his teens on. Went to Durfee. Did you?"

I shook my head. "Packed off to boarding school, I'm 'fraid."

"That's right. You're from the city's aristocracy, aren't you? I met your dad last year at a fundraiser for the Animal Rescue League."

I did not want to discuss my father or his philanthropy. "What does Steve do?"

"He's an engineer. Works in Newport at the navy base. His dad was in the navy so they moved a lot, but he always maintained those navy ties. His job's what brought us here from Indiana. That's where he was born."

"Can I ask you something?" I said, drawing her aside. "Do you know of any reason someone would want to kill Ron?"

For half a minute, she regarded me with grave eyes. "So you think it wasn't an accident?"

"I'm sure of it."

"This is going to make me sound like a traitor, especially here," she said, eyes scanning the room. "But, no. I work with these people every day, Ron's nemeses, I mean. They're xenophobic, narrow-minded and petty, but it's all show. Even Patty's bluster is just that. She talks tough, but she's an old softie. Have to be married to a sweetheart like Ralph. They're wonderful people, salt of the earth."

"But what if Ron discovered something, something someone wanted hidden?"

"If you're talking about some of the questionable business practices around here, we're working on those, but it's slow going. If another Democrat is elected, Dick or Avery Holland, that will make all a difference."

"Who's Avery?"

"He's a contractor in town, the other Democrat on the ticket. He's away at his grandfather's funeral so he couldn't be here tonight." Lowering her voice, she added, "Between you and me, Avery's probably the one who'll get in. Ruth's cronies will work pretty hard to keep a lawyer like Dick off the Council, whereas Avery is a lamb, grew up here. Everybody loves him. Sedgie'll have an aneurysm if Dick gets elected."

At that moment we were interrupted by well-wishers and I left Laura to her public. I sidled off and bumped straight into Alonzo Souza.

"Hello, nice to see you again," I said. "Where's Ramona?"

"Off gossiping and eating, I expect. I just came in. Bobby dropped me off."

"He's not coming?"

"Nope. Betsy and he have a neighborhood clambake or something. Excuse me for a sec, would you? I haven't seen Mona for five days."

I watched him hurry off, pausing to converse with a group of men, suddenly in no hurry to locate his wife. It was okay. I was used to men running away from me. I didn't take it personally.

From behind me, a deep voice purred, "If I didn't know any better, I'd think you were avoiding me."

His hand caressed my back and I pulled away. "If you want to make yourself useful, introduce me to Steve Morrow."

"What do you want with that jarhead?"

"Never mind." I gazed across the room at Laura Morrow's husband, who appeared calmer, less animated now. There was something familiar about him. Where had I seen him?

"Come on," I said, dragging him along. What good was a love slave if I couldn't order him around?

Steve Morrow was the kind of beefy individual I usually avoid. Too clean-cut, too all-American, too jolly. However, once we were introduced, I flirted shamelessly, hoping to make Jay jealous. After playing the "do you know so-and-so']" game for several minutes, we finally made a connection. As a teenager, Steve had worked as a groundskeeper at Aquinessett, my father's country club. While I have spent most of my adult life avoiding the place, as a young child, I had no choice. My parents insisted my sister and I learn how to play golf and tennis. From age five until twelve we were dropped at the club every summer morning for tennis and golf lessons.

The minute golf entered the conversation, I became invisible. The men, Jay included, rambled on about course conditions, handicaps and whatever else golfers talk about. Bored, I wandered off to the buffet in the Chaffees' octagon dining room designed and built by Ralph Boardman. Rebecca was filling her plate with tiny sandwiches and mini-quiches. I grabbed a plate and loaded it up it in record time. By silent agreement, we took our food to the breakfast room off the kitchen, where she sat down with a sigh.

"You look tired."

"I'm beat. Peter insisted we come tonight or, believe me, I'd be home in bed. You probably noticed we weren't on the best of terms getting out of the car."

"Where is he, anyway? I haven't seen him."

"Probably still outside talking tractors with Larry Baylor. Couple of old farmers out of their element. I haven't a clue why he insisted on coming. Had to be on Karrie's behalf. He's crazy about Karrie, and not just 'cause she's his best customer."

How convenient, I thought, wondering if I'd stumbled onto a case of spouse swapping. "Becca, we might get interrupted soon and I have a quick question. Did you and Ron ever discover anything illegal going on with Carl Acevedo's building inspections?"

"No, but that doesn't mean it wasn't happening. Ron was looking into that. I've been too busy. It's probably in his notes if he found anything. We thought it was happening, but only to newcomers. We could never get anyone to talk about it. Once people get settled here and learn the rules, they know damn well who they do and don't want to piss off. They sure as hell aren't going to question Ruth Bowen, scion of one of the oldest families, council president and past president of the garden club, and on and on."

"I went to Carl's farm."

"Lucky you."

"He told me he's about to lose his job as inspector."

"Not on account of bogus inspections. He's losing the job because he's about to go to jail for those clamshells and all the other environmental infractions he's perpetrating out there. Revolting man."

"He loves his pigs."

She made a face. "I heard about Charlie. Awful for all of you."

I nodded. "They're related, Charlie and Ron's deaths."

"So, you still think Ron was murdered?"

"Yes, and so do you."

She looked away, peering out the window into the darkness. "It doesn't matter now. All that matters is he's gone."

"Karen told me about you and Ron."

Startled for an instant, she shrugged. "She would, of course." She pushed her plate aside and took a gulp of wine. "Doesn't matter."

"It might matter to Peter. Does he know?"

Her eyes registered fear. "No! Oh, Ricky, please, don't."

"Relax." I patted her hand, which she pulled back as if scorched. "I'm sorry, Rebecca. I didn't mean to pry."

"Yes, you did. That's why you're here. To uncover everyone's dirty little secrets and dredge up hurts we try like hell to keep buried." Once again, she stared out the window. I noticed her wineglass was empty and asked if she wanted a refill. She shook her head.

"There you are!" Val Ramsey burst into the room, coat over her arm. "Just got here and I was afraid you'd left." She was talking to me. "Oh, Becca, hi, didn't see you there."

Will followed his wife into the room, greeting us both warmly. He took Val's coat and asked if he could bring us drinks. We both declined. While Val went to fill a plate, Rebecca took the opportunity to make her escape. As both Ramseys returned with loaded plates, I caught a glimpse of Peter Morse in the front hall, helping his wife into her coat.

Will and Val ate and I drank, chatting all the while about Dick and Avery's chances at getting elected. By the time Will brought a plate of desserts, I'd consumed too many glasses of wine and things were getting fuzzy. Stupidly, I told myself it was for the best. If Jay Harp was going to have his way with me, I needed to be good and drunk. Then I could either fight him off or succumb without embarrassment. Besides, as my buzz increased, my knee felt no pain.

The three of us dived onto the desserts, somehow finding room even after stuffing ourselves with spring rolls, finger sandwiches and mini-quiches.

"What's new?" Will asked, watching me lick brownie frosting off finger by finger.

"Not much. I've mostly been going around in circles and getting nowhere."

"Here, let me get you ladies another drink." Will rose, taking our glasses to the kitchen. Just what I needed, more wine.

"My white knight," Val said, watching her husband fondly. "He takes good care of me."

"You're lucky." I tried to remember the last time, if ever, I likened a man I was dating to a "white knight."

The white knight returned with the drinks and sat down beside me. "You okay? You look a little funny."

"Too much to drink," I said, taking a healthy swallow from the full goblet he'd handed me.

"Better watch that. Cops in this town are out every night. They're everywhere. You get stopped and Cal will slap you into jail so fast your head'll spin."

I set down my glass, staring at him, trying to focus. "What do you really think about this, Will? Do you think Ron was killed for something he knew? Some deep dark secret someone else wanted hidden? Some million-dollar scheme he was blocking? I mean, what do you really think?"

"I think you need coffee," he said, standing and, giving Val a look before disappearing into the kitchen. I excused myself to use the ladies' room, wobbling along the hall.

"Snap out of it," I lectured myself in the mirror as I splashed cold water on my face.

When I emerged from the bathroom, Dick Chaffee had just returned with his flashlight, after leading a group to their cars. "Ricky, hey, haven't had a minute to chat. How you doing?"

"Truthfully, I've been better," I said, taking his arm to stop from swaying.

"Uh-oh, a little too much to drink? If we were alone, I might be tempted to take advantage of this situation."

What was it about his tone? Even in my fog, warning bells clanged. "Oh, Dick, I bet you say that to all the girls."

His lips came close to my ear, hand circling my waist as he whispered, "No, just nosy ones, who are too damn pretty for their own good."

Steve Morrow stepped into the hallway at that moment, and I pushed away from Dick, lunging forward. As he let me go, I could have sworn I heard, "Watch out, babe," but then he was gone and Steve commanded my attention.

We sat on the hall couch, reminiscing about Fall River days. His clean-cut solid presence was oddly comforting after the exchange with Dick Chaffee. When Jay found us we were nearly cheek to cheek.

"Ricky, Karen wants to go home. I'm gonna give her my car. Can I hitch a ride with you?"

"Sure." I sang, waving my hand gaily.

A few minutes later, Will Ramsey interrupted to hand me a large mug of coffee. "Here, drink this. Val and I are heading out. Can we give you a lift?" His eyes darted from Steve's to mine, wondering if he should say more.

I sat up straighter, meeting his eyes. "I'm fine, Will. Thanks. Jay's coming with me."

At that moment, Laura Morrow came to collect her husband. She gave me a funny look as she said good-night. Oh, dear, definitely time for my exit, I thought, rising unsteadily and heading toward the coat closet.

I had just wrestled myself into my coat when Jay appeared. "All set?"

"Just want to say my goodbyes."

Jay at my side, I sloshed about until I located Myra, my thank-you a trifle over the top. Dick Chaffee had vanished, thank goodness.

"Okay, Miss Marple, time to go." Jay gripped my elbow and steered me toward the door.

We met Dick on the doorstep, flashlight in hand. "Need a light to your car?"

"We'll be fine," Jay replied, as his hand propelled me forward. Before I could react, Dick leaned forward, pecking my cheek. I recoiled in horror as Nurse Ratchet practically carried me down the stairs.

"Night, Dick. Thanks a lot," he said.

CHAPTER 54

As we neared the jeep, I fished the keys from my pocket and made a move toward the driver's side. Before I could react, he snatched the keys. "Thanks, I'm driving."

I opened my mouth to protest, then closed it, knowing he was right. All I needed right now was Skip Burrows hauling me in on a D.W.I. As we started off, I stuck my head out the window. Like a little old granny, Jay maneuvered the jeep down the drive, a lumbering hulk compared to his B.M.W.

"Jeep hard to handle, Tiger? Never get stuck in a ditch with this baby."

Eyes focused on the road, he smiled. "May never get home, either."

As we reached the main road, I began thinking about death—animal and human. Something was connecting all these deaths, I was sure of it. "Jay, did you know about Ruth Bowen's pig? Don't you think that's odd? All the dead animals, I mean."

"We're in the country. What'd you expect?"

"Well, what about Karen's peacock? Someone killed Jambalaya just like they did Hattie Pauls's cats and maybe even Ruth Bowen's pig."

"I don't know about the pig, but teenagers do nasty stuff like that sometimes."

"Not the teenagers I know."

"Everyone doesn't grow up in a *Leave It to Beaver* world, Ricky. If people went around crying murder every time a pet died, Hank Mendoza would be asking for time and a half. When my parents' dog was found dead they didn't cry foul play."

"What happened?"

"They figured he got hit by a car. Found him at the end of their driveway. Must've dragged himself as far as he could, then collapsed. Poor old guy was stiff as a board, frozen up, when they found him."

"Someone could have deliberately run him over."

He turned and gave me a look. "Nobody's that nasty."

"Nasty. That's it, Jay. Don't you see? It's not the secrets at all. It's revenge. He wants revenge!"

"Who?"

"Her kid. Quick, turn here and drive to the police station. I need to talk to Roger."

"It's Roger now, is it?"

"Oh, hush and drive. Please, it'll only take a minute."

He pulled over and stopped the car, taking my hand. "Ricky, this is a *really* bad idea. In your condition you could—"

"I'm fine!" I pulled my hand away and stared straight ahead. "Either you drive me or I'm getting out and walking."

"Oh, for Christ's sake." Shaking his head, he gunned the engine and pulled back onto the road. "Don't go complaining to me tomorrow after you make a fool of yourself."

There was no one at the desk when we arrived, so we made our way down the hall to the last office, a shaft of light from it bisecting the darkened corridor. Demaris sat behind the desk, a mug of coffee in hand, a stack of papers in front of him. He looked up, eyes traveling from me to my companion. Jay's arm circled my waist, the only reason I was still vertical. "Well, this is a surprise."

Uh-oh, big mistake. Even in my woozy state, his face told me I'd done something really stupid, not to mention insensitive. Since the damage was already done,

I pressed forward. "Roger," I said, grasping Jay's coat sleeve as I moved closer. "It was revenge, I know it was."

"Say what?"

"It's the son, don't you see? He's here, in the Harbor. He's getting back at people. Killing them and their animals. It's so obvious, why didn't we see it?"

Resigned, he listened patiently, as if he was indulging a spoiled child who had stayed up past her bedtime. "Who are we talking about here?"

"You know, Ruth Bowen's son. We've got to check, see where people come from. Who's moved here from somewhere else, who's the right age. There are lots of people—Dick Chaffee, Alonzo Souza, Steve Morrow? Who knows how many guys fit the description?"

"Look, I'm trying to finish up and go home and you're in no condition to—"

"Roger, please listen to me." I stumbled forward, tripping over a chair. Jay caught me just as I was about to take a nosedive into the wastebasket. "This is really important and we don't have much time."

He sighed, gazing up at me with furrowed brow. "What do you want me to do?"

"Find him. Do a search. Look into everyone's background that fits the age till we—"

"Go home, Ms. Steele. I don't have time for drunks tonight."

"But—"

"Okay, Ricky, we're going." Jay propelled me toward the door. "Sorry to bother you, Detective."

The last glimpse I had of Demaris was his sad, puppy dog eyes. "No problem." But of course, it was a problem, a problem I had created.

Jay carried me into the house, undressed me and tucked me into bed. Eventually he must have slipped in beside me because that's where I found him in the morning when a pounding headache woke me just before seven.

CHAPTER 55

A shower and three aspirin started me on the road to recovery. My knee throbbed, pain shooting to my eyeballs with every step. Surgery would be coming sooner rather than later, I thought morosely. Through bloodshot eyes, I caught a glimpse of Jay as I padded out of the bathroom, wrapped in a towel.

"Don't say a word. I know, I screwed up. Did I make a dreadful scene at the Chaffees'?"

"Not really. The only people who noticed were the Ramseys and me, and maybe Laura Morrow, who caught you pawing her husband in the hallway."

"I was not!"

"I believe you were calling him your 'oldest and dearest friend' when I found you. That would be right before Laura appeared and took him home."

"Oh, Lord," I said, sinking to the bed, head between my knees. "It's time for me to go home."

"Don't beat yourself up. The Chaffees and Morrows could care less. It's your detective friend you should be worried about. He looked pretty confused when we left. What's going on with you two, anyway?"

"I don't want to talk about it."

"Well, I do." He grabbed my arm, pulling me closer. He felt warm and comfortable. A hint of his aftershave lingered. "What's going on with you and the good detective?"

His hand traveled under the towel and up my thigh, sending shivers from head to toe. It would have been so easy to slip under the covers. Instead I pulled away. "Down, Tiger. I've got things to do."

He stood, not bothering to cover himself, revealing every gorgeous aroused inch of him. "I'll come with you. I'm yours all day. I'll fix breakfast, then drive you wherever you want to go."

I leaned over and kissed the top of his head, my hands resting briefly on his shoulders. "Thanks, but I need to do this alone. If you get dressed, I'll take you to Karen's to get your car. If you'd rather rest, I'll come back later."

Hopping up, he dressed quickly and was waiting in the living room a good ten minutes before I was ready. We drove the three miles to Karen's in silence. I stopped by the barn and waited for him to get out.

"Not coming in?"

I shook my head.

"Ricky, we need to talk. Something like Saturday night happens, we just don't go on our merry way, do we?"

"This is all I can manage right now."

"Is this because of your detective and whatever's going on with you two?"

I shook my head.

"Come on, I'm not asking you for a long-term commitment, but I'd like to at least talk, see where we are?"

"Maybe when this is over."

"What's that supposed to mean?"

"It means, maybe when this is over. Look," I added more gently, "I've gotta go. I'll give you a call later. You be at your parents'?"

"Not till later. I'm helping Karrie clean out Ron's clothes this morning."

"I thought you were free all day." My hand caressed his chin, the skin rough with day-old beard.

"Everything's negotiable." He slammed the door behind him.

Complicated relationships, the story of my life. At the rate I was going, they could write it on my tombstone.

CHAPTER 56

I headed into town and stopped at the deli for tea and a bagel. Tripp Bowen sat at the counter, nursing a coffee, a half-eaten blueberry muffin on a plate beside him. He looked pale and sickly, as if he hadn't slept for a week.

I took the stool next to him. "Hi." He stared, trying to remember who I was. "Ricky Steele. We met at the Harps'."

"Oh, yes, hi. How's everyone doing out there?"

"Getting there. You don't look so hot. Are you feeling okay?"

"Head cold. It's knocked me for a loop."

"What're you doing in town, anyway?"

"I'm down to see a friend. He's making a presentation to the Town Council tonight. Came down to lend moral support."

"You mean Kit Reston?"

"You know him?" Light blue eyes searched mine.

"No, just of him. Button's Marsh, right?"

He nodded.

"Have you worked on that, too?"

He shook his head. "Strictly a bystander, especially now. Truth is, Kit and I were partners."

"Were?"

He nodded. "We lived together for two years and I'm still crazy about him, but he's moved on. Probably will hate it when he sees I'm here, but I thought, hey, why not? Come down and take Mother to dinner, maybe catch a glimpse of Kit? Only way that's happening nowadays. He won't return my phone calls."

"I know how that goes."

"It's been horrendous." He sighed, sipping his coffee, appearing on the verge of tears.

"Do you think it's wise following him? When he's moved on and all?"

"No, it's not wise, but when do people behave wisely in affairs of the heart? The minute Mother told me he was on the docket, I knew I had to come."

"And when was that?"

"Last Thursday, I think, maybe Friday. They try to set the agenda a week in advance so they can give public notice. Open meetings law and all that."

"Tripp, were you around when your mother's pig, Dumpling, died?"

"No, but I came right away. It was dreadful. Mother was beside herself. She was crazy about that stupid pig. Loved him more than any dog or cat we ever had. He was housebroken. Slept in her bedroom on a satin cushion, if you can believe it. He was a smart little porker, I have to give him that."

"Did anyone tell you where they found him or what he looked like?"

"Not a mark on him, according to Mother. Neck was a little chafed, I think, like he'd been dragged around by his collar."

Or strangled, I thought, remembering Hank Mederois's notes. Coyotes indeed. "And what did your mother think happened to him?"

"You know, she never said. People kept telling us it was coyotes or that he'd been hit by a car, but Mother never said a word. She was completely numb for about a month. Even missed a couple of council meetings, I think."

"Well, thanks. I hope you feel better and that tonight goes well."

He gave me a rueful smile, no trace of the puffed up, self-important young man of a week ago. In his place sat a lovelorn soul, destined for more heartache.

I pulled into the police station and spotted Demaris's car at the back of the lot. He was in his office, a clean shirt the only indication that he hadn't been there all night. He looked up as I entered, then returned to his work, shuffling papers from side to side.

"Roger, do you have a few minutes? Please?"

"What happened to lover boy?"

This wasn't happening to me. "Roger, listen, last night was very rude and I'm sorry. Did you think about what I said? About the son?"

"Not really."

"Why not?"

"Because I don't put much stock in the ravings of drunken debutantes who run around in the middle of the night instead of staying home in bed with their preppy boyfriends."

"First of all, if you knew me better, you'd know that I'm about as far from a debutante as you can get."

"Not like I'll ever have the chance."

"Excuse me?"

"To get to know you better."

"I don't know how to respond to that."

"Then don't." He stared at the wall, his expression unreadable.

"Roger, I am sorry, but please don't let last night interfere with this."

"With what? What do you think's been happening between us? Were you freaked out so you dragged pretty boy in to push me away?"

"This is insanity. There's nothing happening between us. I'm decades older than you and we're working together. Period, end of story. I needed to talk to you last night because I figured something out. I'm sorry I wasn't as coherent as I should have been, but can we please put that aside and talk about the murders?"

"I'm busy."

He looked tired and I was pretty sure I looked like hell.

"Five minutes, please."

He shoved the papers aside and met my eyes. "Five minutes."

"What if everything that's happened has happened because Ruth Bowen's son wants revenge? Revenge on his father, Charlie Higgins, on Hattie Pauls, the principal who sent his mother away? Revenge on his mother by killing her pig?"

"What in the hell are you talking about?"

"Dumpling, Ruth Bowen's pot-bellied pig."

"What about Ron Harp? What's the motive there?"

"He might've found out who he was. I haven't completely figured that out yet, but never mind. We've got to trace this person, find him. He'd be in his forties, by my calculations, maybe forty-four or forty-five? Can we contact his adoptive family? Did you find out anything about them when you got the information about his birth?"

"Nope."

"But, you can. Or, I'll start a search. I know it's him and he's living in Windy Harbor. Please, Roger, please help me."

He took a deep breath and leaned back in his chair, staring at me as if I'd just informed him Martians had landed on the village green. "Even if I believed your crazy theory—which I don't—I don't have time to be running around on a wild-goose chase. I'm going to be honest with you, Ms. Steele. I shouldn't, and I'll probably regret it, but I'm gonna anyway. I have concerns about some of the shit that goes on around here. I know damn well certain people have their fingers in the till, but that's small towns for you. My interest in this case has been more personal.

"Close your mouth, let me finish. First time I saw you standing in that cottage doorway, I said, 'This is someone I'd like to know better.' So, I played along. Had two nice dinners. Nicest evenings I've spent in years. Would've asked you out again, too, until you paraded lover boy through here last night. But, now, in the words of Rhett Butler, 'Frankly, my dear, I don't give a damn.'"

I gaped, unsure of what to say. The situation was so ludicrous, I almost laughed out loud. Fortunately self-control won out. "Roger, I'm very sorry about last night, I really am. I've apologized twice and I'm not going to do it again. I believe Ron

Harp was murdered, just like Hattie and Charlie, and you do, too. And, I believe it's all connected—Ron and Hattie, the animals, Ruth's illegitimate son. And, just because you won't help me doesn't mean I'll stop. And, if this is the way you conduct police business you're just as bad as the rest of them." I was at the door now, my last words delivered as I ran headlong into Cal Ripler's barrel chest.

"Bad as who, Miss Steele?"

He grinned from ear to ear. Probably heard the entire conversation. Go to hell, I thought, wisely keeping my sentiments to myself as I stormed out of the building and drove out of town.

CHAPTER 57

I caught Giffy Harp on her way out the door, a stack of canvas bags under her arms. "Market day," she said, giving me a hug. "Patty's staying with Jim for a few hours. What a dear girl."

I caught sight of Patty Boardman in the kitchen window and our eyes met, her expression disinterested. "Have you got a sec, Giffy?"

"For you, dear, anytime. Want to come back in for coffee?"

"Not here. Can we chat in the car? I won't keep you a minute."

"Of course, but why all the secrecy?"

"Patty may be a great gal, but she thinks I'm trying to steal her husband, so I may not be her favorite person right now."

We slid into the front seats of her S.U.V. "You and Ralph? What's that about, dearie?"

"Oh, nothing. Just a misunderstanding." I stared at her, wondering if my questions might upset her. Then, as usual, I forged ahead. "Giffy, this is going to sound strange, but I wanted to ask you about your dog, the one that died last winter."

"Pepper?"

"Yes. I'm sorry to bring it up. I know it was hard on you."

"Poor little Pep, he was only a pup, barely two years old. Why do you want to know about him?"

"Did you ever find out how he died?"

"Not exactly, but we thought he probably got hit by a car out on Main Road. Dogs'll do anything to get home when they're injured. Pep probably dragged himself to the driveway before his little heart gave out. We'd been out looking for him all day and must've missed him. He was probably lying hurt in the bushes along the way and dragged himself home after dark."

"I suppose that could be it." My voice trailed off as I stared out the window. Of course, he could have been dumped there, too, but then, this didn't fit with my revenge theory. What had Jim and Giffy Harp ever done to Ruth Bowen's son?

"What's this about?" Giffy's eyes studied me, waiting.

"I'm sorry, Giffy. I shouldn't have bothered you."

"I know Karen hired you to look into Ron's accident, but it might be time to leave it alone, dear. There's nothing to be gained stirring things up. It was an accident, just like poor Jim's last year. We've all accepted that except Karrie. If Ron had been wearing his helmet he'd be hobbling around now with a skinned knee."

I squeezed her hand. "I'll let you go."

"You're a good girl, darling, and a good friend to Karrie. Please think about leaving this alone, now, will you? It's hard on all of us."

"Giffy, I'm sorry. The last thing I'd want to do is to cause you pain, but Ron deserves justice."

Her mouth set, I steeled myself for a lecture. Instead, she sighed. "There is one thing I've been meaning to discuss with you. Bobby tells me you've been asking about Ruth Bowen. Don't be too hard on Ruth, dear. She's a good egg, really, and she works tirelessly for the town."

"So I hear."

"Even though my dear son didn't think so, she's a lovely person once you get to know her. Likes things her way and is a bit of a sober sides in public, but she can be very funny and witty on social occasions. You may not know this, but she was an old flame of Jim's."

My heart skipped a beat, cold awareness crawling up my arm as she went on.

"Oh, yes, don't look so shocked. They were quite the item one summer. A bit of a scandal, really, him being so much older. Ruth's father was outraged, his daughter running around with a college man. Before his accident, they were best buddies, had lunch together couple of times a month.

"A few times over the years, I've seen a little spark there, as if a smidgeon of the attraction still lingered. Luckily, I'm not the jealous type. Nowadays, poor, dear Jim doesn't know what's going on. Half the time he doesn't even recognize Ruth."

I gave her a quick hug and hopped out of the car. "Giffy, I've got to go."

Suddenly it all made sense, Hattie, the animals, Charlie and Ron. Ron hadn't been killed because he was a gadfly stirring things up, uncovering people's secrets. Ron had been killed because he was his father's son. The father, whose deck had mysteriously collapsed, sending him to the rocks below, crippling him for life. That meant Bobby, Jay and Tripp were all in danger. Ruth Bowen's first son had come home to seek his revenge. He had come home to kill them all.

I fished my cell phone from my bag, praying the battery wasn't dead. Karen answered the phone and I asked to speak to Jay. When he answered, I asked him where Bobby was—out on the boat—then told him to wait for me at Karen's, telling him I'd be there in an hour.

CHAPTER 58

I reached Town Hall, where I found JoJo and another woman having a cigarette on the front step.

"Where is she, JoJo?"

"She's back there, but I'm not sure she's free."

Ignoring her, I rushed inside. Ruth Bowen was on the phone, but hung up as I tapped on her door. Spying me, she scowled. "Get out. I've got work to do."

"You've got to listen to me, please. It's about Tripp." That got her attention. "He's in danger, but then, maybe you already know that."

"What are you talking about?"

"He's here, isn't he? Your son. He's living here in town and you know who he is."

"Get out." Green eyes, cold and furious, couldn't completely hide her fear.

"You have to see it's him doing all this. Hattie, the principal who sent you away, Charlie Higgins, the man who knew all about your pregnancy, knew and helped you cover up the identity of the real father, Jim Harp. Jim Harp, whose strange accident last year destroyed his life, and Ron Harp, his half-brother, who probably hadn't quite figured it out."

"How dare you!"

"He's already come after you once, with Dumpling. Strangled him just like he did the Harps' Corgi."

"You're making this up."

"You know I'm not. Who is he? You have to know. He's got to have approached you at some point, made himself known. He's going to kill them all, then come after you."

"Miss Steele, if you don't get out of this office immediately, I'm calling the police."

"He's going after Tripp, sure as I'm standing here. Have you warned him?"

"Get out!" Her face was a mask of fury, but Ruth Bowen was scared, her eyes rimmed with tears.

"I'll go," I said, quietly backing out. "But if you won't tell me, tell the police. Let someone help you and Tripp." She turned her back on me, staring at the bookshelf behind her desk. There, level with her gaze, was a photograph of her son, and a large, gray animal—Dumpling.

"At least tell Tripp. He deserves to know," I said, turning to walk past the row of desks, occupants staring openmouthed as I passed. Terrific. Within the hour the killer would know all about this little scene and I'd have to start worrying about my own safety, never mind Tripp Bowen and the Harp boys.

CHAPTER 59

I caught Demaris in the parking lot, heading out for an early lunch. "Come on, I'll buy," he said, waving me to his car. We stopped at the deli where he ordered two sandwiches, then drove to the Point, parking in the same lot where I'd had my confrontation with Skip Burrows.

"Come here almost every day," he said, handing me a turkey on rye, extra mustard. "It's the only way I stay sane." He looked sad, but resigned. "Go ahead, eat it. It's not poison. I'm a big boy. I've gotten over you." He gave me a wry smile then took a bite of his corned beef, gazing out to sea. "Okay, I'm listening. Are you gonna tell me why you came racin' outta the Town Hall just now?"

I took a deep breath, set my sandwich on the dash and turned to face him. Willing my voice to stay calm, I related all I'd learned, ending with, "She knows who he is. I'm convinced of it."

"What'dya want me to do? Beat it out of her?"

"You don't believe me?"

He shrugged.

"Your little speech this morning about playing along 'cause you were interested in me. That's bullshit and we both know it. You knew Cal Ripler was listening so you just made that up."

"Is that what your detective nose is telling you?"

"Yes. Now, have you found out anything? Did you check?"

"I made some calls."

"And?"

"And nothing. No one knows anything about that baby. It was forty-four years ago, you know."

"Well, someone adopted him. Have you contacted the agency?" He shrugged, staring out at the sea. "You know something, don't you?"

"A name, that's all."

"Well?"

"Gary Potter. Parents both dead. Died when he was eleven or twelve. Moved east to live with a relative, aunt, we think, but we haven't traced her. I've got someone checking. Look, why don't you lay off this for now, spend some time with your boyfriend, preferably at his place. Where's he live, Boston, right?"

Ignoring him, I chewed on my sandwich, picturing all of the men in their forties I'd met this past week— Dick Chaffee, Will Ramsey, Peter Morse, Alonzo Souza, Steve Morrow, who else? Demaris himself. I gave him a hard look and decided that he bore absolutely no resemblance to either Jim Harp or Ruth Bowen. Truth be told, none of them resembled their supposed mother and father.

"There's got to be something. School pictures, records, something we can use to identify him."

"There are and they're coming. Someone's at his elementary school working on it right now."

I smiled as our eyes met.

He grinned. "Don't look so smug or I'll call the whole thing off."

"Uh-huh."

"I gotta get back."

He started to turn the key, then stopped, leaning over as if to kiss me. I leaned forward, and he shifted, planting the kiss on my forehead instead of my lips. Pulling away, he was grinning, eyes sparkling. He had me. I had leaned into him, ready to return the kiss, and he knew it.

"Friends, right? That's all you want, isn't it?"

"Humph," I said, turning around, staring straight ahead. That was it. I was swearing off men forever.

I was dying to follow him into the station, to see if word had come in, but I had someone I needed to see. After collecting the jeep, I headed out to Maisy Grant's, hoping I'd catch her. No one was around, the A-frame dark and deserted, both cars gone. Noticing the time, I realized it had been hours since I'd begged Jay to wait for me, so I drove to Karen's. A note in the kitchen said that Karen was doing errands, Alex and Carly, the new nanny, had gone to the library, and Jay was "out." He had written the note, which ended with, "Meet you at your house later." Cursing, I headed home, wondering where he'd gone.

Once at the cottage, I paced, trying in vain to piece things together. I called the police station and was told Detective Demaris was out on a call. I called Bobby and Betsy's number. No answer. Finally, I tried the elder Harps.

Giffy answered, sounding groggy. "Oh, hi, dear. Caught me napping. Oh, no, don't worry. Time to get up anyway. No, haven't see Jay unless he came while I was out. Patty didn't mention it. Bobby? He won't be back till tomorrow night. Went back out this morning, the last overnight cruise till spring, thank goodness. I wish he'd find a job on dry land. Of course, dear, I'll have Jay ring you. Is anything wrong? You sound upset."

I assured her all was well, hung up and resumed my pacing. Finally, I grabbed the phone book and located the Grants' number. Maisy answered on the second ring. I asked if I could stop by and she said, "Sure." I wasn't sure what I hoped to learn, but at least I could give her Charlie's treasures. It was time.

CHAPTER 60

This time I declined the coffee and accepted a tepid glass of water instead. When I presented her with the canister, she smiled, taking it from me. "From Momma's old kitchen set. Funny, I didn't notice that first time you were here. Amazing, he kept it all these years." Slowly she examined every item, sometimes offering a comment, mostly thinking her own thoughts about a brother who, despite his shortcomings, she had clearly loved. The last item set on the table, she said, "Thank you for bringing these. Reminders of Charlie before the bad times. Did you learn anything else about who might have wanted to hurt him?"

"It's complicated, but I'm pretty sure it's related to a relationship Charlie had a long time ago."

"What kind of relationship?"

"I'd rather not say till I'm sure. At first, I thought Charlie might have fathered a child when he was a teenager, but now, I don't think that's the case."

"I know it's not the case." She laughed, a joyless sound, her eyes wells of sorrow. "Charlie couldn't have kids. Had a bad case of mumps when he was in fourth or fifth grade. Fifth, I think. Doctor Bates told Momma Charlie was sterile, couldn't ever have kids."

"Did he know that?"

She nodded.

"Maisy, I think he was helping someone, a young girl who was pregnant. He kept her secret, and that's what probably got him killed."

"You're talking about Ruth."

"So, you knew?"

"No, but I suspected. All that about Old Man Simmonds getting transferred. If he got transferred, why was he back in town every other week doing business when we never saw hide nor hair of his wife or Ruthie? They left over a month before he did, too."

"Did Charlie ever talk to you about this?"

"Never."

"Has anyone else ever asked you about Charlie and Ruth?" She shook her head, then stopped. "Well, there was that one time, kind of just came up in conversation. Not about Ruth, but the whole business with Charlie's mumps. I remember because the person who asked was wondering if Charlie had any kids. I never told anyone about Charlie's problem, but, well, I didn't think there was any harm, considering it was only him."

"Who, Maisy?" When she said the name, my blood ran cold and I saw his eyes. No wonder they looked familiar. Gary Potter had his father's eyes, eyes that now stared helpless and glassy-eyed at the world around him. I asked to use her phone and dialed the cottage number. Nothing. Demaris was still out, no answer at Karen's.

I thanked Maisy and hurried out headed to Town Hall.

"She's gone, Ms. Steele," Jo Jo said, staring aghast at the wild vision in front of her. "Took her son to dinner."

"Do you know where?"

"Sorry, but she loves the Moulin Rouge."

CHAPTER 61

I was hurtling down Main Road when I spied Jay's B.M.W. turning into Red Gate Farm. Beeping, I followed him down the drive and leapt out of the jeep and into his arms. "Thank God, you're safe."

"And I was beginning to think you didn't care." He nuzzled my neck, sending shivers to all the right places. "What's up?"

I shook myself and ordered him back into the car. On the way to the police station, I filled him in. Demaris was still out, but expected momentarily. The only person on duty was Skip Burrows and I wasn't about to tell him anything. "Let's go. He might still be working."

As I dragged Jay toward the car, he stopped, turning to face me, hands on my shoulders. "Ricky, this is a bad idea. If what you say is true, we need to tell the police."

"Not Skip Burrows. Come on. I'll keep calling Roger on my cell." He drove and I pushed buttons with no luck at the other end. When we were unable to find Gary Potter at work, I directed Jay to drive to his house. "Now, that's a really bad idea," he said, nonetheless heading the car in the right direction. No one home, both vehicles missing.

"Ricky, let's grab some dinner. The Hearthstone, okay?"

"No, the Moulin Rouge."

He regarded me as if I'd just escaped from the asylum. "Okay, the Moulin Rouge it is."

"Good. Drive there."

His eyes roamed over my attire, dirty jeans and ragged wool sweater. "You don't want to change first?"

"I don't want to eat, I just want to go there!"

"Fine. Want to tell me why?"

"Because that's where Ruth and Tripp Bowen will be eating and I want to make sure they're safe."

"You what? That's it. I'm stopping this car until you call the police and tell them the whole thing."

"Fine." I dialed and was put on hold. Several minutes later, Demaris answered and I blurted out the entire story, ending with, "and we're on our way to the Moulin Rouge where the Bowens are probably having dinner."

Silence. I tapped my cell phone thinking the battery had died. "Roger?"

"I'm here. Now, listen to me. Tell Harp to turn the car around and go home. I'll drive over to the Moulin Rouge and take a look around. Do you understand me? Go home. Ricky, do you hear me? Let me speak to Harp."

"Thanks, Roger, I hear you. Don't worry." I hung up the phone and dropped it into my bag.

"So?"

"So, he said for us to go to the restaurant and he'll meet us there."

"Liar."

"Here, call him yourself if you don't believe me."

"I don't, but what the hell." He pulled back onto the road. "This is what we're going to do. I'm going to drive up, see if the Bowens are there and ascertain if everything's hunky-dory. Then I'm taking you home."

"Fine, thank you." I eased back into the seat, hoping we weren't too late. Potter knew it was over. He would want to finish what he started before the police closed in.

The parking lot at the Moulin Rouge was packed. We parked in the rear, which necessitated walking round the building to the front entrance. I opened my door and he reached over and grabbed the door handle, slamming it shut. "You, stay." What did he think I was, a dog?

"I will not!"

"Think about it for a second, will you? Your leg's killing you. That's right, I have eyes. Don't you think I've noticed your wincing with every step? You're no use to anyone, hobbling around like that. Besides, savior or not, you're the last person the Bowens want to see. Let me check it out. I'll come get you if there's any excitement. You wait here and watch for Demaris. And, if you don't agree to stay in this car, I'm driving you home right now."

"Fine, go." I turned away, staring straight ahead. He was right, of course, I'd only cause a scene, but, I sure as hell wasn't going to let him know it.

Jay disappeared and I waited at least three seconds before I got out. Couldn't hurt to take a quick peek. I sidled up to the building. The first windows I peered into were the kitchen. It's never a good idea to see the kitchen of a restaurant.

Halfway around the building, I peeped through a small arched window to a side alcove off the main dining room, where two tables of diners enjoyed their meal. Beyond the alcove I could see the foyer and Jay's back. He appeared to be talking to a man I didn't recognize. Craning my neck, I peeked around, hoping to catch a glimpse of the Bowens.

No luck. I'd have to find another window. Creeping along, hugging the walls, I was scratched and clawed by pricker bushes. The next window afforded a view of the main dining room. I had just spotted the Bowens at a corner table when I felt his hands around my neck. Gagging, I staggered forward, managing one rap against the window pane before he yanked me backward. As I was dragged away, I saw one diner look up, quizzically eyeing the window.

As he pulled me along, I clawed and scratched, but with his heavy leather gloves he was impervious. As we emerged from the bushes, one of his hands clutching my neck, he staggered. Off balance, he was unable to get the grip he needed to finish the job. For an instant I imagined we might both go crashing to the pavement. I knew I had seconds until I lost consciousness, and very soon after, my life. Thrusting my good leg to the side, I gained a foothold round a gnarly trunk. My leg holding fast, I flailed out wildly.

Chuckling softly, he kicked both legs out from under me and yanked me onto the pavement. Steady now, he held me like a limp rag doll, hands tightening round my scrawny neck. As my limbs grew weaker and I fell into the blackness, I heard her voice from a great distance calling, "No, Ralph, no," and then nothing.

When I awoke I was half lying, half sitting on a couch, looking up at a red-painted ceiling, my throat dry and throbbing. Was this hell?

"Hi there." Jay's eyes, soft and concerned, gazed down at me, his hand cool as he smoothed dampened hair from my forehead. "Don't get up. Rescue'll be here soon."

"I don't need Rescue." I rose, stars dancing before my eyes, my right leg buckling. Groaning in pain, I slumped back. "What happened? Where is he?"

"Out there. That's why Rescue's coming. Patty gave him a good bop on the head.

"Patty?"

"Yup. She saw us leaving town and followed. Patty saved your life. I'd have never gotten there in time. In fact, I thought you were still in the car."

"Where is she?"

"Out there, with Ralph, or Gary, or whatever his name is."

"Poor man," I said, thinking back to our lunch at the cottage. "Ralph Boardman had made a new life for himself with "his Patty." If only he could have let go of the rest.

I stood and asked Jay to help me to the parking lot. He swept me up and carried me out. We arrived just as they loaded him onto the stretcher, "his Patty" at his side. As they took him away, his eyes met mine. I stared into the eyes of a stranger, no trace of the man I knew as Ralph Boardman. Gary Potter's hatred and rage had completely subsumed the warmth and kindness of the other. I started to speak, then caught myself. Ralph was gone. I had nothing to say to Gary Potter.

Epilogue

I refused to be taken to the hospital. Instead, I insisted Jay take me to the cottage, where I strapped on my heavy-duty brace and called my orthopedist. With Jay's help, I packed the next morning. Karen asked me to stay one more night, but I couldn't. Too many things to sort out. I needed to get home.

I'd missed Demaris the night before, so I stopped in at the police station on my way out of town. He told me that Ralph, or Gary, had admitted to all of it—the animals, Hattie Pauls, Ron and Charlie. Ralph had apparently lain in wait for Ron, waving as he approached, then throwing a stick through the bicycle's spokes, finishing the job after rider and the bike flipped over. He had removed the stick and carried it into the nearby woods to hide. His truck parked on a side road leading to Bridle Falls, Ralph had watched as Ron was carried off. Then, when all bystanders had disappeared, he threw the bike into his truck and took off. What he hadn't foreseen was Charlie Higgins coming along just as he climbed the hill, the mangled bicycle rattling in plain view in the truck bed. Charlie, who knew Ruth Bowen's secret, but did not know the son, had accepted a ride, only to meet his death shortly after. Ralph had waited several days before dumping poor Charlie's body off the Ledge.

"What about Jim Harp's accident?"

"That was Ralph, or Potter, too. He knew the deck was rotted so one night last summer he loosened the boards near the steps. He knew Jim's routines, knew it'd be him going out for the paper."

"So sad."

He nodded. "By the way, I found your phantoms in the night."

"Who?"

"White van, remember?"

"You bet I do."

"Belongs to Skip Burrow's younger brother. I confronted him and his buddies. They admitted the whole thing."

"You're kidding."

"It's your call. You want to press charges?"

"You're damn right I do. Big brother probably put him up to it. Model citizen, indeed."

"There's a bunch of paperwork you'll need to fill out and—"

"No." I was tired and I wanted to go home so badly it hurt. "Just forget it. I'll take this up with Officer Burrows at another time."

"Be too late by then." His eyes were weary, resigned, and I knew he wasn't talking about Skip Burrows or his brother.

"Not for what I have in mind." I grinned maliciously. "Goodbye, Roger, and thanks."

He shrugged, shaking my hand, smiling back at me. "All in a day's work, Ms. Steele. All in a day's work. You need help getting out?"

I shook my head. "Thanks, but I think I can make it."

"See ya around sometime?" His gaze was neutral, one citizen to another.

"Count on it."

"Take care of yourself."

I was headed out of town when the jeep just drove itself to the common, where I parked alongside the Lunch. As I entered, she rose from her booth in the back. Tippy, Al and George were with her. The gang. I stopped short and met her eyes, waiting to gauge her reaction. Patting George's shoulder, she approached me, passed by, and headed out the door. I followed. Once we were out of view of the restaurant's windows, she stopped and turned back. "So?"

"I came to say goodbye."

"You want me to thank you for what you did."

"No."

"He wouldn't have hurt us, you know. Not Trippie, and certainly not me."

"How do you know that?"

She shrugged. "Mothers know these things."

"What about the others? You knew and yet you didn't stop him."

"Now that's where you're wrong. I knew about Ralph. Have known who he was for a number of years. But I never thought he'd hurt anyone. And I don't believe he killed Dumpling."

Ralph had admitted killing the pig, along with all the other animals, including Bobby's sheep, but I didn't feel it necessary to rub it in. "Well, I won't keep you. I'm glad you and Tripp are safe."

She nodded. Ruth Bowen had aged twenty years since our confrontation in her office. "Yes, safe."

"Charlie Higgins was a good friend to you, wasn't he?"

"Yes, he was. Goodbye, Miss Steele." She turned away, shoulders stooped as she made her way across the green to the Town Hall, never once looking back, never once looking from side to side to enjoy the beauty of the town she worked so hard to preserve.

***

Keep reading for a sample from *Lost in Spindle City!*

Acknowledgments

Thank you to my friend and neighbor, Sgt. Jason Pacheco of the Fall River, Massachusetts, Police Department, for talking with me about police procedures. Any missteps in this area are entirely mine as he is always clear and professional.

I would also like to thank my publisher, Larry Anderson at Quicksand Chronicles, for his generosity and willingness to take my books on. To Dona Burke, I am indebted for her formatting wizardry and good humor as we grappled together to bring forth the first version of *Gadfly*. If not for Dona, my novels would still be languishing on my computer or in my basement. And to the Formatting Fairies, who took up where Dona and I left off to copyedit, revise and format *Gadfly* so beautifully! Most importantly, I would like to thank my dear family and friends, who are always there, no matter where life's travels take me. They make every day a gift.

A Note from the Author

Thank you so much for taking the time to read *Gadfly*! I had a great time writing it, exploring small-town life from a purely fictional point of view, of course! I was happy to set this adventure in a New England village very much like one where I spent a number of years. Although I now live on a river, I return to the seaside often. It was fun to drop in a few local details, as I do in all my novels, even if actual persons and places are figments of my imagination!

Gadfly is the second mystery featuring Ricky. Her third and fourth adventures are *Lost in Spindle City* and *Poof!* Many authors have a favorite character, and, I must confess, Ricky is mine. Her strength, spunk, resilience, and tenacity at this stage in life make me smile, laugh, and applaud her sometimes bumbling, but always heartfelt investigative style. I've always envisioned the Ricky Steele series as films and can think of some wonderful, *mature* actresses to play Ricky and her cohorts. The physical comedy would come alive on screen in the way it does when I picture scenes in my mind, but perhaps am not quite able to capture on paper.

If you liked *Gadfly* and would be willing to write an Amazon review, I would be so grateful! If you would like to hear about future book releases and occasional news from me, please visit my website http://www.mleeprescott.com/ and sign up for my newsletter. I promise I will not share your address, nor will I flood you with emails. Do visit my http://www.mleeprescott.com/ and email me any time – mleeprescott@gmail.com -- as I LOVE to hear from readers!

Finally, this book has been revised, proofed and edited many, many times, but I, and my intrepid assistants, are human so if you spot a typo, please email me at mleeprescott@gmail.com and I will fix it. If you'd like to know more about my other books, please scroll ahead to the next section, which is followed by sample chapters of *Lost in Spindle City*.

Warm wishes,

M. Lee

Chapter 1

Some days have less than auspicious starts. This was one of them. My third floor office seemed light years away as I dragged myself up the stairs. My head was fuzzy, legs wet noodles, stomach churning.

Last night was one of the truly dumb ones where I forgot that I'm fifty-eight, not twenty-eight. I had just wrapped up a crappy case, and despite my best efforts to breathe deeply and let go, my shoulders and neck were locked tight. Instead of taking a bath and hitting the sack, yours truly had to play tough PI, belting back beers with the guys at the Rainbow.

A little hole-in-the-wall bar frequented by the locals, the Rainbow is a block from my house. A small cardboard sign taped to the inside of the grimy front window, "Food and Spirits, do drop in," is the only indication that it's a place of business. The sign, brown and curling at the edges, was penned in red. The ink, now faded, coordinated nicely with the grayish-pink peek-a-boo half curtains, frayed and dusty, after many smoky years. One glimpse of its subterranean façade and no stranger would dare "to drop in."

Once I got started on the beers and shots of tequila, it was all over. My neighbor Vinnie and I play cribbage or maybe dice. There used to be an ancient pool table, but Jack, the owner, had it removed the previous year, fearing its imminent collapse might injure one of his valued patrons.

The walk home a dim memory, I had slept in my clothes, never a good sign. I woke at 6 a.m. and the phrase "death warmed over" sprang to mind. After three aspirin, a shower, juice and muffins, I felt better, but that's not saying much. I'm supposed to have oat bran and lots of fiber to combat high cholesterol and triglycerides, but after ingesting platters of grease and empty carbs the previous evening oat bran didn't stand a chance.

A run? Out of the question. My daily yoga? Probably not wise to invert my body. Better to wait until dark to see stars. Maybe a short walk, and then later in the day when my stomach stopped roiling, I'd treat myself to a coffee cab. The rest of the world calls them milkshakes, but around Spindle City, we call 'em cabs or cabinets. Yum!

I'm not crazy about coffee. I prefer tea, mostly Earl Grey and Yerba Mate, but I love coffee cabs and occasionally coffee ice cream, both of which serve as my primary treatment for the occasional hangover I experience as a middle-aged nincompoop. I keep a coffee maker in my office for clients and I've been known to swill a cup to be friendly, but coffee has never been part of my daily routine.

My name is Ricky Steele, given name, Dorothy. I've been married and divorced, have one sister and a father who I see every so often. No children, my one regret. I recently had what, for me, was a serious relationship, which lasted about five months. It ended when he went back to his former girlfriend, again. I had a history with Jay Harp, the lothario in question, and should have known better than to trust my heart to him a second time. We had a brief fling years earlier when we were both members of a wedding party. As best man and maid of honor, we spent many hours together and one thing led to another. We kept things up for a month or two post-wedding, but then Jay disappeared, never to be seen again, until last year.

I was investigating the murder of his brother, Ron Harp, when Jay and I met up again, and our former spark turned into a blaze. We spent some passionate, intense months with one another, and even discussed moving in together. Then Jay confessed that he had "unfinished business" with his former fiancée, Marty. What is it with men and "unfinished business" with old girlfriends? My reaction to his confession was to storm off and refuse to see him or talk to him. We speak on the phone every so often. I have to admit that I miss him. Our breakup hurt. My friends tell me I have a gift for choosing men who are dishonest and narcissistic, but maybe I'm not "girlfriend material?" Who knows? I try to stay positive and hope that the right guy will walk into my life someday.

I have many odd jobs, from newspaper columnist for our local paper to waitress and craftsperson. Most recently, I've been working as a private investigator, a profession I fell into thanks to my own foolishness. To my surprise, I found I liked it enough to put in the hundreds of hours interning with two local PIs that were required in order to get my license. I'm a private person and this life suits my personality, if not my overall health, and I've been able to let some of the odd jobs go—waitressing, in particular.

While I've stumbled into several murder cases, most of my work is fairly routine. A good friend, Bud Dixon, runs his own insurance business and throws me a fair amount of work. Insurance fraud is a full-time occupation for lots of folks, so Bud's jobs help make ends meet. I also pick up a fair amount work trailing errant spouses, since infidelity is epidemic. About half of this work is accomplished in the real world, the other half online, since the Internet is a cheater's best friend.

Over the past months, I've become the PI of choice for a certain Newport set. Having hubby followed and photographed as he goes about his tedious daily routines seems to be the "in thing" for bored housewives and those who have a vested interest in keeping close tabs on the checkbook.

My last case, which I tried mightily to stay out of, nearly got me killed. There are certain cases one does not take in this city if one wishes to remain among the living. I was out of physical danger now, or at least for the next decade, but I was still emotionally shaken, hence last night's idiocy. I'm not a big drinker—the occasional beer and glass of wine is about the extent of it—but sometimes the amnesia of alcohol can be therapeutic. A day spent indulging myself with junk food and sugar and I'd be ready to face the world again.

As I reached the top of the stairs, my stomach flipped. Increased heart rate, beer and tequila definitely do not mix.

My office is in a restored mill building in the heart of the city's Flint District. It's a beautiful structure, the façade still strong and proud, despite acres of advertising splayed across its granite walls. In the city's heyday, its cavernous rooms once roared with the machinery of textile production, hundreds of workers toiling twenty-four hours a day. For years, the abandoned mill had sat, gutted and empty, left to ponder its fate as the once-thriving city slipped into poverty, neglect and high unemployment. Now, although silent, the halls and passageways had been "repurposed" and housed a variety of enterprises.

The ground floor hummed with a ragtag collection of outlet stores and bargain kiosks hawking every type of merchandise, but right now the second floor is vacant, providing a buffer between Outlet Central and offices on the third floor. Bud, my insurance friend, began his business here and dragged me along, but as his client list grew, he moved to fancier digs downtown, leaving me with several other tenants on the partially renovated third floor. Not exactly a classy location, but it suits me. I have my own rear entrance, insulated from the comings and goings of the outlet crowd.

At the moment, there are four of us on the third floor. I'm in 308, a real estate appraiser I rarely see is in 312, and a salesman for *Boats Afloat* or some nautical magazine is in 316. The writer in 320 comes most days at 10 a.m. and departs shortly before 3 p.m. He told me last week that 320 is his sanctuary, an escape from the bedlam at home. The remainder of the floor is vacant. An acre of empty is a lot of empty. They tell us there are sixty to eighty potential office spaces, but it takes a certain type to locate here-- cheap and bizarre. It's relatively quiet and fairly secure, at least during the day, since they've hired extra security to keep the bargain hunters' thievery in check. Apparently for some, no price is low enough.

I slid open the heavy metal fire door and headed down the hall. The walls were painted dull, asylum gray, but they had left the beautiful woodwork alone. I ran my hand along the dark mahogany chair rail collecting dust. Unfortunately, the renovators had made no attempt to match the old with the new, so my cubicle and others had been slapped together, minus mahogany trim.

As a middle-aged spinster set in her ways, I have a little routine I like to follow that involves a cup of tea, a little bill paying, or ignoring, depending upon the status of my bank account, a little office tidying, record keeping, and whatever puttering I find to occupy me as I drink my tea. I do not like to be interrupted before 11 a.m. I have found this ritual to be important to my sense of well-being and willingness to face the day. I was not to enjoy my routine today.

CHAPTER 2

She was curled up against my door, a tangle of arms and legs. Her spindly legs were covered in snagged black netting that had been patched in several spots with nail polish. Bright red pumps, from all appearances several sizes too large, adorned impossibly long feet.

Street people often camp out in buildings when they can slip by the airtight security. In other words, they're regulars. I've kind of adopted one little lady, Irene, whom I suspect is around my age, but looks to be about one hundred. She's been sleeping in my hall for the past six months. If I forget to lock the office door, I often find her stretched out on my couch, catching up on her beauty sleep. Irene snores. Loudly. She's short and pudgy, not scrawny like this little gal with her bony limbs sticking out all over the place. I definitely did not have room on my couch for two.

I was contemplating how I might slip around my slumbering guest, when Terry, the appraiser, banged open the fire door and startled her awake. I turned to give him an icy glare, but he had already banged into his office without so much as a glance in our direction. Turning back, I found her rubbing her eyes, looking disoriented and none too happy. That made two of us.

She gathered herself up and ineffectually endeavored to smooth her hair as she inched up the wall like a spider. Her light brown hair, the consistency of my childhood dolls' after I'd styled their tresses, stuck up in odd clumps, coarse, wiry and clearly in need of a wash. She wore a red skirt and matching ribbed top, the entire ensemble made of 100% unnatural fibers. Over her skimpy getup, she wore an oversized man's gray sport coat in a herringbone pattern, brown suede patches on the sleeves. I wondered if she had grabbed it from the outlet dumpster on her way in to ward off the April chill.

Several strands of brightly colored beads hung from her skinny ostrich neck, and she sported matching dangly earrings. Her left earring was missing its bottom red bead, giving her an off-kilter look, and I found myself listing to the side as I regarded her. As I gazed into dark, round eyes rimmed with think black eyeliner, I gulped. I was looking at a child, twelve at most, maybe younger. Bud's fifth grader looked older that this sad little bird.

"Miss Steele?" She spoke tentatively, voice husky.

I nodded, thinking, *At least she can read.* My office door has my name emblazoned in stick-on black-and-gold letters. Very classy.

"I'm sorry to be crashed here."

I shrugged. "No problem. Happens all the time. Must've been a rough one last night, huh? Shouldn't you be in school?"

"Not today. Sometimes we go, but not today. I needed to see you and I snuck in before the guard locked up so I could catch you first thing."

She began fussing with her hair again, pulling at her skirt, smoothing out the jacket. Clearly nervous gestures, a way to occupy her tiny, shaking hands until I responded.

I smiled. "Well, you caught me. Come on in."

I didn't have a good feeling about this, but what could I do? Besides, my solemn routine had been broken now, so what the hell?

Chapter 3

My office is two small rooms, no bathroom. The bathroom's down the hall and pretty grungy. About once a month, I scrub it out, as building cleaning service is practically nonexistent. Every couple of months I work on the plumbing. My fellow tenants don't seem to care about maintenance, but then, I've never set foot in the men's room, and never intend to.

My outer office has a couch, or guest bed, as some would call it, super comfy if you ignore the moths that fly out of the holes in the arms. I keep a woven basket of old magazines, mostly donated by Bud. As a waiting room, it needs work, but I rarely have clients waiting. There's also a small refrigerator. The table beside it holds a coffee maker, an electric tea kettle, and a few assorted canisters filled with sugar, coffee and tea bags.

My inner office has two tall windows that look out over the parking lots and rows of mills beyond. In its heyday, the city had over a hundred granite mills dotted along the river. An incredible view, in the morning the sun streams making the office warm and comfortable. It gets a bit nippy in the late afternoon. I have a huge oak partners desk that I discovered in one of the yet-to-be-renovated spaces. The landlord sold it to me for ten dollars and Bud helped me drag it down the hall. After I cleaned it up, polished the wood and fixed a couple of broken drawers, it gleamed. Sitting behind it makes me feel established and solid, as if my business had a long, illustrious history.

A four-drawer file cabinet, three chairs, a gray metal locker, and two steamship prints on the wall complete my décor. I store valuables and my camera equipment in the locker, but any two-bit crook could pop the lock in thirty seconds. I wasn't sure I should offer coffee to my visitor. Didn't it stunt growth or something? Instead I invited her in and she took the comfiest chair. I sat in my swivel chair, and scooted it around the desk to sit beside her.

"So, what's up?"

"I'm sorry to bother you so early in the morning, but Mrs. Silva said you could help me and I really need help."

Ebbie Silva, a friend of a friend, had hired me a few months earlier to track down her brother-in-law. He had skipped out on her sister and Ebbie wanted a word with him. A few quick phone calls and I managed to dredge him up. When I handed Ebbie his address, I almost felt sorry for the guy.

"How is Ebbie?"

She shrugged and fidgeted. "Don't know her too well. Lives near us, that's all. She told me you can find people. I need you to find someone for me."

"Oh?"

"My friend. She's gone missing."

"What did you say your name was?"

Her face reddened and she gave me a shy kid's smile. "Oh, sorry, it's Natalie, Natalie Remy. I been so stressed about Lisa. That's who I'm lookin' for, my friend, Lisa. I'm so worried, I'm kinda out of it, you know? It's just she's been gone for a couple of days and I'm getting freaked."

She was trembling now, rubbing her hands together. I caught a glimpse of an incredibly thin arm inside her coat sleeve. I knew with certainty I was way out of my depth.

"Hey, are you hungry? I think better with food and a cup of tea."

"Well, I—"

I rose, smiling down at her. "My treat. I'll put it on my expense account. Come on, Dino's is right around the corner. We can talk while we eat."

She followed me out of the office and down the stairs, her heels clattering on every step. The buildings and lots along Quarry Street were quiet as we walked side by side, maintaining the silence except for the drumbeat of Natalie's high heels. She hovered close, occasionally brushing against me the way good friends do as they walk and talk. This was a needy child. Where was her mother?

CHAPTER 4

Dino's Diner is a long, dark, narrow affair with high-backed oak booths, their seat covers upholstered in green, faux-marble Naugahyde. The booths run along one wall, a counter along the opposite wall with ten swivel stools in gleaming chrome, same Naugahyde seats as the booths. There is a mirrored wall behind the grill. I make it a point never to sit at the counter. That's all I need at 7 a.m. -- a good long look at myself. How to ruin a day before it even begins.

Dino was full of his usual early morning cheer, which I find amusing, endearing, or irritating, depending on my mood. This morning I found it disconcerting. Clearly, solicitous attention unnerved my companion when she wanted nothing more than to blend into the woodwork, or Naugahyde. She clung to me as we retreated to a rear booth, Dino on our heels.

"How can a man be so lucky? Two of the most gorgeous creatures in the city, right here in my restaurant! Did they go to Lizzie's, The Pier, the Q-Club? No, they came to Dino's!"

"We love you too, Dino. How's Lois?"

Lois, his wife, worked the lunch shift, keeping his fraternizing in check. At breakfast he was on his own.

"Why bring Lois up when we're having such a good time, just the three of us?"

"Dino, my love, we're in kind of a hurry, and real hungry, so could we please just order?"

"No problem, doll. We'll get back to this later."

He winked at Natalie, her mouth agape. I had the maternal urge to say, "Close your mouth or the flies 'll get in," but I bit my tongue.

"What'll it be for you and your gorgeous friend?"

"Go ahead," I said, "anything you want."

Natalie ordered a full breakfast, eggs, sausage, toast and juice. She refused Dino's offer of coffee and asked for a large milk. At least some of her is still a kid under all that. I ordered tea and English muffins, jelly on the side. Dino winked, then swaggered off, leaving us in peace.

"So what's up?" I asked as Natalie slipped out of her overcoat and began shaking, rubbing those bony little arms. "Are you sick?"

"No", she shrugged, "just a nervous habit, I guess." She forced her hands to her lap, "I'm not sure what to tell you. My friend, Lisa, she's just gone, no message, no phone call, no nothing. It's not like her. We always tell each other everything, you know? If we're in trouble, we always turn to each other. We ain't got anyone else really."

"What about your parents?"

"Lisa's mom hasn't seen her in a while. I mean, she's pretty much out of it anyway."

"What about your parents?"

"It's just my dad and he doesn't know Lisa very well or me either, for that matter. Actually, I live with Lisa. My dad's kinda busy, you know? He didn't need a kid around, if you get my meaning."

I didn't, but I left it alone. "So the mom hasn't seen her. Anyone else who might know where she is?"

"Only her brother, but I can't find him either."

"How old is this brother?"

"Ten."

"Great. And how old are you and Lisa?"

"Fifteen, almost sixteen."

"Bull."

"Okay, so we're almost thirteen, but who gives a shit? We've been taking care of ourselves for years. We earn a living and take care of our place. That counts for something, doesn't it?" She screwed her face into a pout, hands on her hips. She was tough little bird.

"It counts for something." I struggled to maintain a neutral listening face, forcing back the urge to either grin or cry.

"Okay, dolls, here you go!" Dino brought everything at once, sparing us repeated interruptions. We ate in silence for a few minutes. She was obviously starving and devoured her entire plate before I picked up my second muffin.

"You want more? Go ahead if you're still hungry. Dino loves people who eat a lot."

"No thanks." She smiled. "I need to use the bathroom. Where is it?"

I pointed. "Right behind the counter on the end. It's not the cleanest, but it works."

I watched her teeter off, wondering if she was going to bolt on me. She had left her coat. Anyway, why would she want to run? There was something furtive about her wish to use the bathroom. Drugs?

"Little early for Halloween, isn't it?"

Dino slid into the booth for one of our early morning heart-to-hearts. These chats took several forms depending on Dino's mood. He either flirted shamelessly or pretended he was my father, lecturing me on the hazards of my lifestyle. He has been at this since my days volunteering in the South End, so it wasn't the PI work that he objected to. He just hated that I was alone. No husband, no kids, no anyone.

"Enough Dino. And don't you dare say anything when she gets back. She's anxious enough without you giving her the third degree."

"Hey, you know me, Rick. But I ask you, what's the world comin' to, kids runnin' around like that? What's up with you anyway? You look like shit."

"Too much to drink last night. Dumb."

"Drunk? Better watch yourself, doll. 'Specially at your age."

"Our age, thank you. No lectures, okay? I've learned my lesson. Can I have another tea, please?"

"Sure. But, you betta come back at lunch and Lois will fix you a coffee cab. Stay away from that McDonald's crap. All chemicals, no milk."

"We'll see." I smiled, thinking about Lois's coffee cabs, so creamy and delicious.

Lisa Brown, a routine missing persons case, probably a runaway, probably mixed up with drugs, prostitution, and who knows what else? The usual shit that neglected, abused city kids got into these days. I'd seen too many of them the past few years. Sometimes it appalled me, but none of it shocked me anymore. Maybe in my hungover state, the wall I'd erected was kicked away, allowing me to feel. Whatever, my gut wrenched thinking about these two kids and I didn't every know them.

I polished off my second cup of tea and she still had not returned from the john. Out of the corner of my eye, I spied Dino headed my way. *Here we go*, I thought, bracing myself for further effusions.

"Hey Rick," he said in a low voice, "I think there's something wrong with your friend. Sounds like she might be sick in there."

I followed him and we tried the bathroom door. It gave way, and I spied Natalie crouched near the toilet wiping her face with a paper towel. As the dry paper scraped across her checks like sandpaper, I shivered. "You okay? What happened?"

"It's nothing." Her face was pale and streaked with tears, eyes bloodshot and watery.

"Did you make yourself throw up?" I asked, trying not to sound accusatory, but probably failing miserably. My roommate in college spent four years doing this, so I was well acquainted with bulimic purging.

"No, it just happens sometimes after I eat a lot. I have kind of a funny stomach, you know?"

"Natalie, you need to see a doctor. This is nothing to fool around with, and you're pretty thin. I can take you to my doctor and he'll look you over." *What was I saying? Too involved, Steele, too involved.*

"No, I'm okay. If I rest, I'll feel better."

I lifted her up and half carried her out of the bathroom. Dino brought her coat and we wrestled her into it. After handing me my bag and Natalie's sack, he helped until we reached the door, muttering about "kids today." He refused the money I dropped on the counter and since my hands were full, I let the bills stay in my jacket pocket where he stuffed them. I would settle with him later.

We staggered back toward the office. She collapsed on the sidewalk outside the building, so I heaved her over my shoulder and toted her up the stairs like a sack of potatoes. All three flights. Fortunately, my back is stronger than my stomach, which was feeling even queasier now. I deposited her, none too gently, on the couch, and threw an old overcoat I keep in the office over her. As I paced around wondering what to do, she opened her eyes.

"Sorry about this. I've had the flu. I'll be okay. Can I sleep here? I'll feel great in a few minutes. You'll look for Lisa, won't you?" She rambled on, not waiting for my reply. "Her mom's address and phone number are on a paper in my purse. Maybe she's seen her. I doubt it, but it's worth a try. And there's Teddy, her brother. Please, I'll just crash here a while, then take off. I can pay, no problem. I mean, I got money, you know. Not on me, but I can get it. I'll just take a nap." With those words she closed her eyes and drifted off, leaving me standing with my mouth open, stomach in knots.

I rifled through the psychedelic carpet bag she called a purse and unearthed a scrap of paper.

"Oh, for Christ's sake."

I grabbed my bag and headed out again, locking the door behind me.

OTHER TITLES BY M. LEE PRESCOTT

Contemporary romances and mysteries by M. Lee Prescott include:

The Ricky Steele Mysteries
Book 1: Prepped to Kill
Book 2: Gadfly
Book 3: Lost in Spindle City
Book 4: Poof!

Also featuring Ricky Steele:
Jigsaw

Roger and Bess Mysteries
Book 1: A Friend of Silence
Book 2: In the Name of Silence
Book 3: The Silence of Memory

Contemporary Romances
Well-Loved Romances
Widow's Island
Hestor's Way

Morgan's Run Romances

Book 1: Emma's Dream

Book 2: Lang's Return

Book 3: Jeb's Promise

Book 4: Rose's Choice

Book 5: Hope's Wonder

Book 6: Ruthie's Love

Young Adult Historical Romance

Song of the Spirit

About the Author

M. Lee Prescott is the author of dozens of works of fiction for adults, young adults, and children, among them **Prepped to Kill, Gadfly, Lost in Spindle City, Poof! (Ricky Steele Mysteries), A Friend of Silence, In the Name of Silence and The Silence of Memory (Roger and Bess Mysteries), Jigsaw,** and **Song of the Spirit**, and her newest contemporary romance series, **Morgan's Run.** Three of her nonfiction titles have been published by Heinemann, and she has published numerous articles in the field of literacy education. Lee is a professor of education at a small New England liberal arts college, where she teaches reading and writing pedagogy. Her current research focuses on mindfulness and connections to reading and writing. She regularly teaches abroad, most recently in Singapore.

Lee has lived in southern California (loved those Laguna nights!), Chapel Hill, North Carolina, and various spots in Massachusetts and Rhode Island. Currently she resides in Massachusetts on a beautiful river, where she canoes, swims, and watches an incredible variety of wildlife pass by. She is the mother of two grown sons and spends lots of time with them, their beautiful wives, and her amazing grandchildren. When not teaching or writing, Lee's passions revolve around family, yoga (Kripalu is a second home), swimming, sharing mindfulness with children and adults, and walking.

Lee loves to hear from readers. Email her at mleeprescott@gmail.com, and visit her website to hear the latest and sign up for her newsletters!

AUTHOR WEBPAGE AND NEWSLETTER SIGN-UP:

www.mleeprescott.com

Follow me on BookBub:

www.bookbub.com/authors/m-lee-prescott